ALSO BY KATHY REICHS

Adult Fiction

Déjà Dead
Death du Jour
Deadly Décisions
Fatal Voyage
Grave Secrets
Bare Bones
Monday Mourning
Cross Bones
Break No Bones
Bones to Ashes
Devil Bones
206 Bones
Spider Bones
Flash and Bones
Bones Are Forever
Bones of the Lost
Bones Never Lie
Speaking in Bones
The Bone Collection
Bones: Buried Deep (coauthored with Max Allan Collins)
A Conspiracy of Bones
The Bone Code
Cold, Cold Bones
The Bone Hacker
Fire and Bones

Novellas

Bones in Her Pocket
Swamp Bones
Bones on Ice

Young Adult Fiction
(with Brendan Reichs)

Virals
Seizure
Code
Exposure
Terminal

Novellas

Shift
Swipe
Shock

EVIL BONES

A TEMPERANCE BRENNAN NOVEL

KATHY REICHS

SCRIBNER
NEW YORK AMSTERDAM/ANTWERP LONDON
TORONTO SYDNEY/MELBOURNE NEW DELHI

Scribner
An Imprint of Simon & Schuster, LLC
1230 Avenue of the Americas
New York, NY 10020

First Scribner hardcover edition November 2025

Manufactured in the United States of America

1 3 5 7 9 10 8 6 4 2

The Library of Congress Cataloging-in-Publication Data has been applied for.

ISBN 978-1-6680-5147-4
ISBN 978-1-6680-5149-8 (ebook)

For

Paul Reichs

who has been there from the beginning

EVIL BONES

PROLOGUE

Don't panic!

Don't you dare panic!

Wind rocked the ancient Buick. Rain drummed millions of tiny missiles against its hood and roof.

Her fingers ached from maintaining their ten–two o'clock grip on the wheel. Her neck burned from the strain of craning forward. Pointless. The altered posture did nothing to improve her cataracts-clouded vision.

Beyond her little bubble, the world was a swirling maelstrom.

Please, dear Jesus!

Protect me!

When no deity appeared to offer guidance or aid, Bella eased off the gas but maintained enough pressure to continue her agonizingly slow forward creep. Terrified of going faster. Terrified of coming to a stop on the blacktop.

Bella alternated between chastising and defending herself.

You should have checked a weather report. You should have told the kids you were going out.

You should have stayed home.

Bella usually listened to her children when they told her to wait. Sometimes they came. More often they forgot, too busy with their jobs and their lawns and their kids.

She needed eggs for the angel food cake promised for the church bake sale. What could go wrong? The trip to the Publix took only twenty minutes.

Unless something unexpected happened to alter the usual script.

This predicament really wasn't her fault, Bella panic-reasoned. The storm had come out of nowhere, a dark monster racing across the late afternoon sky.

Bella squinted hard behind her thick trifocal lenses, frustrated that the car's high beams seemed not to be penetrating the thick curtain of rain.

Have mercy, dear Lord!

A fast-food wrapper winged out of the gloom, danced across the glass, then whipped off in an airborne pirouette.

Fresh tears ran down Bella's wrinkled old cheeks.

More rapid heartbeats, then a glow lit the far-off horizon. Bella watched the approaching brightness contract and separate into two orbs. Moments later, a pair of headlights in the opposite lane flashed past.

The blast of air and spray of water triggered a new round of palpitations and prayers.

Twice, headlights took shape in the rearview mirror, looming like creatures with fiery eyes. Twice, the creatures swung wide to pass. Twice, Bella watched taillights recede into the wet void.

More supplication.

Please!

More self-castigation.

This is your own fault, you idiot.

Another blustery gust almost dislodged Bella's hands from the wheel.

Brake now! A cluster of panicky neurons bellowed.

Wait until you can safely pull off! a more rational gaggle countermanded.

Bella's frontal lobe pounded. Her hands felt numb.

The Buick kept crawling.

Time passed.

An epoch.

Maybe ten minutes.

Then, as if in answer to her prayers, the deluge began easing in interrupted bursts.

The interruptions yielded fleeting glimpses of the outside world. A narrow two-lane. Fenced farmland. A brown horse with a white muzzle patch shaped like a rat.

The horse was a mare. The mare had a name.

Glenda.

Bella's spirits soared.

Praise be, Heavenly Father!! Thank you for the sign.

The horse lifted and shook its soggy head. Noted Bella's slow passing with little interest.

Unhurriedly, the pockets of light expanded and merged. The sky brightened and the rain appeared to lose interest.

Ahead and to the right, a tree materialized in the murky wetness, its height far greater than that of its brethren.

Bella yelped with joy.

The pasture. The horse with the rodent-shaped mark. The majestic old oak. The world was recognizable and as it should be.

Shifting her foot from the gas to the brake while doubling down on her viselike grip, Bella rotated the wheel a few degrees to the right, aiming for a strip of gravel barely wide enough to qualify as a shoulder.

The treads were worn. The pavement was coated with oil-slicked rainwater.

Easy. Not too much.

Too much.

The right front tire dropped off the edge of the asphalt, pulling the vehicle in that direction. Terrified, Bella jerked the wheel hard to the left and gunned the engine. The Buick fired across both lanes and slammed into the trunk of the oak.

Bella's head snapped forward and hit the wheel, jumbling her thoughts. Righting herself gingerly, she settled back against the headrest, allowing her gaze to slide skyward through the spiderweb cracks in the windshield.

When questioned hours later, Bella wouldn't remember losing consciousness.

She *would* recall waking up.

The leaves rustling.

The birds singing.

The engine hissing.

The scream rising from deep in her chest.

The EMTs listened with disbelief as Bella described the horror she'd spotted in the branches above.

CHAPTER 1

I was thinking about frogs. Specifically, about the one living in the fountain outside my town house.

Every summer, the creature took up residence there. Based on the depth and resonance of its dawn and dusk croaking, I guessed the amphibian was of fairly good size.

Why *there*? I wondered. What was the appeal of that tiny basin?

Where did the frog go in winter? Palm Beach? Key Largo? Did it leave at all or just hunker down in leaves somewhere and sleep?

Did the little fellow fear birds? Lawn mowers? Off-leash dogs?

Was it actually the same frog year after year?

I know what you're thinking. But my office at the MCME was warm and stuffy, encouraging wandering thoughts, and I'd been awakened at sunrise by yet another polliwog serenade.

My sleep-deprived mind was meandering.

Also, the task at hand was beyond tedious.

At the request of my boss, Dr. Samantha Nguyen, Mecklenburg County's chief medical examiner, I was compiling an inventory of the reports I'd written during the first six months of the year. Every MCME professional was doing this. The pathologists, the odontologist, the radiologist. *Moi.*

An *annotated* inventory.

Had the case involved a human or an animal? Had the remains been fresh, putrefied, mummified, burned, mutilated, skeletal, or other? Yeah, other. I'll skip detailing the possibilities.

Had the examination focused on establishing identity? On analyzing trauma? On determining cause or manner of death? On reconstructing the method of body disposal? On estimating postmortem interval—the time that had passed since the victim's death?

Some entity above Nguyen's pay grade had requested the data. Maybe the governor's office. Maybe the chief ME in Chapel Hill. Maybe God.

The questions I was answering could have served as descriptors for my job. I'm a forensic anthropologist, a specialist in the human skeleton. My expertise is requested for cases in which a normal autopsy is impossible, and all observations and conclusions must be derived from the bones.

Primarily, I'm employed by coroners and medical examiners in my home state of North Carolina, and by the Laboratoire de sciences judiciaires et de médecine légale, the main medico-legal lab in the province of Quebec.

Charlotte and Montreal.

Long story.

Long commute.

One I've been making for decades.

Trust me. I have a mother lode of frequent flier miles.

More on that later.

I love my job and can't imagine doing anything else. I love giving names to the anonymous dead and providing next of kin with closure. What I don't love is informing families that the person they're searching for has died.

I despise doing paperwork. Keyboard work?

That day I was on the Carolina end of my geographically complicated professional arrangement. Finally addressing the chore I'd avoided for weeks.

I'd been staring at a computer screen for hours. My eyes burned and a headache was bullying my frontal lobe.

Resting my elbows on the desktop, I circled the tips of my fingers on my temples. Sighed. A pointlessly theatrical performance given that I was alone in my office.

It was late morning on a Wednesday deep into August. The weather had been low-country hot and muggy for weeks, so I was hoping for a brief getaway soon, a jaunt to the mountains with Ryan, my significant other. Nothing big. A leisurely drive to Asheville, some hiking, a couple of nights at an inn with way too much chintz in the room.

I was clicking open yet another file when I sensed a change in the light filtering in from the hall. I looked up.

A small woman stood framed in the open doorway. Dark, almond-shaped eyes. Olive skin. Black hair gathered into a bun at the nape of her neck.

"Tempe." Nguyen's voice carried hints of Boston and some other far more exotic locale. "You are well?"

"I am. Thanks for asking." Knowing the boss hadn't come to query my health.

"I have just had a call from the Stanly County sheriff's office. An elderly woman named Bella Abato was involved in a single-car accident late yesterday near the town of Frog Pond."

"Is this a joke? Were you reading my mind?"

"What?"

"Never mind." Knee-jerk reaction on my part. Nguyen was not a kidder.

"A trucker called to report the crash. Abato was concussed and hysterical when officers arrived. They couldn't make much sense of her rambling. But they persuaded her to go by ambulance to an ER."

I was clueless why Nguyen was telling me this.

"Abato calmed overnight but is still insisting she was driven off the road by a sign from Satan."

"The devil."

"Yes."

"Is she on pharmaceuticals?"

"She is. But when a tow truck arrived at the scene this morning, the driver, too, encountered a sight that unnerved him."

Nguyen hesitated, unusual for a woman perpetually cool and unruffled. I waited for her to continue.

"The driver claims he saw a painted human head nailed to the tree."

An image popped in my forebrain.

"Was the head wearing a hat, wrapped in fabric, and decorated with glitter and feathers?"

"Yes."

"It's probably another of these sick animal displays showing up around the county."

"Perhaps it *is* another snatched pet." Nguyen didn't sound convinced.

It was clear she expected me to swing into action. I summoned my best bright-eyed-and-curious expression. "I assume the driver called the sheriff and that the sheriff called you?"

"Yes," replied Nguyen. "The sheriff's name is Hattie Spitz. Finding the man's story quite bizarre, but wanting to take no chances, she drove out to see for herself. She says the item in question is about ten feet off the ground and that it's something she doesn't want to touch. She's ordered a deputy to stand guard until personnel from this office arrive."

I vaguely remembered Spitz, a thin woman with a jowly hound dog face. An overly earnest type who'd approached me after one of my "call in the experts and don't contaminate the evidence" lectures at some regional law enforcement conference.

Advice I was now mildly regretting.

Nguyen studied my expression, which by this point was considerably less than bright-eyed. A scene visit wasn't in my pre-weekend plans. In the event our mountain holiday panned out, I had to organize my cat, Birdie, for delivery to the neighbor, have the air pressure checked in my tires, make a pharmacy run, buy the drinks and munchies Ryan and I would want for roady snacks, and pack.

A trip to the boonies to collect a putrefying raccoon or opossum held absolutely no appeal.

"You want me to go out to Stanly County?" I asked with zero enthusiasm.

"I think that would be best. Sheriff Spitz has offered to send a vehicle and driver to transport you."

"Can't this—"

"The deputy has been on site for several hours now." Then, almost as an afterthought. "He was instructed to bring a ladder."

"Do you have precise directions?" I asked, resigned.

"I do."

"I prefer to drive myself."

"As you wish."

Before setting out, I hopped onto the net. Learned that Frog Pond was an unincorporated community of roughly five thousand souls located in the eastern part of Stanly County. That the town's variety store sold everything from iPads to diapers. That area Airbnbs rented for as little as twenty bucks a night.

After entering the coordinates Nguyen had provided, I followed the nice WAZE lady's navigational directions. Once out of Charlotte, she sent me east on Highway 24, also unhelpfully labeled Highway 27. Beyond the city and its suburban sprawl, the landscape yielded to rolling farmland dotted with convenience store–gas station combos, rural churches, and the homes of citizens wanting distance from their neighbors.

I passed through several small communities. As was my habit, I played mental games with the colorful town names so common in Dixie. Midland. Locust. Red Cross.

Frog Pond was one of those speck-on-the-map burgs one could blow through without taking notice. The Abato crash scene was just beyond the town limits, on a two-lane shooting off Molly Springs Road.

An hour after departing the MCME, I spotted the tree in question, a massive oak whose best days were far in the past. Pics forwarded to me courtesy of Spitz and Nguyen made the ID easy.

As did a pickup idling on the shoulder opposite the tree. A logo on the side of the cab declared *Sheriff* in bold black above, *Stanly County* in smaller font below. A five-point gold star topped the lettering.

A tired-looking deputy sat behind the wheel, ubiquitous cop Aviators shading his eyes. Sun winked bronze off the lenses as they followed my car's progress from the pavement onto the shoulder in front of him.

In my rearview mirror I saw the deputy's head tilt and his lips move, assumed he was reporting my arrival by radio. Then the truck's door opened, and the man emerged.

The guy was small, maybe five six, and weighed less than he probably would have preferred. His hair was blond and buzzed close to a scalp the same bright pink as the Hello Kitty purse my daughter, Katy, had owned as a kid.

Buzz Cut wore black pants and a blindingly white shirt sporting one of the largest shoulder patches I'd ever seen. Pinned to his chest's left side were a small brass plaque and a gold star identical to the one on his vehicle.

Heat enveloped me as I climbed from my car, the lack of any breeze cueing my sweat glands for serious action. I said a silent prayer that this outing would be brief.

While striding toward me, the deputy positioned a hat on his head and adjusted it twice. The hat's brim was black and large enough to shade a schoolyard. Hand shielding my eyes, I read the inscription on the man's plaque: "*F. Torgeson.*"

F. Torgeson stopped five feet out and nodded, offering one quick birdlike dip of his chin. His face was flushed, his nose and cheeks badly in need of sunscreen. I guessed his age at maybe twelve.

"Ma'am." Neither smiling nor frowning.

"Deputy." I dug out and proffered my MCME ID.

F. Torgeson studied the small plastic rectangle, then my face.

"Anthropologist," he said, voice flat.

"I am." Feeling no desire to elaborate. "Dr. Nguyen sent me to evaluate remains in a tree."

"Yes, ma'am."

"Do I need PPE?" I was asking about personal protective equipment.

F. Torgeson's brow creased, but he said nothing.

"Can I expect snakes, wasps, black widows, poison ivy?"

"I wouldn't know that, ma'am."

"Have you walked to the tree?" I asked, an edge to my voice.

"Just to set down a ladder, ma'am." Jabbing a thumb over his shoulder, he added, "It's there, yonder by that oak."

Wordlessly, I unlocked the trunk of my car, removed my recovery kit, and turned back to F. Torgeson.

"Lead on."

Our feet crunched on the gravel bordering the pavement, went silent as we entered the knee-high scrub beyond. Flying insects rose up and swarmed my face and whined in my ears. Now and then, a loner kamikazed into one of my eyes. I batted the nasty things away as best I could.

The air was thick with the smell of petroleum, heated asphalt, and sunbaked vegetation. Rivulets of sweat began running down my back.

Up close, the oak looked almost primeval, its branches semi-nude and terminating in clawlike twigs. Its scabby bark was black in patches, green with moss in others.

Nailed to the tree's trunk, roughly ten feet above the ground, was the reason for my visit. Before climbing up, I set down my case and took pics with my iPhone, then expanded and studied the enlarged images.

Faded blue fabric partially wrapped the object, obscuring some detail. But just beneath a weathered old ball cap, within the shadowy folds, I spotted the curve of a cheekbone, the dark recess of an orbit, the yellowed enamel of dentition.

An eight-foot stepladder lay on the ground below the tree. Together, F. Torgeson and I lifted, spread, and maneuvered it into position. He stood at the base as I climbed, a spotter at the ready should his teammate tumble.

One rung. Two. Three.

Somewhere in the distance, a dog barked. Otherwise, the only sound was that of my boots hitting the aluminum rungs.

Halfway up, I paused. Surprised.

The smell of decomposing flesh is like no other, sweet and fetid and rank. The odor hung there on the hot, midday air, faint but unmistakable.

Yanking a latex glove from the back pocket of my jeans, I inflated, then snugged it onto my right hand. Probably overkill for an animal DOA, but what the hell. Best to follow protocol.

Two more rungs, then I encountered the flies. They swarmed and darted, whining in protest at the intrusion, the sun iridescent on their blue-green bodies.

Their presence at that height also surprised me.

Shooing the flies with my gloved hand, I mounted the final rung.

And got my first good look.

Holy bloody hell.

CHAPTER 2

My Charlotte home is part of Sharon Hall, a nineteenth-century estate-turned-condo complex adjacent to the Queens University campus. The property's centerpiece is a redbrick manor house with a wide front porch, white shutters, pediments, and columns. The grounds are accessed via a circle drive cutting through acres of lawn shaded by enormous magnolias. A naïve tourist might mistake the place for a set from *Gone with the Wind*.

My little abode is just inside the estate's eastern wall, next to a gnarled old pine. The odd little two-story structure is called the Annex.

Annex to what? No one knows. The building appears on none of the estate's historic plans. The hall is there. The coach house. The herb and formal gardens. No annex. Clearly, the tiny edifice was a postscript to the original design.

Friends and family used to play games guessing my home's initial *raison d'être*. Hothouse? Smokehouse? Playhouse? Kiln? I'd play along. But I'm not much concerned with the architect's intended purpose.

The Annex's livable space measures barely fifteen hundred square feet. The kitchen faucet drips. Two staircase treads are warped. Nevertheless, the place suits my needs just fine. Bedroom, bath, and wee study up. Kitchen, dining room, and parlor down.

Why live in a tiny unit with bad plumbing and wonky flooring, you ask? Why not a slick high-rise condo like the one with your name on the deed in Montreal? Or a town house with modern wiring, a Sonos sound system, maybe a Toto toilet?

Attachment? Laziness? Lack of motivation? I'm not sufficiently introspective to probe my reasons for staying put. Maybe it's the backstory that keeps me rooted.

Eons ago, finding myself suddenly single and needing a rental stat, I chose the Annex as a stopgap measure. My plan was to take my time, find something bigger and more up-to-date, and move on. Turned out I loved the place, warts and all.

I've made some modifications over the years, expanded the second floor when Ryan and I decided to try cohabitation. Splurged on new appliances. Upfitted the primary bath. I no longer think about leaving. Well, not often.

At seven-forty that evening I was sitting on a lawn chair on my small porch, tired but satisfied with the outcome of my trip to Stanly County. The specimen, which still baffled me, would be waiting at the MCME for analysis in the morning.

I was sipping a Perrier with ice, wishing the drink was vodka with lime. Another long story, colorful, but neither original nor pretty. Let's just say that, for me, every bottle is permanently corked.

My cat, Birdie, was curled in my lap, mostly dozing, sporadically raising his head for a halfhearted sniff. Or to remind me that I should keep stroking his back.

Ryan had said he'd phone at eight. I was looking forward to that call. To making plans together for his upcoming visit.

The sun was low, the breeze cautious but managing an occasional frail gust. With each anemic puff, the grass shifted in soft undulating waves, momentarily going from green to bronze.

Two cardinals—each male and flamboyantly crimson—were arguing loudly high above my head. An unclaimed seed? A female? A coveted position on a branch? Whatever the dispute, both birds held strong opinions.

It was one of those velvety summer nights unique to Dixie. I felt relaxed, happy to have no obligations that evening. Pleased that Ryan might be with me soon.

Ryan, you ask?

Lieutenant-détective Andrew Ryan, recently retired from the homicide division of the *Sûreté du Québec*, the provincial police service for the Canadian province of Quebec. Tall and sexy in a younger Harrison Ford sort of way, the French version, Ryan has been my cop partner for decades. My romantic partner for a few years less.

Canada and North Carolina? It wasn't easy but, at the moment, we were making it work.

Ryan and I had been apart for almost two weeks. I'd been stuck in Charlotte with commitments at the MCME. Bones discovered by a hunter stalking quail. A torso washed ashore along the Catawba River. An attic skull that turned out to be a "borrowed" museum specimen.

Ryan had been stuck north of the border working a PI job involving surveillance of an employee suspected of skimming from a family-owned business. The case, boring as mud, was typical of many he'd accepted since his retirement.

At seven-fifty-five my iPhone rang.

Sang. It's dorky, I know. The teasing from Katy is brutal. Still, I program my mobile to alert me with musical ringtones. Currently, it was Fleetwood Mac singing about dreams.

"Hey, big guy," I answered, certain it was Ryan.

"What?" Katy blew one of her trademark snorts. "You're stealing material from Rachel Feinstein, now?"

"Who?"

"Never mind."

"I'm expecting a call from Ryan," I explained, a bit defensive.

"How is the old dude?"

"He's not old."

"How is the young buckaroo?"

"He's good."

"In every way."

Katy's sense of humor leans hard toward sarcasm. Occasionally, I have no idea of her meaning.

"What's up?" I asked, wanting to move the conversation along.

"Have you left yet?"

That caught me off guard.

"Nooo." Neutral.

"Good. Can you pick up a baguette on your way? It seems I'm supposed to serve bread with mussels. Who knew?"

"Any particular kind?" Buying time as I swiped the phone's screen to open my calendar app.

"The recipe says it should be crusty. Aren't all baguettes crusty?"

Mental head slap.

Eight p.m. Dinner with Katy and Ruthie.

"Got it. That may delay me a bit."

"No prob."

"How's it going with Ruthie?"

"We can talk about it."

With that cryptic comment, she disconnected.

So much for my leisurely evening solo.

Racing inside, I dumped Birdie on the sofa, flew up to my bedroom, and yanked on fresh jeans and a tee. After a quick redo of my very questionable ponytail, I fired off a text to Ryan, then hustled back down to the first floor.

The cat watched with dubious eyes as I checked his kibble and refilled his water fountain. Or maybe he was still sleepy.

Grabbing my purse and keys, I hurried out to my car.

We Charlotteans insist on labeling every square inch of our burg. Dillworth. South End. NoDa. Opinions are split concerning the city center. Some call it Uptown, others prefer Downtown. Battles have been fought over this matter. Mannerly battles, of course.

My neighborhood is called Myers Park. Think surgically manicured gardens and lawns; sidewalks buckled by tree roots older than the Valley of the Kings; churches on every corner—Baptist, Presbyterian, Methodist, Catholic. Except for the steeples, each pious complex looks like a small college campus.

Myers Park's charm comes with a price. Her southern gentility is fiercely guarded against any resident who might consider going rogue. Paint your shutters orange? No way. Cut down that willow oak? Not a chance. The fine ladies of the MP homeowners' association could give Stalin pointers on authoritarian rule.

As predicted by the largely traditional architecture, the populace is mainly white and Christian—the golf at the club, martinis at five, church on Sunday crowd. During elections, most yard signs feature Republican candidates.

Why do I choose to live in such a conservative enclave? Typically, the quiet on my block is disrupted only by lawn mowers, leaf blowers, and the occasional barking dog. *Tsk-tsk* and call me boring. What can I say? I like the serenity.

Katy lives roughly ten minutes away in Elizabeth, Charlotte's only neighborhood named for a woman, though a regal one. After a quick stop at the local grocery to buy its finest baguette, I was mounting the steps to Katy's front porch a few minutes later.

My thumb had barely hit the buzzer when my daughter opened the door. Her honey-blond hair wasn't exactly chaotic. It was cut far too short to rise to that level of disarray. But it was seriously tousled. I was unsure if the look was a fashion statement or the result of agitation.

The tension in Katy's face suggested the latter.

"Hey," I said.

"Hey," she said

Not a shared warning. That's how we Southerners greet.

Katy stepped back and held the door wide. I entered, followed her down a narrow hall to a shockingly large kitchen, and laid the baguette on the table, which was set for two.

That surprised me. Tonight's dinner was arranged so that I could spend time with my sister Harry's granddaughter, Molly-Ruth Howard. Perhaps I should unravel that little bit of the family tree.

My younger sister, Harriet Brennan Howard Daewood Crone, has been married and divorced three times. Or is it four? In all honesty, I don't bother keeping track since the score sheet could change at any moment.

Harry, who lives in Texas, has a grown son named Christopher "Kit" Howard, the result of her second, and very lucrative, marriage to Howard Howard. Kit, a veterinary researcher living on an island near Beaufort, South Carolina, has two daughters born fifteen years apart. Go, Kit.

Victoria "Tory" Brennan is the older of the half sisters. Kit first learned of Tory's existence when the kid was fourteen years old. The Brennan-Brennan surname match is a weird coincidence. Tory's mother, sadly deceased, was from a clan of Massachusetts Brennans.

Unlike Tory, Kit's younger daughter is the fruit of a long and relatively stable marriage. Molly-Ruth, called Ruthie since birth, was now seventeen and, according to Harry and Kit, pissed off with everything in life. And letting the world know about her unhappiness.

When the grandmother-father-daughter dynamic became intolerable, Katy took pity and invited Ruthie to spend the end of her summer in Charlotte. Ruthie gladly accepted and had been in town for two weeks. I thought the visit was going well.

"Where's Ruthie?" I asked.

"Gone."

"Gone where?"

"If I knew that I would have said." Removing a lid from a steamer pan on the stove and slamming it onto the counter. "Gone to class. Gone to the pharmacy. Gone to the park to shoot up."

"What?" Unable to keep the alarm from my voice.

"Forget it. I shouldn't have said that."

"Is Ruthie being difficult?"

"She's being Ruthie."

"What does that mean?" I was pretty sure of her answer but wanted to allow Katy the chance to vent.

"The kid elevates moody to a whole new level."

"She's not really a kid anymore," I corrected.

"Exactly. I'd welcome some of that gag-me-with-a-spoon adolescent angst. Instead, she talks like she's going on thirty. Do you know what her favorite book is?"

I shook my head.

"*Sleeping, Dreaming, and Dying* by the Dalai Lama."

Katy crossed to the sink. Returned to the stove and emptied a colander of mussels into the pan.

I waited for her to continue. When she didn't, I prompted,

"What do you mean by moody?"

"She's all sunbeams and rosebuds one minute, sulky the next. She'll want to talk about something, I mean, TMI to the max. The breakup with her boyfriend, the reason she barely graduated because of a D+ in algebra, the definition of consciousness. But if I ask the simplest follow-up question, she shuts down like I'm a cop trying to rubber-hose a confession."

"That kind of unpredictability can be hard." Hiding a smile at the irony. My daughter had been prickly as hell during her teens. Still was, at times.

"It's always fucking eggshells with her."

Katy ladled out two servings of mollusks and carried the bowls to the table.

"Let's eat."

I took my place, tore off and buttered a segment of bread. Opened a mussel and scooped out the soft, gray flesh.

We ate in silence for a while, the only sound the rattle of our shells hitting the discard bowl.

I spoke first.

"Is Ruthie still working at the shelter?"

Years back, Katy had been gutted when her fiancé was killed by an IED while on a Peace Corps mission in Afghanistan. Though she had no legal claim to his estate by virtue of their relationship, his will had left her a large sum of money and she'd used it to establish a charity for homeless veterans. She'd named the organization the Aaron Cooperton Foundation in honor of her lost love. She'd also founded the Charles Anthony Hunt Center, a home for unhoused vets, named in honor of one of my friends who'd also died tragically young.

The organization and the shelter remained Katy's two passions. She put in long hours daily, overseeing the running of each.

"Mmm," Katy offered through a mouthful of seafood.

"That's working out?"

"Reasonably well."

Several moments passed. Then I tried again.

"Is Ruthie still refusing to consider college?"

"Yes."

"I'm good with that." I was. Not everyone is meant to go that route, at least not right out of high school.

Katy offered another noncommittal "mmm."

"She can always change her mind."

"I don't see that happening."

Though I wasn't certain of Katy's meaning, I let it go.

"Do you know if Kit's on board with Ruthie's decision?" I asked.

"Ruthie says he is."

"How's Harry taking it?"

Katy's response was an Academy Award–level snort. This time I had no doubt regarding the message.

Harry hadn't pursued any education beyond high school, preferring parties and booze to English 101 and a cramped dorm room. Decades, marriages, and careers down the road, she still feels inadequate over her lack of a degree. Ruthie's refusal to attend college was a flamethrower issue with my baby sister.

We passed the rest of the evening engaged in amiable conversation. I didn't mention my mutilated animal corpses. Katy didn't talk about her soldiers damaged in body and soul.

The tranquil interlude was a well-timed blessing, given the events about to unfold.

At ten, I headed home.

Not having spoken to Ryan.

Not having laid eyes on my great-niece.

CHAPTER 3

The next morning dawned unapologetically hot. And the humidity was going along for the ride.

I'm a person whose moods are strongly influenced by weather. Give me high temps and sunny skies and I'm happy as a lark. Let clouds gather or the mercury edge toward freezing and I'm grumpy as hell.

And, for the record, I'm not big on the white stuff. Unless I've gone seeking it deliberately—to ski, sled, or ride a toboggan—I'm good with snow for about twenty-four hours. Which is roughly the lifespan of the occasional dusting we get in Charlotte.

But the forecast would be irrelevant that day. I'd be spending every minute inside the sterile walls of the MCME.

Still, I was feeling upbeat as I left the Annex. Until I rounded the building and saw an Amazon driver drop a package on my neighbor's front porch. Literally. Drop it with a loud thud.

"Gently, please," I admonished, smiling. "That box could contain her grandma's crystal goblets."

"Yeah, lady? I could leave it at the curb." The guy was pale and lumpy, with limbs that might have worked well on a spider monkey. A short roll-your-own bobbed on his lower lip as he spoke.

"There's no need to be rude," I said.

"There's no need for you to be telling me my job."

Removing, crushing, and dropping the butt into his uniform shirt pocket, the man strode to his truck and roared off.

I stood a moment, offended and angry. Debating whether to report the incident. Knowing I wouldn't.

Then I got into my car and drove away.

By eight-thirty I was in an autopsy room outfitted with a razzle-dazzle ventilation system designed to combat the most pugnacious of odors. There is a similar setup at the lab in Montreal. On both ends, the specially equipped space is referred to as "the stinky room." In different languages, of course.

But the razzle and dazzle are never fully effective. Nothing is. The stench of putrefied, decomposed, bloated, or scorched flesh always manages to outwit the blowers and fans and disinfectants.

A stainless-steel table occupied the center of the room, surrounded by glass-fronted stainless-steel cabinets overhanging stainless-steel countertops. Tile floor. Overhead mic and video camera for recording every move and observation.

Since many employees opt to vacation in summer, August can mean reduced staff at the MCME. That day, one autopsy tech was in the mountains harassing trout, and another had taken a personal day to tend to a sick goat. Expecting to encounter nothing more complicated than a squirrel or a rabbit—nonhuman remains, case closed, specimen sent for incineration—I'd offered to work unassisted.

While I'd changed from street clothes to scrubs, the thing from the tree—now designated MCME-701-25—had been wheeled from the cooler to the stinky room. Upon entering, I took a quick look.

Lying on the gurney was a black plastic bag concealing a relatively small bulge. The size of the bulge squared with my recollection from the Frog Pond oak.

I began by dictating contextual information—the case number; the day's date; the name of each transporter; the name of the analyst performing the examination; the name of the assisting technician; the condition of the remains upon recovery; the location at which the remains were found. All the tedious details that could later become relevant in a court of law.

When finished, I shot a few backup pics. Then I secured the ties of a plastic apron behind my neck and waist, pulled on latex gloves, and raised a mask to cover my nose and mouth.

Properly garbed, I stepped to the gurney. Using a pair of heavy shears, I cut the bag with four smooth strokes and laid the segments of plastic flat. Splayed out on the stainless steel, they brought to mind the unfurled petals of a rose.

Au contraire, the smell slowly filling the room was far from floral. My olfactory lobe registered moldy fabric with a hint of something organic. Feathers? Fur? Traces of degraded tissue or blood?

On a scale of autopsy aromas, this one wasn't all that rank. That, too, was consistent with expectations. Mummified flesh can be relatively odorless.

The fabric was some sort of heavy cotton or canvas duck. Its color, once bright and probably called "royal" blue, was now soiled and bleached by exposure to the elements. The material was nothing special. Except that it was so very familiar.

I took another round of pics, feeling the usual prickle of heat in my chest. Sadness for the helpless dead animal victim. Fury at the perpetrator. Anger at the existence of such cruelty.

Focus, Brennan.

Do your job so the cops can nail this fruitcake.

Peeling back the final layer of wrapping, I had my first good look.

As anticipated, the skull wasn't human. And it wasn't large. I estimated cranial capacity similar to that of a cocker spaniel.

Also, as anticipated, the skull had been converted into some peculiar animal version of a death mask.

I ran a quick mental inventory of details.

Patches of desiccated and discolored tissue adhered to the bone.

The eyelids had been stretched wide and stitched above and below the orbits.

Wadded tinfoil filled the hollows where the eyeballs had been.

Specks of glitter still adhered to the ectocranial surface.

A bundle of feathers projected from each ear opening.

The mandible had been rearticulated and glued in place, leaving the mouth agape in a rictus snarl.

All four canines had been removed.

The same bizarre motif had been observed on the other creatures turning up in Mecklenburg and the surrounding counties.

I'm no expert on mammalian cranial anatomy. Far from it. But I know the basics. Something about this specimen looked off.

Leaving the skull on the gurney, I swiveled to the terminal behind me and entered a number into the MCME computer system. A few more keystrokes, then I opened a file and began running through a series of images.

Rat. Squirrel. Rabbit. Skunk. All mutilated and decorated in the same manner as MCME-701-25.

All missing at least one body part.

I was viewing a close-up of the base of a rabbit cranium when I heard the door open. Curious, I turned.

Officially, Erskine "Skinny" Slidell is no longer a cop. But Skinny spent decades with the Charlotte-Mecklenburg PD Felony Investigative Bureau/Homicide Unit, and leaving the "murder table" wasn't easy for him.

Apparently, the parting of ways wasn't easy for the CMPD, either. Skinny is often called out of retirement to lend a hand with his extensive, though not always orthodox, investigative skills.

I've worked with Slidell over the years. Frequently. My take? The guy's got the personality of moldy gouda, but good instincts.

Slidell was standing at the open door, one hand on the knob, as though prepared should a quick getaway prove necessary. His cheeks were flushed, his Brylcreemed hair damp at his forehead and temples and separated into oily clumps on his scalp. Having experimented with a crew cut for a while, Skinny had gone back to his signature pompadour-ducktail arrangement of late. It wasn't a good look.

Slidell hates hot weather. Almost as much as he hates autopsies and the rooms in which the cutting takes place. His overheated face radiated displeasure at having to cross from the administrative and office area to the scientific working area of the MCME. From the facility's "clean" to "dirty" side.

"Doc." Slidell greeted me in his usual indolent way.

"Detective."

"I hear you collected another one of these critters."

"I did."

"All decked out like the others?"

"Yes." Thinking the same could be said about Skinny. Today he was wearing a tan-and-yellow plaid jacket over a mint green shirt with blue top stitching. Polyester black pants.

"We got us one weird sonofabitch out there." Delivered without venturing across the threshold.

"We do."

"What the hell is his thinking?"

"Or her."

Slidell made a noise in his throat to acknowledge the point.

A moment of silence, then,

"I read an article about Mexicans decorating dead human heads."

"Calaveras," I said, hiding my surprise. Not at the fact that Skinny knew about "sugar skulls" as they're also called. At the fact that he read.

"Yeah." Jabbing the air with the index finger of his free hand. "Those."

"Skulls were a prominent feature in pre-Columbian societies and cultures," I said, wanting to encourage Skinny in his literary pursuits. "And calaveras—crania decorated to reflect the beauty of life—are still created for the annual Day of the Dead celebrations in November."

Skinny looked unimpressed with this ethnographic morsel dredged up from my grad school days.

"But this is different," I added, gesturing toward MCME-701-25.

"Different how?"

"The skulls being nailed up are forest creatures or stolen pets."

"They're from animals."

Duh. I didn't say it. Didn't matter. Skinny was lost in thought and had tuned me out.

I resumed studying my screen.

A full minute passed, the only sound the click of the keys as I enlarged or reduced an image. Slidell's hot breath on my neck suggested he'd approached and was leaning forward viewing the pics, too.

"What kinda animals we talking, here?"

"They're all mammals."

"What kinda mammals?"

"Once I determined that the remains weren't human, I didn't spend more time on them. I'd have to do research to identify exact species. Why? Do you think that's significant?"

Skinny called on one beefy shoulder to give a "who knows" shrug.

A beat, then he asked,

"How do you know how big these things are?"

I pointed to a flat, L-shaped object lying to the right of the specimen filling the screen—a gizmo I'd explained to Skinny more than once.

"That's an ABFO ruler. It's marked off in centimeter and millimeter gradations and is placed in every forensic shot to provide scale."

"And the others?"

"The others what?"

"Jesus on a pogo." A sharpness to Skinny's voice indicated waning patience. "How friggin' big were the other skulls?"

"Not big. But they were animal remains, so I didn't take measurements." Feeling a prickle of unease. Where was Skinny going with this? Had skipping that step been a mistake?

Again, Slidell made that glitchy noise in his throat.

"I'm viewing a master file that I created. It contains a shot of each specimen," I said. Again defensive. "Would you like to see the whole series?"

"Yeah. Show me that." The terms "please" and "thank you" don't figure prominently in Skinny's lexicon.

I exited the current image and went to the chronologically earliest case. A date was penciled onto the associated ABFO ruler.

"So this asshole began his little hobby at least three years ago," Slidell mumbled under his breath. Then, to me, "Keep going."

More keystrokes, more images—frontal, lateral, and basal views of mammalian crania showing variations on a common evolutionary theme, the bones and dentition modified over eons for adaptation to varying niches. Before photography, each skull had been cleaned of the curious embellishments recently adorning it.

"The shitpot's going bigger." Again, Slidell seemed to be talking more to himself than to me.

"Sorry?" I asked, not sure of his meaning.

"Run back through. Check your ABFO thingy."

I did.

The skulls had been photographed full frame. Each was relatively small, so size differences weren't glaringly obvious in the close-ups.

But Slidell was right. Each skull in the series had come from an animal larger than its predecessor. MCME-701-25, which I guessed was from a canine of some sort, was the biggest so far.

"Do you think the increase in body size is significant?" I asked, basically reframing the question I'd asked about species.

"Hell if I know. Could mean the perp's getting bored. Could mean he's getting better at catching game. Could mean fuckall."

"Or maybe," I said slowly, considering an idea, "targeting bigger and bigger prey indicates an escalation in whatever twisted impulse drives the guy."

Slidell just looked at me.

"Maybe he needs increasingly larger kills to satisfy whatever fantasy he's acting out."

"Or maybe the sick bastard just hates animals," said Slidell.

"So he decorates their skulls, sticks feathers in their ears, and nails them to trees?" A bit strident on my part, but, as usual, Slidell was starting to annoy me. "Oh. And one other thing. I think the guy's keeping trophies."

"What does that mean?"

"Something's missing from each set of remains. You might ask why he'd do that."

"Sounds like a question for a shrink," he said.

I couldn't disagree with that.

We both fell silent as I rolled through the images a second time.

"Or maybe the bastard's got a hard-on for *certain* animals." Again, Slidell was thinking out loud.

"Might identifying species or breed of dog help nail the guy?"

"Couldn't hurt."

"I know a local veterinarian who does forensic consults," I said.

"Yeah? Who's that?"

"Ralph Balodis."

Slidell snorted, surpassing any volume Katy had ever achieved. "You talking about the guy down in Weddington?"

"I am." I didn't really *know* Balodis, had exchanged a few words with him at a charity event in Charlotte several years back. *You also do forensic work? You must know so-and-so?*— that sort of thing.

"Balodis won't do it," Slidell said.

"Why not?"

"The guy's a friggin' train wreck."

"What makes you say that?" Cool.

Slidell brought a thumb to his lips and pantomimed chugging from a bottle.

I said nothing.

"Way I got the story, Balodis screwed up and killed a horse," Slidell added. "Quit practicing and lives like a goddam hermit now."

"Balodis has a reputation in the forensic community as an excellent vet."

"The guy could be Doctor Doolittle, but he wants nothing to do with nobody."

"Fine," I said. "I'm about to change that." I resisted saying to Slidell what I was thinking.

What if the sicko creating these grisly displays decides animals don't satisfy anymore? What if the next kill is human?

CHAPTER 4

I left the MCME and hurried out to the parking lot. *Wheep-wheeped* the locks of my Mazda and slid behind the wheel.

Immediately shot forward.

The interior temp had to be at least 120 degrees, the vinyl seats double that. For the billionth time, I reminded myself to buy one of those windshield sunshades designed to keep a car cooler. Knew that once the AC kicked in, I wouldn't remember.

Recognizing that the drive to Weddington might take longer, but not wanting to divert out to the beltway, I decided to follow Providence Road, a city street, the full distance. Bad call. Cars and trucks clogged the lanes in both directions, slowing my progress and souring my mood.

As usual when jammed up in traffic, I thought about all the things I could be doing with the wasted time. Reports on the three sets of bones in my lab. Birdie's overdue checkup. Dirty laundry cramming my hamper.

Mostly, I thought about Ralfs Balodis. Ralph.

I'd met Balodis at an Allegro Foundation fundraiser. I was there with my husband Janis "Pete" Petersons, soon to be my ex. Sad but clichéd story involving his partying with women other than *moi*. Painful then, but time heals. Pete and I are on good terms now.

Pete and Balodis had spoken to each other in Latvian that evening, but I'd caught that they shared a connection through a camp both had attended as kids. As adults they'd maintained contact for a while, but

Pete went into law and Balodis became a vet. Their lives diverged. You know how that goes.

Over the years, I'd learned through Pete that Balodis operated a veterinary clinic in Weddington, one of Charlotte's southernmost burbs. That he'd married a woman named Marcia, maybe Marcy or Marve. That the marriage had ended after about three heartbeats. No kids.

My ex has made a lot of mistakes in his life. I guess I'm one of them. But Pete's a good guy. And a good judge of character. Though he disapproved of the switch from Ralfs to Ralph, he liked and trusted his fellow Latvian. We'd bumped into Balodis sporadically back in the day.

Weddington, once a sleepy southern town surrounded by farmland, was sucked into Charlotte's orbit as developers began casting their nets farther and farther south in search of buildable land. Today it's a mélange of parks and malls and churches and schools. Of McMansions and small tract homes. Of pools and jungle gyms in large backyards. Of shiny new SUVs in three-car garages and not-quite-late-model cars at curbs.

Forty minutes after setting out, I went left onto Sunset Hill Road, left again into a cluster of shops featuring a lot of red brick. Scrolly lettering on a sign indicated that Balodis's clinic, optimistically named Happy Tails, was located down a narrow strip of asphalt cutting between a dental office and a Bojangle's chicken joint.

I made the turn and twenty yards farther came to what looked like a modest two-story brick home topped by a satellite dish and fronted by a patch of asphalt marked with diagonal yellow lines. Closed blinds obscured what lay behind every window, up and down.

A doggy comfort station had been set up to the right of the asphalt. Artificial turf. Faux fire hydrant. Water bowls half full of what had to be very warm water. Nice touch.

After parking I got out and walked to the door. Philodendra in large ceramic crocks sat to both sides. The wood, though alligatored in places, had been freshly painted a bright Kelly green. The potted plants looked discouraged at having to compete.

A sign hung at eye level.

Sorry. We're Closed.

Below, in smaller font, a phone number accompanied the words: *For emergencies.*

Did my desire to speak with Balodis qualify?

No.

I dialed.

My call was answered after two rings.

Thank you for contacting Happy Tails. The clinic is closed until further notice. For urgent veterinary needs please phone Dr. Michaela Horowitz.

Another number followed that message.

I stood a moment, perspiring and considering options. Which seemed nonexistent.

Frustrated, I tapped a name on my Favorites list.

Pete answered with his usual affable greeting.

"Tempe, how's it going?"

"Sorry to bother you, Pete."

"No bother at all. It's always great to hear your voice."

"I've got an odd ask."

"Hit me."

"Do you remember Ralph Balodis?"

"What is this, a senility test? Ralph and I were cultural soulmates back in the day. You know, fellow patrons of the opera and ballet."

"More like the bars and beer joints."

"Tempe." Faux disappointment.

"Anyway, are you still in contact with Balodis?"

"I haven't spoken to Ralph in years."

"Do you have a phone number?"

"Probably. Hold on."

I waited as Pete scrolled through his contacts, my shirt now feeling like wet tissue wrapping my skin.

"Babe, you're in luck."

I entered the digits into my Notes app as Pete read them off.

"Last I knew, Ralph was living in an apartment above his clinic," Pete said. "The guy always had an inertia problem, so he probably still is."

I almost did a hand pump at hearing that.

"What's up?" Pete asked, undoubtedly curious about my desire to talk to a ghost from the past. To a guy who'd really been *his* friend, not mine.

Instead of answering, I asked, "Are you in Charlotte?"

"Pittsburgh. I'll be home tomorrow. Katy and I have a date for the Knights game Saturday."

"Sounds like fun."

"You're welcome to join—"

"That's so nice of you. But I already have plans."

"Another time."

"I'd like that."

"Take care of yourself, Tempe."

"You, too."

I disconnected.

Wondered. Had Good Time Pete sounded wistful?

More to the point, I wondered what to do now that I had Balodis's number.

Slidell said the vet had become an alcoholic. A recluse. Not using such a poetic term, of course.

Balodis had a reputation as a kind and caring doctor. I'd heard that back in the day he was an honest and conscientious forensic consultant. Why such a dramatic retreat from life?

Had the man suffered some trauma greater than that of losing a horse? Weren't animal deaths a sad part of every veterinary practice?

Could my request for Balodis's expertise function to reestablish his sense of self-worth? Could it help draw the man out of his funk?

Worth a shot.

And I did want his opinion on the bizarre animal carcasses arriving at my lab.

But how to approach him?

If I phoned and Balodis told me to take a hike, I couldn't then brazenly waltz up and ring his bell. If I appeared at his door unannounced, he might slam it in my face.

Despite the sign, I tried the clinic's main entrance. As expected, found it locked. Putting my nose to the glass, I saw that the waiting room was dark.

Deciding that it was better to annoy and apologize later than to be rejected in advance, I circled the building. Spotted a set of exterior stairs connecting a backyard patio to a second-story landing.

Again shielding my eyes from the sun, I scanned up the risers. At the top, beyond waist-high iron fencing surrounding a tiny porch, was a door leading into the rear of the house. Kelly green like the one at the front of the clinic.

Brushing sweat-damp bangs from my forehead, I drew one deep breath and began to climb. A bird who'd been vociferous about some victory or injustice went silent at the sound of my sneakers slapping the rubber runner covering the treads.

A button hung to the right of the door. I thumbed it. A muted buzz sounded deep inside the apartment.

Seconds later, a man posed the expected question, voice muted by the cheery green wood.

"Who's there?"

"Temperance Brennan."

The name was met with a very long pause. Balodis was either running through his mental Rolodex or formulating a reply to send me away. Maybe both.

"Tempe?" With an added frisson of apprehension. "Has something happened to Pete?"

"Pete's fine. But I need your help, Ralph. On a forensic case."

"I don't do—"

"I know you're retired, but this is important."

"I'm sorry but—"

"Some psycho is torturing and killing animals, then mutilating and displaying their corpses." I wasn't certain about the first half of that statement but needed something to hook Balodis.

"Oh my."

"May I come in so we can discuss it?"

I heard the *snick* of a deadbolt. Then the door swung inward.

I remembered Balodis as, well, unmemorable. Not tall, not short. Average build. Brown eyes. Mousy hair. The only thing notable were his enormous "what-me-worry?" ears, appendages that made one wonder how the man fared in strong winds.

Balodis was still in there somewhere. Same features. Less hair and more forehead. But the man standing before me was a mere remnant of his former self.

His face was gaunt, his shoulders so rounded it took two inches from his height. His frame was hung with the minimum amount of musculature needed for upright posture and ambulation.

I hid my surprise. I think.

"Hey, Ralph. Sorry to barge in like this."

Ralph dipped his overly prominent chin, then stepped back.

I entered. After closing the door, he led me down a short hall to a surprisingly roomy parlor.

At his direction, I sat on the sofa. Balodis remained standing.

"Would you like something to drink? Coffee? Soda?"

"Water would be good," I said.

Balodis disappeared back into the hall, heading, I presumed, to a kitchen. In seconds, I heard the *whoosh* of a refrigerator door, then ice rattling against glass.

I looked around.

In addition to the sofa cushioning my butt, the room held two armchairs, all three upholstered in a burgundy-and-green floral print. The side and coffee tables were blond, probably oak. I guessed the last updating of decor had taken place sometime in the sixties.

Framed pictures crowded the top of a sideboard by the far wall. I was idly scanning the collection when one image caught my attention.

Two men stood holding hands facing each other in front of an altar. They wore corsages in their lapels and gold bands on their fourth fingers. Ringman, we'd called the digit as kids.

Beyond the couple, a preacher clutched a Bible and beamed her approval. Above them curved an arch made of flowers. It was a classic wedding shot.

The man on the right was Ralph Balodis.

Clarification of the implosion of marriage number one?

My gaze was still lingering on the photo when I heard a throat clear.

I turned.

Balodis didn't say a word. Just watched me.

"It's a lovely picture," I said.

"His name was Michael Fielding. We were married a very short time."

I waited, hoping he'd reveal more. He didn't.

"Was?" I queried his use of the past tense.

"Michael died four years ago. Cryptococcal meningitis."

"I'm so sorry."

Balodis's withdrawal from life made sense now. It wasn't because of a dead horse. It was due to the loss of his partner.

As usual in situations of heightened emotion, I didn't know what to say. Though I empathize with the sorrow of others, I'm lousy at expressing condolence or comfort.

Didn't matter. Balodis was already moving on.

After handing me the glass of ice and a bottle of Evian, the vet sat in one of the flowery chairs and said, "You say someone is disfiguring animals."

I told him the whole ugly story.

He listened without interrupting.

"This abuse is still going on?"

"Yes," I said.

"What would you have me do?"

"We'd like you to examine each kill. For the earlier ones you'll have to work from photos."

"The goal being?"

"To determine exact species or breed and note anything of significance."

A deep inhalation, out through his nose.

"Yes. I will do this."

We were halfway down the stairs when my iPhone buzzed in my pocket. I pulled it out and checked caller ID, hoping it was Ryan. It was Slidell.

I answered, suspecting the conversation wouldn't be pleasant. And the news wouldn't be good.

I was right on both counts.

CHAPTER 5

As expected, Slidell skipped any of the greetings typically used to open phone conversations.

"They found another goddam dog. *Maybe* a dog."

"Good afternoon, detective." In the background, I heard the soft sputter of a police scanner with the volume turned low. Beyond the static, muted traffic sounds. I assumed Skinny was in his car.

Slidell offered one of his guttural non-responses.

"I hope your day is going well," I said, chipper as Mr. Rogers.

"I spent the last two hours risking a stroke standing out in this freakin' heat. So, we gonna waste time chewing the fat, or you wanna listen?"

Having reached the bottom tread, I stepped onto the patio and moved off a few feet, making room for Balodis, who was clomping down behind me.

"Go on," I said.

"The nine one one came in around noon. A counselor from an outfit called Thundercloud or Thunderclap or something."

"Thunderbird? The YMCA camp outside the entrance to River Hills?"

As a preteen, Katy had spent parts of her summers at Thunderbird, grooming horses and sweeping shit from their stalls. Riding them, too, I assume. Currently, my best friend, Anne, lived in River Hills, a lakeside community down the road from the camp.

"Yeah. That's it," Slidell said. "The kid, Huggy Ronstall—who the hell goes by Huggy? Anyway, Ronstall was out in the woods hiking or smoking weed or whatever it is those nitwits do and came across what he thought was a human body. He went home, considered his options, then dimed it."

I heard the pop of a plastic water bottle being gripped too tightly. Waited out the glugging as Slidell rehydrated.

"The captain had me listen to the audio. The mope sounded like he expected to see his face on *Dateline* for nabbing the next Charlie Manson."

"Ronstall seemed believable?" I prompted, hot and sticky and wanting to wrap this up and get into my air-conditioned car.

Slidell ignored my question.

"The case being of subterranean priority, the assignment fell to yours truly. I got the pleasure of schlepping out to south bejeezus."

A bee, maybe attracted by the scent of my rose hips shampoo, maybe by the earthy reek of my sweat, began circling my head. I batted it away with my free hand.

"Ronstall was right, and he was wrong." I heard rhythmic clicking, figured Skinny had activated his turn signal. "His fifteen-minutes-of-fame discovery was a headless corpse, all right. But it wasn't human."

"He'd found a decapitated animal."

"Give the lady a cigar."

"I assume the scene was processed properly?"

"I knew you'd ask that, what with this sicko beautifying the county with parts of Fido and Lassie."

"And?"

"We took videos and stills and the techs collected everything that looked suspicious. I did the overseeing. Which was about as much fun as fuc—"

"Where are the remains now?"

"Making their way to the morgue."

"Thanks, detective. You did good."

Not at all sure that he had.

The Mecklenburg County Medical Examiner used to be housed in uptown Charlotte, an easy ten-minute drive from the Annex. The facility is now located farther out on Reno Avenue, so the trip from Weddington took almost an hour.

That's where my mind was. Tallying lost minutes like a taximeter tallies up miles.

Anyway, it was after four by the time I pulled in behind the building, a featureless box with all the architectural whimsy of a Stalinist apartment block. One upside. The structure is surrounded by enough asphalt to pave Cincinnati, so I lost no time searching for a parking place.

I killed the engine, and we got out of my car.

Yeah, we. To my surprise, Balodis had offered to accompany me.

During the trip, I'd explained that the cops were now involved in investigating the animal killings. Balodis nodded sadly, then asked if the lab would allow him access to a laptop and scanner.

Assuring him those items would be available, I asked why they might be needed. He responded with a single word. "Chip."

My car's AC tries hard but often fails to live up to its job description. Nevertheless, emerging from the semi-cooled auto interior was like entering a plasma field around a black hole. Heat rose from the pavement in rippling waves, creating the illusion that my sneakers were underwater.

The lot held few vehicles that late in the day. An ancient black Chevy suggested that Joe Hawkins, the oldest of the death investigators, was still clocked in. Nguyen's Volvo was nowhere to be seen.

Balodis and I mounted a few stairs and entered the eco-friendly brick building through centrally positioned doors and crossed to a reception window on the left. A woman, aptly named Mrs. Flowers, beamed us all the way to the glass. Her over-bleached hair was permed into curls tight enough to cushion the reentry of a Titan 2 missile. Her teeth weren't great.

Mrs. Flowers had been a fixture at the MCME for as long as I'd worked there. When first we'd met, I'd guessed that she was pushing sixty. The severe perm. The wonky dentition. Actually, she hadn't yet closed out her forties.

Of late, Mrs. Flowers was in what I thought of as her "blush" phase. Today's cardigan was a shade of pink that matched the rosy flamingos in her shirtwaist dress. Her nails featured a polish probably named Miami Beach Sunset.

"Dr. Brennan." Vowels broader than grits and pecan pie. "What a lovely surprise."

"Something came up unexpectedly."

"Involving another unfortunate pooch?"

"Mm."

"My goodness, it's hot out today."

"It is," I agreed.

Mrs. Flowers's eyes drifted to Balodis. Returned to me.

I asked what number had been assigned to my new case.

The Beach Sunset nails worked a keyboard.

"MCME-727-25."

"Joe is still here?"

"He is, but I believe he's preparing to depart."

Of course he was. Joe Hawkins was like a German train. He arrived every morning at precisely 6:50, left every afternoon at precisely 4:20. Had for decades.

"Could you phone and ask Joe to bring the remains to room four?"

"Certainly. Shall I register your guest?"

"Please."

Balodis provided ID and was issued a pass saying *VISITOR* in large block letters.

"You attach it to your shirt with that little clippy thingy," Mrs. Flowers offered with a flick of one manicured finger. In case Balodis couldn't figure out the obvious.

"You two just come on in."

I scanned my badge and the lock buzzed. Balodis followed me through.

We crossed into a small vestibule and continued through a second set of doors. To the left was Mrs. Flowers's command post and four work carrels. To the right, groupings of upholstered furniture and wooden tables. Magazines. Plastic plants. The universal waiting room motif. At that moment, no one was waiting.

Behind Mrs. Flowers's desk was a mountain range of gray filing cabinets. Opposite the cabinets, on the far wall, hung an erasable board divided into a grid.

Numbers and dates filled some of the grid's cells, the digit-letter combinations representing suicides, homicides, accidents, flukes. Deaths that had earned tickets to Y-incisions.

One corpse had been designated MCME-727-25. The letters *NH-B* had been penned beside that. *Nonhuman. Brennan.*

The MCME went digital years ago. Every case is now entered into the computer system upon intake, every detail added to the file as the cold process of death examination unfolds. Still, Nguyen keeps the old-style display. Explains that she likes eyeballing the visual summary every day upon her arrival. I do, too.

I showed Balodis the door to the men's locker room, then proceeded to the smaller one reserved for women. Minutes later we reconvened in the hall, both suited up in surgical scrubs.

Room four was as I'd left it the day before. With one exception.

A different black plastic bag lay on a different gurney. The bulge it contained was significantly larger than the one created by yesterday's Frog Pond skull.

I dictated the basics. Marked an ABFO ruler. Took the standard pics.

Balodis waited, face neutral, arms crossed on his chest. His body language suggested anxiety, but I hadn't a clue what the man was thinking.

Preliminaries completed, I gloved and withdrew a pair of scissors from a drawer.

"Ready?" I asked.

Balodis nodded.

Raising my mask to my face, I cut the plastic and spread the segments flat, exactly as I had the day before. It felt like Bill Murray's *Groundhog Day,* except for two differences.

One, Balodis was there peering over my shoulder.

Two, the stench of putrefaction was as powerful as any odor I've ever encountered. It caused my eyes to burn and my breath to catch in my throat.

Behind me, I heard Balodis inhale sharply.

I stared at the thing I'd exposed, considering how to describe it.

For a full minute, I dictated nothing.

Then I began.

"The remains are those of a headless quadrupedal male mammal, probably a dog.

"The coat is wavy and of medium length. Though matted and blood-caked, the color appears to be a solid chocolate brown.

"Both forelimbs and the left hindlimb terminate in claw-tipped paws.

"The right hindlimb is missing distal to the mid-femur.

"The claws are densely black and appear to have been mechanically ground down.

"The tail is short—"

"It's a spaniel," Balodis said. "Probably a Boykin."

"You're sure?"

"On the spaniel part, yes. As to the Boykin, this dog's body is longer and rangier than that of a Cocker, and more compact than that of a Springer. I'd estimate the animal weighed around forty pounds and stood about sixteen inches at the shoulder."

"Measurements consistent with yesterday's Frog Pond skull?"

"Absolutely. As are the color and length of the coat."

Before I could respond, Balodis stepped forward and lifted the left hind limb for my inspection

"Look at the paws. See that slight webbing between the toes?"

"I do."

"Boykins were bred to work in lakes and swamps. That webbing allows them to swim well."

"Bred by whom?"

"Waterfowl and wild turkey hunters down in South Carolina. For years nobody outside the state knew about Boykins. Now the world loves the breed because they make great pets."

"You think this dog had an owner."

"Its nails have been trimmed."

"Meaning someone had him groomed."

Balodis crossed to the counter, on which a tech had placed a scanner. The thing was about three inches wide and six inches long, white, with a round antenna at one end, a screen and orange buttons below on the handle.

When powered up, the screen offered four options: *Scan; View History; Clear Records; Upload.* Choosing the first, Balodis ran the gadget in a slow, S-shaped pattern over the dog's upper body, just tailward of the putrid tissue edging the truncated neck.

I know how scanners work; still Balodis felt compelled to explain. Sensing the man was firing on nervous energy, I let him talk.

"A microchip is a small glass tube roughly the size of a rice grain that functions as a tiny transponder. When its radio waves are picked up by a scanner, the chip is activated and transmits an identification number, which is displayed on the scanner's screen. We'll know we've hit pay dirt if we hear a beep."

Nothing.

Balodis moved down each of the dog's front legs.

"That would be an odd place for insertion," I said.

"Indeed, it would. Microchips are implanted directly under the skin, usually between the shoulder blades. But the little buggers often migrate."

The words had barely left his lips when the scanner gave off a high little chirp. Balodis raised the device to his eyes.

"Bingo."

"This is a first," I said.

"So you *are* familiar with the technology?"

"Actually, we did scan the others."

"Forgive my mansplaining, then. None of the other displayed animals had chips?"

"Nope."

Balodis turned the scanner so I could see. A nine-digit sequence filled the screen.

Opening his laptop, Balodis brought up a website called *Petmicrochiplookup.org,* entered the number, and checked a list. Shifting to one of dozens of registry sites, *AKCreunite.org,* he input the number again.

"Bingo bingo!" Stepping back to allow me a better view.

The dog's name was Bear. His color was brown. His gender was male. As suspected, his breed was Boykin Spaniel.

Bear's owner was a guy named Crawford Joye. Joye lived on Archdale Drive in Charlotte.

"Good God in heaven."

I turned.

Balodis's right hand covered his mouth. All color had drained from his face.

"What?" I asked, surprised at such strong emotion.

"I know that man."

"Crawford Joye?"

Balodis nodded. "Joye's a cigar smoker. I met him through a group that gathers at McCranies."

"The pipe shop at Park Road Shopping Center."

Balodis nodded again.

"What's his story?"

"He's a lawyer. A solo practitioner, as I recall. Does mostly divorce work. That's about all I know."

"Were you aware that Joye had a dog?"

"He never spoke of a pet."

I was considering that when my gaze fell on an irregularity in Bear's neck. Unnoticed until now, the dark cleft seemed wrong amid the ravaged flesh.

Using one gloved finger, I palpated, then probed the small hollow.

Sonofabitch

I knew what had happened to Bear.

CHAPTER 6

The bullet looked dark and deadly in my gloved palm.

Questions ricocheted in my brain.

Had Crawford Joye killed and decapitated his own dog?

Was Joye the person mutilating and displaying animals throughout the region?

Why?

"Some bastard shot this good boy."

Balodis's voice brought me back.

"Is Joye capable of doing this?" I gestured at the headless corpse on the table.

Balodis's shoulders rose, dropped.

"Who knows?"

The Archdale address was in Montclaire, a residential neighborhood behind the Park Road Shopping Center. The house, like most lining the street, was a flat-roofed, single-story affair. Its brick exterior, once red, was painted white. Probably built on the cheap back in the sixties, the place would now be marketed by realtors as midcentury modern.

I pulled to the curb. Balodis and I got out and followed a walkway bisecting a browned-out lawn. On the small porch, two Adirondack chairs flanked a smokeless bonfire pit, the kind you buy at Costco to make s'mores when camping.

Three steps connected the walk to a concrete stoop. The off-center front door was gray and had six small square windows stacked on the right. A sticker affixed to the uppermost said *No Soliciting.*

We mounted the stairs. Balodis waited as I thumbed the bell.

A single *bong* sounded deep inside.

No one spoke up. No one appeared.

I rang again.

"Yes, yes, yes. I'm here." Though muted, the voice was obviously male, its owner obviously annoyed.

Locks clicked, then the door cracked open a few inches. A manicured finger jabbed at the sticker.

"Do you not see that sign? Are you unable to read English?"

"Am I speaking to Crawford Joye?" I asked, flashing what I hoped was an engaging smile.

"No solicitors!"

"I'm not a salesman."

"Good. Go away."

"We've—"

"Get lost."

Screw engaging. I cut to the chase.

"Do you own a spaniel named Bear?"

"What?" Sharp with surprise.

"We think we've found your dog, sir."

A beat, then the door swung inward a few more inches.

A man stood in the widened gap, fingers gripping the outer edge of the wood. I guessed his height at six feet, his weight at maybe one-forty.

The man's eyes were a startling cornflower blue that eclipsed every other feature on his pallid face. Thin lips and nose. Weak jaw ending in a pointy chin. Wispy blond hair in swift retreat from an unnaturally smooth forehead.

"You have Bear?"

"We think so, sir."

"Thank God!" With a smile so big it split the unimpressive face in two.

Lifting his chin, Joye craned to look past us, cerulean eyes scanning the windows of my car.

As a member of countless death investigation teams, I'd performed that moment's task far too often, delivering news that would usher in pain, perhaps change a life forever. The job never got easy.

Even if the tidings concerned a pet.

"My name is Dr. Temperance Brennan," I began, as gently as I could. "I work for the Mecklenburg County Medical Examiner."

"Where's Bear? Where's my dog?"

"I'm afraid I have bad news, sir."

Joye's eyes whipped back to mine. For a moment he said nothing. Then, reading the signs, he mumbled,

"Bear is dead."

"I'm so sorry."

"You're sure it's Bear?"

"We found an implanted chip identifying the dog as yours."

"Yes. I had that done."

Joye's jaw tensed as the significance of my self-introduction wormed through his grief.

"The medical examiner. Like, the coroner?"

"Yes."

"Why would the coroner care about a dead dog?"

"May we come in, sir?"

"Who's he?" Joye chin-cocked Balodis.

"Dr. Balodis is a veterinarian," I said, surprised that Joye didn't recall the man from their cigar-smoking days. Assumed it was due to the vet's altered appearance.

A moment of hesitation, then Joye stepped back.

Balodis and I entered a postage stamp foyer. A framed mirror hung on the wall to the right. A bench with a hinged seat occupied the space to the left.

Pegs ran in a row above the bench, three of the four holding canine paraphernalia. A leash. A harness. A cable-knit sweater with the name *Bear* embroidered across its turtleneck collar.

Joye led us down a narrow hall to a kitchen at the rear of the house. Pointed to a pine table with four matching chairs.

Balodis and I sat. Our host remained standing, arms crossed on his chest.

"I should offer you something." Delivered with zero enthusiasm.

"We're good, sir."

Joye drew one breath.

"Okay," he said tonelessly. "Give it to me straight."

"Tuesday, an elderly woman found canine remains near the town of Frog Pond."

I studied Joye's reaction as I spoke, alert for any sign suggesting involvement in the atrocity. I knew Balodis was doing the same.

"Big fellow, long wavy brown coat?" he asked for verification.

"Yes, sir. I'm so sorry. I know how hard it is to lose a pet."

"Bear's a great dog." Joye was barely audible now. "He likes long walks. We took one on Tuesday."

"In Park Road Park?"

"Yes. Bear loves going there." Joye's chest gave an involuntary hitch. "Loved going there."

"You and Bear came to be separated?"

Joye nodded. "It's my fault. Bear prefers to run off-leash. Occasionally, when few people are around, I allow him to do so. That day, we were alone on the trail."

Joye's expression moved through a range emotions. Sorrow? Guilt? Regret?

Balodis and I waited a full thirty seconds for him to continue.

"It was never a problem. Bear would dart off into the woods, chasing a squirrel or a rabbit, the way dogs do. But he always came back when I whistled. For some reason, he didn't. I searched for hours, whistling and calling his name."

"Did you report the dog missing?"

"Seriously?" With a derisive snort.

Joye had a point. A lost dog would hardly top a police priority list.

"Then what happened, sir?"

"I finally gave up. Figured I'd either get a call from some Samaritan, or Bear would find his way home."

"Would you like the ME to handle the disposal of—"

"What happened to him? Was it a car? A coyote? Did he swim too far out and drown in the lake?"

"He was shot."

Joye flinched as though slapped.

"That dog didn't have a mean bone in his body. Who would do such a thing?"

"We don't know."

Then the question I'd been expecting.

"Who found him?"

I slid a sideways glance toward Balodis. The vet's gaze met mine, quickly dropped to the hands folded in his lap.

The subtle exchange didn't go unnoticed.

"What?" Joye's eyes flicked from me to Balodis and back. "What is it you're not telling me?"

Sharing the minimum amount of detail, I described the circumstances surrounding the discovery of Bear's remains. The wrapped and decorated head nailed to the oak outside Frog Pond. The decapitated corpse discarded in the woods near Camp Thunderbird.

Joye listened, face growing harder with each particular.

"Where's Frog Pond?" he asked when I'd finished.

"Stanly County."

"How the blazes did Bear get all the way out there?"

"We don't know, sir."

"This is so messed up."

"It is," I agreed.

"Where's my dog now?"

"I don't—"

"Where. Is. My. Dog." Staring at me hard.

"At the morgue."

"I want to collect the body for burial. Him. Collect him."

Sweat dampened Joye's hairline, and a wide crescent darkened each of his pits. I was suddenly aware of the man's BO. Of the rage he was struggling to suppress.

"Of course," I said.

"Do the authorities have any idea who shot him?"

"Not yet. But the situation is under investigation."

"This was murder, you know. Pure and simple. But the victim's just an animal, so the police won't give a crap."

"That's not true. I know the detective assigned to Bear's case."

"CMPD?"

"Yes." Sort of.

"Why would the cops care who killed my dog?"

I chose my words carefully.

"Bear's death is not an isolated incident."

"What do you mean?"

"Other animal corpses have been treated in a similar manner."

"Dogs?"

"No. Bear is the first."

Silent throughout the interview, Balodis spoke up for the first time. "Mr. Joye, do you have any idea who might have harmed your pet?"

"Are you asking do I have enemies?"

"Do you?"

"I'm a divorce attorney. Rarely do both parties walk away happy. Often neither does."

"Has anyone been exceptionally angry with you of late?"

Joye thought about that. At least appeared to.

"This past year I represented the wife of a man named Jerome Sunday."

Joye stopped, perhaps considering the ethical implications of disclosing privileged information.

"Go on," Balodis urged.

"What the hey. Sunday wasn't *my* client. And the man was a real piece of work."

"Explain that, please."

"I'll give you one example. At the close of proceedings, Sunday swaggered up and put his face this close to mine." Joye held a thumb and index finger two inches apart. "Promised to sever my balls with a hacksaw and shove them down my throat. A poet he wasn't."

"Do you think Sunday is capable of violence?" I asked.

"Aren't we all if pushed hard enough?"

"Do any other possibilities come to mind?"

"How about I send over a list."

"That would be helpful."

"Keep me looped in?" Joye asked as Balodis and I rose to leave.

"You have my word," I said. "And, again, I'm sorry about Bear."

We were at the front door when Joye made a request that seemed out of character.

"Do me a solid?" His eyes were neon lasers on mine.

"I'll try," I said.

"Find who did this to Bear."

"As I said—"

"Kill the fucker."

CHAPTER 7

Arriving home a little past six, I showered, then slipped into a sundress and sandals. After gathering my hair into a wet bun, I slapped on lipstick, then hurried downstairs. Surprised by the sound of voices, I diverted to the kitchen.

Loitering there were Katy and Ruthie, who'd swung by the Annex hoping to cajole me into joining them for dinner at Southern Pecan followed by a movie. I begged off, saying truthfully that I already had plans to meet with a friend.

A ten-minute drive brought me to a Japanese restaurant featuring open cooking on robata and yakitori grills. Not my first choice. No matter what I ordered, it seemed my bill always came to two hundred dollars.

But the food was good. And I'd told my dinner companion she should feel free to book anywhere.

Hot damn! I scored a parking place right by the door. Stepping from the early-evening brightness into the restaurant's cool, dim interior was like crossing from a sun-drenched beach into an underground cavern.

A cavern with a vigilant gatekeeper. Before my eyes could adjust to the lack of ambient light, a voice welcomed me and asked if I had a reservation.

Blinking, I picked out a face in the darkness. Below the face, a white ceramic cat on a bamboo-fronted counter.

The face belonged to a blond woman with blue eyes and skin as melanin challenged as the fur on the cat. No name tag, but I'd have pegged her as an Astrid, not a Mitsuki.

I introduced myself and answered in the affirmative. Mitsuki-Astrid smiled and ran a lacquered nail down a list. Frowned.

"I'm so sorry. Could the booking be under another name?"

"Try Kumar."

"Of course. How lovely. The lady is already seated."

Entering the main dining area, which held maybe twelve tables and a row of booths along one wall, I spotted a woman waving from a far corner. I wove my way through the room to join her.

"Dr. Temperance Brennan," she said with a playful sing-song cadence.

"Dr. Adina Kumar," I sing-songed back while sliding onto the bench seat opposite hers.

What to say about my dinner companion?

Adina Kumar isn't exactly beautiful. Her nose is a bit large, her eyes deeply shadowed and set too close together. But I've noticed that men straighten and stand taller in her presence. Maybe it's her five-foot-eleven height. Maybe her soldier-on-parade posture.

More important than her appearance is Adina's brain. Her work has appeared in every major periodical in her field. *The American Journal of Psychology. The Journal of Applied Psychology. Frontiers in Psychology.* Though these publications don't exactly fly off the bookstore shelves at the mall, her inclusion in their pages is a testimonial to her brilliance.

Adi and I were Best Friends Forever in high school. Went our separate ways in college, married, divorced. Well, she did. Neither Pete nor I ever bothered with paperwork. Several years back she and I discovered that we'd both ended up in Charlotte. One coffee, and the friendship had rekindled as though uninterrupted.

The two of us met monthly now, for lunch or dinner depending on our schedules. Sometimes we discussed our professional lives. A patient that worried her. Bones that troubled me. We'd each listen to the other, on rare occasions offer input. Some was useful. Most wasn't. It was the airing of concerns, not the advice, that helped keep us both sane.

More often, we talked about mundane matters. Our kids—she had two, both doctors living out of state. Movies, books, clothes, hair disasters. Now and then, sex. Some of Adina's anecdotes were as funny as anything in the history of comedy.

"So. What's up in the world of putrefied flesh?" she asked after we'd ordered drinks and edamame and exchanged some small talk.

"My job involves more than decomposed bodies," I responded, feigning offense.

"Right. I forgot the incinerated."

I rolled my eyes. "Do we really want to go there?"

"I plan to share the story of a man who eats his wife's feces."

"What's wrong with his own?" I asked.

"He prefers hers."

"Revolting, but not exactly evil."

"Ah, evil. What *is* evil?"

"Yeah," I said. "Let's talk about that. How do psychologists define evil?"

"An evil act or an evil person?"

"You pick."

"The former is easier."

"Go with that."

Adina shelled, then popped another bean into her mouth. Chewed, taking time to organize her thoughts.

"First—remember these are just *my* views."

"Jesus, Adi. You're not on the stand."

"First, the act must be truly horrific."

"Like kidnapping and torturing a child."

"I think everyone would agree that qualifies as evil. Second, the act must be intentional."

"Malice aforethought." I used the legal expression.

"Yes. The act must be preceded by some degree of planning."

"Not triggered by sudden emotion, like jealousy or rage. In other words, the violence isn't impulsive."

"Exactly," she agreed. "When did you complete your psych degree?"

"Yeah, yeah." I circled a wrist for her to continue.

"Third, the level of suffering inflicted must be extreme."

An image of Bear flashed in my brain. Mercifully, he'd been shot.

"Finally, the nature of the act must seem inexplicable."

"Incomprehensible to normal people," I said.

She nodded. "Beyond what the average Joe can imagine or understand."

"The average Joe." I picked up on her phrase. "Do you believe that the ordinary person is capable of this type of premeditated violence?"

"Many violent acts are committed by the mentally ill. Nevertheless"—she raised a finger to emphasize her point—"I'd give that a yes."

"What do you mean by the 'mentally ill'?" I hooked air quotes around her words.

"Persons with psychosis."

I looked a question at her.

"Those with schizophrenia, which primarily affects thought processes, and those with manic depression, which primarily affects mood."

"It seems the term 'psychosis' covers pretty broad territory."

"Indeed. It's kind of a catchall for any condition that disturbs one's grip on reality."

Our food arrived, tempura and sushi platters. We fell into a companionable silence as we dipped and ate.

Adina broke it.

"Don't get the wrong impression, Tempe. Most mentally ill people go their whole lives never hurting anyone."

"Are you and your colleagues able to predict who among the mentally ill might become violent?"

"There are known risk factors."

"Such as?"

Adina thought a moment. "Command hallucinations."

"Hearing voices that urge violent acts."

"Yes. Also, delusions of persecution."

"Thinking someone is out to cause them harm."

Adina ticked off points on her fingers. Which were sticky from handling the nigiri.

"Fantasies of revenge. Alcohol or drug abuse. Paranoia. Antisocial behavior. A history of violence. The recent purchase of a weapon or camouflage gear."

She froze in mid-tick and her dark eyes narrowed. "What gives? Are you dealing with someone who fits the bill?"

"Maybe."

"Spill."

"Okay," I said. "You asked for it."

I told her about the animal remains being found nailed to trees. The pilfered body parts. Finished with the most recent case, Bear.

She was quiet for a very long moment. When she spoke again her tone was grim.

"Let me tell you about John. Not his real name, of course. I interviewed John as part of my thesis research. Unimposing guy, looked like anyone's uncle.

"John had a normal upbringing. His father was strict, but not abusive, his mother timid and unassertive. Early on, John began exhibiting troubling behavior."

"Troubling?"

"In lower school he started setting fires and torturing animals."

"Always endearing qualities in a kid."

"He'd capture random pets, kill them, then bury their bodies in his backyard."

"Must have made him popular with the neighbors."

"It gets worse. Though John dated in his teens, his peers described him as creepy. He abused drugs, especially grass and LSD. He was impotent. A high school psychologist thought he had serious issues but stopped short of recommending hospitalization.

"John grew more bizarre as he moved into his twenties. He lost interest in his appearance. He nailed his pantry door shut, thinking aliens were living behind the shelves. He presented at hospital ERs with strange complaints. Once, he said that his right lung had been stolen. On several occasions, he claimed his heart had stopped beating. Though he lived with his mother, he repeatedly insisted that he was being poisoned.

"Thinking his impotence was due to insufficient blood, John drank that of the animals he killed. He'd catch rabbits, eviscerate them, and eat their innards raw. He tortured dogs, cats, squirrels, even a horse.

"Eventually, John escalated to murdering and disemboweling humans, at first women and children, since they were easier prey. Ultimately, grown men. He'd shoot some, stab others. He'd cut the nipples from some and stuffed them into the vics' mouths."

"Doing his vampire thing in hopes of curing his sexual dysfunction." I couldn't keep the disgust from my voice. Didn't really try. "Did John rape his victims?"

"Not always. And in those cases, only after the victim was dead."

"So these weren't considered classic serial sexual homicides," I guessed.

"True."

We stopped talking as the server cleared our dishes and brought tea.

"Murder and necrophilia," I said, when she'd gone. "John's behavior would probably classify as evil in anyone's mind. But what's your point?"

Adina bunched and tossed her napkin onto her place mat. Leaned back and asked a question that had occurred to me, too.

"Though seemingly not sexual in nature—nonhuman vics, no posing of the body, no semen present, et cetera—could there be a sexual *component* to your animal displays?"

"Nothing's off the table."

"You should mention the possibility to the detective working the case."

"I will."

I would. Despite knowing Slidell's tendency to become channeled on theories that appealed to his narrow view of human nature.

"Though I suspect Slidell will be contacting you directly," I added.

"Happy day."

We exchanged wry smiles.

"One other thought," Adina said after a pause. "Driven by some sick perversion or not, from what you've said, your doer is escalating, I suspect."

"His prey are getting larger."

"Which means he's growing bolder."

"Or more skilled."

"Or that," she agreed.

I felt a low buzz in my chest. My friend agreed with the unsettling suggestion I'd made in my conversation with Slidell. My friend with a doctorate in psychology from Harvard University.

"Shall we thirty-second volley this dolt?"

Adina referred to a sparring game we often played, a shotgun back-and-forth using the known facts of a case.

"You start," I said.

"The perp is a psychopath driven by feelings of inadequacy and rage."

"By a sense of powerlessness in controlling factors in his life."

"That powerlessness makes him angry."

"But he *can* control animals, so he takes that anger out on them," I said.

"Or *she* does."

I raised a palm, acknowledging Adina's correction, the same one I'd made to Slidell. "For some reason, that feeling of powerlessness is escalating."

"The perp sees life spinning out of control."

"Might this nutcase follow a trajectory similar to John's?" I asked.

"Nutcase. Nice gender-neutral term."

"Thank you."

"My professional opinion?" Adina floated both brows.

I nodded.

"That's already happening."

"Do you think he or she might move up to humans?"

"I believe that's highly likely."

A moment, then the shadowed eyes locked onto mine.

"If this 'nutcase,' as you call him, isn't stopped, I fear people may die."

CHAPTER 8

While driving home, I phoned Slidell, not really expecting him to pick up.

He did.

"Yo."

"It's Tempe."

"Yeah? A name's helpful. You know, 'cause I don't have caller ID or nothin'."

Ignoring the sarcasm, I relayed the gist of my conversation with Adina Kumar.

Slidell listened, now and then interjecting some quaint Skinnyism. At one point, I thought I heard a woman's voice in the background.

When I'd finished, he let loose with a particularly colorful reference to a duck and its mother, the vehemence of which startled me. I braced, expecting the usual blow off to follow.

"You're talking about that psychologist chick?"

"Dr. Kumar."

"You think she's solid?"

"I do. She asked a lot of good questions. Especially about the earlier cases for which I had no pics." The cases for which my approach had been a bit cavalier. Not human? No big deal.

"Like what?" Slidell pressed.

I had to think a moment.

"Like, how far from a drivable road were the remains located? Were they positioned for easy viewing? Was there a pattern to the way the bodies were displayed? Which parts were removed?"

"Go on."

"She also asked about the places from which the animals went missing."

"Not sure we've got that intel."

"We know about Bear."

I waited out a round of nasal breathing. Then, Slidell surprised me.

"CSU's been all over the spot that dog was *found*. Maybe Kumar's onto something. Maybe we should go at it ass back ways. Scope out the place the dog *disappeared*."

"I'm in," I said.

My first surprise. Slidell pulled up at the Annex at exactly seven a.m., the agreed time.

The weather hadn't cooled. If anything, the heat and humidity had upped their game. My outdoor thermometer already read eighty-two degrees.

I hurried out and slid into the passenger side of Skinny's Chevy Trailblazer. The AC was in polar ice cap mode, blasting air cold enough to goose-bump my arms.

Slidell's company usually brings with it a range of odoriferous delights, the particular mix depending on his prior engagement. A night of surveillance followed by a skipped morning shower. A lunch of pastrami with garlic kraut. A beer in a joint that, forget health regs, still allowed smoking.

My second surprise. That morning, Skinny smelled as flowery as the cologne section in a Sephora. His hair was parted hard on the right and slicked into a greasy swirl on top. His shirt, a madras plaid that looked like an escapee from the sixties, was pressed into creases sharp enough to make surgical incisions.

Though curious, I made no comment on his appearance.

We exchanged our usual effusive greetings.

"Doc."

"Detective."

"Another scorcher."

"It will be."

"Park Road Park?"

"That's where Joye said Bear disappeared."

Skinny's jaw muscles bunched, and his fingers tightened on the wheel. I wondered the source of such agitation. Made no comment on that, either.

Traffic ground to a halt two blocks back from the light at Woodlawn Road.

"What the hell."

"It's morning rush hour," I said, unnecessarily.

"They can rush this up my sweet cheeks." Skinny flipped a bird to no one in particular.

I didn't bother to reply.

Minutes dragged by.

Five.

Ten.

Skinny drummed a staccato beat on the wheel.

Sliding my phone from my shoulder bag, I skimmed my email. Two items had landed in my inbox since last I'd checked. That day's *New York Times* crossword puzzle and a politician's plea for money.

I saved the former, deleted the latter.

"You submit all those goo-gaws from this latest mutt?"

"Sent to the crime lab and waiting in the queue."

"Don't guess an animal hit will get high priority."

"Don't guess it will."

I was pondering a four-letter word for *pouch* when Skinny surprised me with another stab at conversation.

"You still seeing Monsieur le stud?" Pronounced "miss-your."

"His name is Ryan." Skinny knew that. In fact, despite all odds, the two men had become friends. Of a sort. "And yes, I am."

"How's that work, him being from the North Pole and all?"

"He lives in Montreal."

"Yeah, like I said."

"We take turns flying back and forth."

"Guess that makes for sizzling *bone-jour* nookie." I doubted Skinny was clever enough to realize his pun.

Didn't matter. No way would I discuss my sex life with him.

"Your niece still around?" he asked, after another round of silence.

"Ruthie. She's mostly staying with Katy."

"The kid's how old now? Ten? Twelve?"

"Seventeen."

"Time sure as shit flies. I remember when she was a scrappy little runt with scabs on her knees. What's she up to?"

"I suppose you could say she's taking a gap year."

Slidell slid me a sidelong glance, the cant of his brows suggesting no comprehension.

"She's trying to figure out what to do with her life," I translated.

"Today's kids are pampered little assholes." As the brows re-angled, "When I was coming up, we didn't get no goddam gap—"

"How's Doris?" To shut down a critique of modern youth, I asked about Skinny's long-term on-again-off-again girlfriend.

"Doris and me are stepping back."

Nope. Not going there.

"You look especially nice today." Now I *was* curious about Slidell's slicked-up appearance.

Color crept up Skinny's neck and into his cheeks.

"I got a lunch date."

"Oh?"

"Name's Lyric. She's an entertainer."

"That's quite unusual."

"Eeyuh." In a tone suggesting the subject was closed.

Taking the hint, I refocused on my puzzle.

Twenty minutes later, we'd finally made it to our turnoff. Hooking a right onto a park service road, Slidell asked,

"When?"

"When what?" I asked, clueless to the new thread unspooling in Skinny's brain.

"Jesus H Christ. When did the goddam dog go missing?"

"Tuesday."

"So this asshole didn't keep it long."

"No."

We passed the tennis complex on our right. A dozen women were warming up for doubles. Probably a league.

I'd played on those courts many times. Wished I was heading to do so now, not to revisit a site where a dog had gone missing before turning up dead.

"Maybe it ain't the mutilation what gets his rocks off." Slidell's voice brought me back. "Maybe it's the killing."

"We don't know who shot Bear. It's possible whoever decapitated and displayed his remains did so after finding him dead."

Again, Slidell made that crotchety sound in his throat.

Park Road Park is an urban oasis offering hiking trails, wooded picnic areas, open green spaces, sports fields, and a lake called the Duck Pond. Just before the small body of water, Slidell pulled onto a grassy strip paralleling the pavement.

"Anything else turn up when you did your cutting?" Shifting gears, he made another of his disjointed segues.

"Besides the bullet, no."

Skinny swiveled toward me, a look of disgust on his broad, florid face.

"Honest opinion, doc. You think the same doer what's been nailing up body parts also capped that dog?"

"I don't know."

"Either way. I catch this shit weasel, he's gonna wish he died in his mama's womb."

Slidell released his seat belt with a one-thumb jab, hit the door handle with his elbow, and hauled himself from the car in one surprisingly swift move for a man of his bulk.

Donning shades and a ball cap, I alighted also. Scanned my surroundings.

The lake was to my right. The ducks gliding on its surface seemed not to care that the water was green and murky. Or perhaps they preferred it that way.

"Where's the goddam trail?"

"There."

The woods to our left were a mix of pine and hardwood. Recognizing the trailhead from Joye's description—the weathered utility shed, the pump, the tree stump—I indicated a point among the oaks, more a gradation in shadowing than an obvious gap.

Slidell set off at an unusually fast clip. I followed, half running to keep up.

By the time we reached the trees, Skinny was panting like a marathoner finishing a race. Sweat dampened his hairline and rivulets streamed down his temples. The greased pompadour lay flat on his crown.

At his winded direction, I brushed past him to take the lead. Ten yards into the woods, I spotted a scrap of red cloth tied to a low-hanging branch. Recognizing Joye's marker, placed during his search for Bear, I veered from the path.

Skinny's wheezing told me he was close behind. As did the occasional whiff of BO, now overpowering the cologne. Moving through the dense vegetation, I handed off low-hanging branches to prevent them snapping back in his face.

In less than five minutes, we reached an enormous oak.

"This is the last place Joye had eyes on Bear. According to his statement, it was here that the dog shot off into the trees."

Slidell was bent at the waist, hands on his knees. When he straightened, his face was the color of claret.

"Show me those Frog Pond scene pics," he managed to pant.

I dug my phone from my pocket and pulled up the compilation file. In it, I'd created a folder for every case for which we had photos of the remains still in situ.

As Skinny flipped through the images, I walked the area, following a loose grid pattern. Several minutes passed with no words exchanged.

"Spot anything shouldn't be here?"

I turned. Slidell had finished with the photos and was now watching me.

"Not yet," I replied.

Casting me one baleful look, Slidell started walking a grid to the left of mine. Again, the only sounds were his heavy breathing and the shuffling of dead leaves underfoot. Not a single forest creature had anything to say.

Then, in my peripheral vision I noticed Skinny stoop to pluck something from the ground. Bringing his hand to eye level, he inspected his find.

"Yo."

"What?"

He curled impatient fingers with his free hand, indicating that I should join him.

I walked over.

"Let me see those pics again."

I reopened the file and handed him my phone.

He scrolled through the photos, eventually paused. Moved on. Stopped again. Continued scrolling.

"Sonofabitch." With feeling.

"What?"

"What's your take on that thing down among the roots?"

I retrieved the phone and enlarged the image with a finger-thumb spread. Studied the item on the screen.

"No idea." I said. "What is it?"

"Fuck if I know. But check this out."

Slidell extended his upturned palm. Lying on it was an object resembling the one he'd spotted in the earlier scene photo.

"You found that here?" Stupid question. I'd just seen him pick it up.

Tight nod.

"So far we don't have much tying this whole freak show to one perp," he said, with none of the derision I'd expected. "Or leading us to him. I mean, there's no pattern to the type of animal, the type of tree, the type of pose. The creep changes his MO slightly every time, except for nailing up some poor critter and keeping a body part."

Slidell was composing his voice into a careful monotone, masking an underlying anger I didn't fully understand. Why such a high level of emotion?

I said nothing.

Slidell raised his upturned palm.

"But he messed up with this. And it's going to put his sick ass in the can."

CHAPTER 9

"What's your take?"

Slidell was asking about the thing he'd plucked from the tangle of tree roots.

"Hold it out," I said.

He did.

Activating my phone's magnifier app, I brought the screen close and slid the yellow button to the right. The image exploded and detail emerged.

I could see that the outer margins were ragged, suggesting the object had once been larger in size. Though mud-speckled and discolored, it had also been lighter in color. One side was edged with blue rubber.

"Lemme look."

"Did I hear please?"

"Yeah, yeah."

I handed Skinny the phone.

"Looks like part of it's rawhide, the rest rubber. There's indentations along one edge. A round hole at the top."

Slidell offered the phone back as he extended his palm.

"The indentations are tooth marks," I said, staring at the magnified object as he had done.

"Human?"

"No."

A moment of silence, then he snapped and pointed a finger at me.

"It's a dog toy."

"You think so?"

"Yeah. That's why I said it."

"How do you know? You don't have a dog."

"I've had more dogs than you've had girlie cramps."

I let that go.

"Maybe the guy used this to lure Bear," I suggested, pointing at Slidell's palm. "Manufacturers infuse them with a smell that appeals to the canine brain."

Slidell said nothing.

"How common are these things?" I asked.

"Hell if I know."

We stood a full minute, swatting at flies and considering options.

"Maybe we could ID the perp by finding where he bought the toy?" I suggested.

"Maybe."

Slidell's plan was simple.

Visit every pet store on the planet until we hit pay dirt.

Three hours later we'd been to a Pet Palace, a Pet Wants, two PetSmarts, and a canine café. I'd seen enough geckoes, guinea pigs, goldens, and guppies to last a lifetime. And heard enough grousing about a lunch date in peril to set every one of my nerves on edge.

The early-morning cloud cover had burned off, and the sun was blazing with white-hot intensity in a clear-blue sky. I had no doubt the mercury had clawed its way into the low nineties.

Slidell's mood hadn't improved with the rise in temperature. Nor had his appearance. His cheeks were flushed and the capillaries flanking his nose looked ready to burst.

"This is horseshit. After this, I'm done."

I shared his sentiment but said nothing.

"What's the name of this next joint?" Slidell asked as he turned from North Tryon Street onto a patch of concrete fronting a one-story strip mall.

"All Creatures on Earth."

"Pure poetry." With a snort that would have made Katy envious.

The mall's exterior had been painted yellow sometime in the Eocene and never touched up. It housed three stores in all, each with bars on the windows and doors.

All Creatures took up a big chunk of the square footage on the building's south end. To its right was a beauty shop called Belezza Salon Sylvia. Beyond the salon, a currency exchange boasted *Ready Cash* in blue-and-red neon.

Popping his seat belt and swinging his body left, Slidell heaved himself from the Trailblazer feetfirst. I followed him to the pet shop's front door. Which failed to budge when Skinny pulled on the handle.

"You have to ring." I pointed to a button to the right of the barricaded glass.

"What the hell's wrong with this country when a citizen can't enter a freakin' store without a shakedown?"

"It's hardly a shakedown."

"Eeeyuh."

"I'm guessing they've been robbed more than once."

Slidell's anger wasn't directed at the shop's owner. He knew the crime stats for that part of town. He was hot and sweaty and frustrated by the morning's lack of results. And anxious to move on to lunch with Lyric.

A beat, then a buzzer sounded, and the lock clicked. Slidell yanked the door wide. A bell jangled us into the store.

Shelving filled the center of the room, holding items organized according to animal. Cat. Dog. Reptile. Feeder. I was unsure the makeup of the latter category. Worms? Crickets? Rodents? Whatever. I felt sympathy for the members of that group.

Fish tanks lined the left-hand wall, casting an eerie glow over that half of the room. Birds twittered in cages somewhere out of sight. A counter projected from the right-hand wall at the rear, its front painted red, its top shiny black.

Hanging beside the counter was a cork bulletin board. Tacked to it were dozens of homemade flyers. Pictures of lost pets. Ads for adoptable kittens. A poster offering a parrot named Buster for re-homing.

Standing behind the counter was a skinny man with bulging eyes that tracked our progress with interest. A lack of wrinkles and firm jawline suggested an age under thirty. Challenging that youthful estimate was one of the worst comb-overs I'd ever seen.

"May I help you?" Comb-over beamed a welcome. "We have some adorable wee kitties needing forever homes."

Slidell badged him.

"Oh, my." The smile underwent a significant decrease in wattage. "Has there been another break-in?"

"How 'bout we start with your name."

"Jeremy Dahmer." Two slender hands came up, palms pointed at us. "I know what you're thinking. The dreadful monster who cannibalized people in Wisconsin. I get *sooo* much ribbing about having the same name."

Dahmer referred to a serial killer and sex offender who'd murdered and dismembered seventeen men between 1978 and 1991.

I flashed back to my conversation with Adina about the nature of evil. Dahmer truly qualified. But I wasn't thinking of him at all.

"But I'm *Jeremy*," Dahmer continued his unsolicited explanation. "Not Jeffrey. So—"

"I don't care if you're Vlad the Impaler," Slidell said. "I need information."

Dahmer swallowed. An Adam's apple the size of a plum rose and fell in his skinny throat.

"Show him," Slidell demanded, half turning to me.

I drew a Ziploc from the side pocket of my shoulder purse and laid it on the shiny black wood.

Dahmer glanced down but made no move to touch the baggie.

"Pick it up," Slidell ordered. "Take a look."

"I'm not going to, I don't know, contaminate evidence or something?"

"Who said it's evidence?"

"You're a police officer." Dahmer blinked, one hand now pressed to his sternum.

"Pick. It. Up." Slidell demanded in a low and very even voice.

Using a thumb and forefinger, Dahmer lifted the bag gingerly by one corner. His expression suggested anticipation of a dead spider or a stool sample.

"So?" Slidell prodded.

"So what?" Dahmer sounded genuinely confused.

"So, what can you tell me about it?"

Dahmer peered at Slidell's find through the clear plastic. Turned the baggie this way and that.

"It's a chew toy," he said without hesitation. "For dogs."

"We know that. What else can you say?"

Stiffening at Slidell's brusqueness, Dahmer bent and withdrew a handheld magnifier from below the counter. Raised and lowered the glass over the baggie.

"It's part of a Doggieflex chew toy," he said when several seconds had passed. "The Dragon model."

"Are they common?" Slidell asked.

"No."

"Do you carry them here?"

"Not anymore."

"But you did."

"Yes."

"When did you stop?"

"About six months ago. We received notice that dogs were choking on bits of rubber that became detached, so we discontinued the product. We would never sell anything that could harm—"

"Did you keep records on who bought the things?"

"It's a six-dollar item, officer."

"So that's a no."

"It is."

Slidell began rolling his shoulders. I knew his body language well. He was frustrated and considering his next move.

"But I remember the customer who purchased this one," Dahmer said.

Slidell froze in mid-roll.

"How's that?"

"He asked me to punch a hole so he could hang the toy on his belt. Or on a lanyard. Or on something." Dahmer waggled the baggie. "This one has that hole."

"He?"

"Yes, sir."

"No one else ever asked you to do that?"

"No, sir."

"Describe the guy."

Dahmer shrugged. "He was just a guy."

Slidell's cheek muscles bunched just south of his temples. Before he could snap, causing Dahmer to pee his jockeys or to shut down completely, I jumped in.

"Was the gentleman old, young? Tall, short? Heavy, slight? White, Black, Hispanic?"

The Adam's apple made another round trip as Dahmer gave thought to my question.

"He wasn't all that tall. And he might have been blond, though I'm not sure—he was wearing a hat. But there was something weird about the way he looked at me."

"What do you mean?" I asked.

The bulbous eyes shifted from me to Slidell and back.

"I don't know. Forget it. The guy was like anyone you'd see walking down the street."

Katy texted as Slidell and I were en route back to the Annex. She and Ruthie were taking the Southern Charm Haunted/True Crime golf cart excursion around Charlotte that night. She invited me to join them.

I'd never heard of the tour. Had to admit, it sounded fun.

Nevertheless, I declined. First the outing to Park Road Park. Then the zillion pet store canvassing romp. The day's agenda, accompanied by Slidell's constant sarcasm, had left me exhausted.

After parting from Skinny, though, I did find enough energy to run a series of pesky errands—purchased printer cartridges, returned an unfortunate impulse-buy sun hat to Nieman's, filled a prescription, picked up a bag of wild bird seed for my feeder—and arrived home to an extremely petulant cat. It was well past Birdie's evening mealtime and he showed his annoyance by ignoring me.

"Sorry, Bird. My bad."

An accusatory stare came my way from atop the fridge.

"No kibble tonight, big guy. How about we crack out one of your faves?"

The cat watched me open and empty a can of seafood pâté into his bowl. Made no move to descend from his lofty perch.

Pushing through the swinging door into the dining room, I heard the soft *thup thup* of paws hitting the granite countertop, then the hardwood floor. Couldn't help but smile.

A quick change to cutoffs and a tee, then I returned to the kitchen. For my dinner I zapped a Stouffer's chicken and mashed potatoes combo.

Yeah, I know. Sodium, sugar, saturated fats, preservatives. But frozen dinners are *uber* quick and easy. Haute cuisine when paired with fresh-squeezed supermarket lemonade.

I hate to cook. That's a given. More important, I wanted time to relax—maybe take a bubble bath—before Ryan's call.

By nine my skin was flushed, my fingertips puckered from a very long immersion in very hot water. Odd choice, given the heat still gripping the city. Don't care. A soaky bath tops my list of methods to chill.

I was propped against a mountainous heap of bed pillows, watching CNN, when my mobile sounded.

"Bonjour, ma chère." Ryan's eyes looked even more intensely blue on my phone's little screen than in real life.

"Bonjour."

"Comment ça va?"

"Ça va bien."

Once we'd greeted each other and given assurances that all was well, Ryan asked his usual question.

"Where are you?"

"In bed."

"What are you wearing?"

"Panties and an old PETA T-shirt."

"Show me."

"No."

"Sounds hot."

"It's so sexy, if you saw me in person, I'd have to sedate you."

"No need for drugs, *ma chère*. Your charm and beauty knock me out every day."

My eyes rolled with no input from me.

"I can't wait to see you," I said.

"My flight is booked, and I should wrap up my investigation shortly."

"What's the issue, again?" He'd mentioned his most recent case briefly, but I'd forgotten.

"A guy got canned for skimming at a car wash where he works. Says he didn't do it. Wants me to find the bastard who did. What's up with you?"

"It's been relatively quiet on the forensic front."

I updated Ryan on Bear and the other animal remains. Balodis. Joye. Kumar. My happy time with Slidell trying to track the dog toy.

"Skinny's probably pissed at being demoted to paw patrol."

"Actually, I'm surprised at how committed he seems to be."

"The guy's a marshmallow center when it comes to animals."

"How do you know that?"

"Not important. Look, Slidell can be a boor and a loudmouth, but he means well."

"He does. But—"

"But what?"

Good question. What *was* it that had been bothering me?

"Kumar made a comment about the animal displays possibly having a sexual component. Slidell called and grilled her on the theory. I think he's become a bit channeled on that."

"Who cares his motivation? If Skinny's fired up to put the bust on this whacko, just go with the flow."

"You're right."

"As always."

"What about those Kelly-green seersucker pants you bought?"

"A momentary lapse in judgment."

"You wore them."

"Only once."

"Ciao," I said.

"Ciao," Ryan said.

"And don't worry," I added. "Paw patrol will be sorted by the time you arrive."

If only that had proven true.

CHAPTER 10

Charlotte has a plethora of trendy breakfast spots. The RedEye Diner. The Flying Biscuit. Café Monte French Bakery & Bistro. Ruthie insisted on the Original Pancake House. Though not a bold choice, I was good with it.

So. At eight o'clock the next morning, I was sitting in a booth opposite my daughter and great-niece, struck by how much they resembled each other. Both were tall and lanky, with green eyes and blond hair, Ruthie's long and braided, Katy's in a practical boy cut.

I sensed tension. The two were largely ignoring each other.

Katy had ordered the apple pancake. Which arrived looking large enough to feed Great Britain. I'd gone with the cherry crepes.

After lengthy consideration involving a great deal of sighing, Ruthie had finally decided on the ham and cheese omelet. Having eaten maybe two bites, she'd planted an elbow on the table, cradled her head in her palm, and commenced macerating the remains of the egg concoction.

I raised my brows in question to Katy.

She raised hers back to me.

"Would you like something different?" I asked Ruthie.

"No." Poking again at the yellow mess oozing over the edge of her plate.

Our waitress reappeared and waggled the stainless-steel coffee pot she clutched in one hand. Her name badge said *Helen*.

We all nodded.

"Would the young lady like to place another order?" Helen asked the young lady with a note of disapproval.

"I'm good," Ruthie said.

"Shall I clear the table?"

"Yes, I think we're done," said Katy, while tapping her iPhone screen to check the time. "Then please bring the check."

We fell silent as Helen stacked plates, balanced utensils on them, and withdrew.

Talk had been sparse throughout the meal, so I gave conversation another go.

"Are you enjoying your stay in Charlotte?"

Jesus, Brennan. What's the kid supposed to say?

Ruthie shrugged.

"She went to check out UNCC," Katy said.

"That is *not* true," Ruthie said. "I've made some friends. They attend UNCC. End of story. I have zero interest in enrolling there. Or anywhere else. So don't suggest otherwise to my lunatic mother."

Alrighty, then.

"College doesn't interest you. Fine. What *does*?"

Ignoring Katy's annoyed tone, Ruthie answered quickly.

"Animals."

"No surprise," Katy said. "Given that your dad's a vet."

"What aspect?" I asked. "Species ecology? Physiology? Taxonomy?"

"Behavior," Ruthie said.

"Aren't you working a string of animal cases?" Katy asked me.

"Really?" Ruthie said, perking up.

Sliding a cautionary glance in my daughter's direction, I said, "You know I can't talk about—"

"Seriously, Mom?" she said, issuing an exasperated eye roll. "We're not asking you to name names. We're good with four-legged aliases."

Katy was right. What could it hurt?

Choosing my words carefully, I provided a brief overview of Bear and the others. Ruthie listened, her emerald eyes showing surprising focus.

"Maybe it's the animal's reaction that triggers this guy's need to act out," she said after a short pause. "You know, the way a squirrel or a raccoon vibes."

"What do you mean?"

"Different species deal with threat in different ways. You've heard of the four f's for dogs?"

I shook my head.

"Flight, fight, fidget, or freeze."

"Fart?"

Ruthie and I ignored Katy's quip.

"Some animals try to make themselves look bigger," she said. "Some can detach limbs or tails if trapped, mostly reptiles, I think. Sea cucumbers can actually eject internal organs."

It was the first time Ruthie had shown enthusiasm for any topic. Wanting to encourage her, I said,

"You know a lot about animal behavior."

"I read books on ethology. If I could work at a zoo someday, that would be a dream come true."

"I've seen her in action," Katy said. "She's like a dog whisperer. Or cat, or toucan, or gerbil. Fill in the blank."

"It's nothing magical," Ruthie said. "I just try to imagine what the animal is feeling. What it's seeing, hearing, smelling. What it's experiencing in that moment."

"What it's vibing." I tried the Gen Z lingo.

"Facts. Then I act accordingly."

Helen arrived and placed the bill squarely between my daughter and me. "Y'all have a good one."

Katy and I both went for the check. Not surprisingly, I won the staged battle that ensued.

"I'm bummed that I have to work," I said to Ruthie. "What's your plan for the rest of the day?"

"I'm going to visit Uncle Pete."

Ruthie and my ex have always shared a special bond. Partly their mutual love of baseball. Partly their offbeat sense of humor. Mostly, they just like each other.

"That should be fun," I said.

"I can't wait to see Boyd." Ruthie referred to Pete's dog.

"Brace yourself. The Chow will be excited."

"Katy has offered to drop me off. Could you maybe pick me up if it turns out I need a ride home?"

"It would be my pleasure."

As we wove our way toward the door, I said to Ruthie, "You have great insight. Have you considered a career in counseling or psychology?"

"As I said, I prefer animals."

"Why?" I asked.

"Animals hit different."

"Meaning?"

"Nonhuman means nonjudgmental."

A summer storm had broken during the ninety minutes I'd spent in the restaurant. Nevertheless, the day felt even warmer than when I'd gone in. The sky was leaden, the humidity somewhere in the Amazon Basin range.

The gravel parking lot was like The Land of Ten Thousand Lakes. Weaving between the puddles, trying to keep my feet dry, I considered my conversation with Ruthie. For someone not yet out of her teens, she was certainly well-grounded. I wondered what had made her so cynical about people at such a young age.

I had my hand on the car door handle when Slidell phoned. As usual, he launched in without greeting.

"Got a forensic report might interest you."

"On the articles associated with Bear?" I asked, sliding behind the wheel.

"No. On fingernail clippings we think might ID the Ripper."

"That was fast." As usual, I ignored Slidell's sarcasm.

"I got friends."

Though surprised that Slidell would call in a favor on an animal case, I said nothing.

"I'm thinking we should visit another of the sites this toad dressed up."

"Why?" I turned on the car and the wipers.

"Jesus take the biscuits. Why the freak not? We scored something the last time we ran a reboot."

I couldn't argue with that.

"When?" I asked, watching the blades flick water from the windshield in matching fan shapes.

"You got a lot on your dance card today?"

"Enough."

"I can go without you." Slidell's tone was totally neutral, suggesting I could take his words anyway I chose.

"Which location?"

"Chantilly Park. That's near your crib. How 'bout I pick you up in thirty."

"I'll be ready."

I lowered the window and set out for home, enjoying the smell of fresh rain as I drove.

Chantilly is wedged between Plaza Midwood and Elizabeth, where Katy lives. Originating with the construction of a few homes in 1913, the neighborhood grew during the 1940s and, for a while, thrived. Eventually, with the expansion of housing options throughout the Queen City, the hood's fortunes began a slow decline.

Then, a renaissance. As with Elizabeth, Chantilly's affordable pricing and proximity to Uptown were recognized as a winning combo by those with limited budgets and by those wanting to avoid the expense and tedium of a long commute. Older homes were purchased for restoration, others for demolition and replacement by more modern construction.

Inevitably, property values climbed. Soon followed the restaurants, funky stores, and art galleries frequented by millennials and Gen Z. Or whatever gen young property buyers were of late.

Bottom line: Chantilly is home to both the run-down and the renovated. And contains some of the hottest real estate in Charlotte.

Slidell's reference to feedback from the forensics lab had been a type of bait and switch. He'd gotten a prelim report, all right. But all it said was that the fabric, feathers, glitter, and other articles decorating

Bear's skull had been unremarkable, items that could be purchased at a Michaels or any handicrafts store.

Slidell delivered that news while driving past brick-and-frame bungalows set behind sodden front yards, finishing as he turned onto Wyanoke Avenue. At the rear of the hood, he pulled into a small parking area by the entrance to the park.

We got out and crossed to a pebbled path barricaded by two chest-high posts to prevent the passage of cars and trucks. Beyond the posts was a wood-chipped playground similar to the one at Park Road Park. Swings. Slide. Monkey bars. All glistening wet.

An elderly woman in a long black skirt and a sweatshirt proclaiming something pertaining to Jesus sat on a bench holding an umbrella and bouncing a pram with one foot. Her red high-topped sneakers reminded me of a similar pair at home in my closet.

A young, blond woman stood by the swings, eyeing her phone while pushing a towheaded toddler buckled into a baby seat. The child's face was red and scrunched. I couldn't tell if it was crying or laughing.

Two teens slouched at a picnic table, elbow leaning, legs outstretched. Dyed black hair, purple eye shadow, and abundant facial hardware suggested they were going for a goth look. Both were soaked and appeared to be stoned.

I wondered briefly if everyone had arrived after the rain. Or weathered the storm under the corrugated tin roof covering part of the playground.

Slidell had nailed it. This trip was a reboot of our previous outing.

Entering the woods via a gap in the trees, Skinny continued a short distance, then veered off to the left. Cursing and swatting at mosquitoes and gnats, he stopped at an ancient elm and pointed upward.

My eyes followed the sightline of his finger. Spotted fragments of yellow police tape caught in a lower branch.

"Let's do that grid thing," Slidell got out between wheezy breaths.

We did.

Found nothing.

As I walked back and forth on parallel tracks, eyes scanning the ground, Ruthie's words again looped in my brain.

I imagine what the animal is feeling. What it's experiencing in that moment.

As a scientist, I like my data hard, not slippery. Evidence I can measure, weigh, dissect, photograph. Thus, my attraction to bones. I suppose you'd say I'm pragmatic by nature, skeptical of out-of-body travel, ESP, clairvoyance, the paranormal. I don't deny that people experience these things. But I believe such phenomena can be explained via logical principles.

Still. Could Ruthie's approach work with humans? With me? In this place of his choosing, could I enter the mind of the psycho we were pursuing? Sense his thoughts? His feelings? His motivation?

Probably not.

What the hell.

I closed my eyes, cleared my mind, and spread a welcome mat for whatever cerebral stirrings might be out there in the universe wanting to come in.

My hindbrain conjured a vision. A man striding the trail I'd just taken, black plastic garbage sack in one hand. The sack's contents appeared to be weighty but not overly large.

Stopping at the elm under which I stood, the man reached in and ear-yanked a dead rabbit out into the open. Raising the limp body two-handed above his head, he tipped his face to the sky, neck tendons bulging and taut.

A heartbeat, then the man's chin leveled. Scowling, he threw the rabbit to the ground, dropped to his knees, and wept.

Unexpectedly, my face went hot.

Electricity fizzed in my chest.

I heard a voice.

No.

The experience wasn't auditory.

It was a feeling, cold and hard as igneous rock.

The unexpected surge of emotion sent a chill down my spine.

CHAPTER 11

"Hey. Doc. You okay?"

Slidell's sweat-slick face looked like a bright-pink peony coated with dew.

"What?"

"You zoned out there."

"I'm fine. It's just—"

It's just what? I had no idea. But I damn sure wasn't going to tell Slidell that I'd flashed into the mind of the perp we were chasing.

That the message I'd received was scary as hell.

But had that really happened?

Or was the heat getting to me?

Slidell and I looked around for several minutes, found nothing. "This is bullshit," Skinny said, yanking a grayed hanky from a pants pocket and wiping his brow. "I'm pulling the plug."

"Suits me."

With that we headed back toward the Trailblazer.

Trudging through the prickly vegetation, accumulating more bites with each step, I couldn't help wondering what the hell I'd experienced. Had my subconscious noticed something that I'd missed? Something that prompted an unsolicited *psst* from my id?

Triggered the sense of foreboding now filling me?

Because in that moment, in that startling peek into the psyche of another, I knew.

The perp had grown bored with nonhuman prey and would inevitably move up to humans.

Unbeknownst to me.

He already had.

Katy and Ruthie spent their last summer days together doing exactly as they pleased. Picnic dinners. Bike rides. Garden tours. Popcorn and old movies on the sofa each night. Life on the edge. I joined in as my work schedule allowed.

On yet another simmering Monday morning, I returned to the MCME to resume the case inventory I'd abandoned to collect Bear's skull. It was Labor Day, I know. But I figured I could work uninterrupted with most everyone gone.

I figured wrong.

I was opening a third file when my mobile rang.

Recognizing the number, I picked up, grateful for the interruption.

"Hey, pookie," I answered, knowing the response I'd get.

"I've asked you not to call me that, Mom."

"I know."

"You can be so annoying," said Katy, sighing.

"I'll work on it."

"Listen, I need a favor."

"Oh?"

"Jesus. Don't sound so apprehensive."

I considered a moment before responding. "I'm remembering some of your past requests."

"Like what?"

"Like the time you needed help collecting horse ejaculate."

"That jizz was from an extremely valuable thoroughbred," said Katy, sounding slightly offended. "I made good money on that gig."

"I'm glad you've changed jobs."

"Whatever." A pop-top whooshed. "I've just had a call from a retired Marine captain down in Greenville, South Carolina, a former resident at the center. This guy was a train wreck when he first arrived, I mean totally butt-kicked by PTSD."

"I'm sorry to hear that."

"He's better now—has a job, a wife. But he's undergoing some sort of crisis and wants me to come see him."

"You shouldn't go alone."

"Bubs is riding with me." Katy referred to a worker at the men's shelter, a kid who was never going to win a brain power competition. "Besides, this guy's never been violent. And he's ancient."

"How old?"

"He's got to be well into his fifties."

"I'm surprised the old geezer is still able to dial a phone."

"Hilarious."

"How can I help?"

"Can Ruthie stay with you for a few days?"

"Of course. I'd love to have her." Not totally true given Ryan's upcoming visit.

"I'll warn you. Ruthie can be"—Katy groped for the proper descriptor—"cantankerous."

"Good word, that."

"Thanks. I'll let you know when I plan to drop her off."

"Sounds like a plan."

We'd barely disconnected when Nguyen appeared at my door. Apparently, she, too, had no social life.

Nguyen's eyes took in the framed 1920s Ireland travel poster hanging on one wall, the plants lining the windowsill, the whiteboard with its jumble of scribbled notes. Her gaze rested briefly on the collection of Ziplocs almost filling the top of one file cabinet. On the bones and body parts inside each.

"How many does this last one make?" she asked, nodding in the direction of Bear's skull.

"Eight."

"Unfortunately, now it's nine. Same decorative elements. Slightly different MO. Instead of being nailed high up on the tree, these remains were found at its base."

"Where?"

"The Stevens Creek Nature Preserve. Down by Mint Hill."

Nope. No way.

"I'm sorry, Dr. Nguyen. My niece is staying with me for a few days, so I'd rather not go all the way out—"

"There's no need for a scene recovery. The remains are here."

"In the morgue?"

"Yes. The gentleman who found them is a birder named, are you ready for it?"

I nodded.

"Devlin Finch. Mr. Finch stated that he collected the material hoping for avian specimens. Ultimately, he boxed everything and called the police."

"Why the change of heart?"

"He said when he got the bones home and spread them out something didn't look kosher."

"Meaning?"

"I've no idea. That's what the officer told me when he delivered the box. Anyway, they're here. But it's nothing that can't wait a few days."

Two emotions fought for supremacy. Relief that I wouldn't have to go on another recovery trek. Dismay that Finch's actions, though well-intentioned, may have compromised a scene and possibly led to the loss of evidence.

Probably no biggie since the deceased wasn't human.

It was a supposition that would prove incorrect.

By eight the following morning, I was in autopsy room four, suited up in gloves and scrubs. A mask hid the expression of shock on my face.

Bones and mummified tissue lay separated into groupings on two gurneys. Contrary to my initial plan, I'd ended up viewing each scrap using every means possible. By gross observation. Under magnification. Via X-ray.

Though damaged and badly eroded, sufficient anatomical detail had survived. My conclusion was undeniable.

Case MCME-741-25, initially logged in as *collection of animal bones*, contained elements that were clearly *Homo sapiens*. Rib and limb segments. A hunk of pelvis, including a portion of pubic symphysis. A partial sternum. Numerous skull fragments.

Since I'd worked unassisted, there'd been no one with whom to share my startling discovery. No one with whom to speculate. Questions whirled unvoiced in my head.

How had the remains ended up at the tree? A lack of redundancy in parts along with compatibility between all elements suggested a single person. Had that person been killed, then his or her remains placed below the oak? If so, When? Why? Who was the victim?

Had the corpse been disinterred from a local cemetery? If so, Which one? Was the act random? Or had the individual been specifically chosen?

How had the remains become mixed with those of several animal species?

Murder? Grave robbery? Something altogether different?

For a moment, I just stood there, fluorescents buzzing fitfully on the ceiling, clock humming softly on the wall.

Snap out of it, Brennan!

Setting the animal remains aside, I opened a file and began moving through my standard protocol with the human material.

A skeletal inventory showed that the remains did, in fact, represent a single individual. Biological indicators pointed to female gender and an age estimate of thirty-five to fifty years. Cranial and facial anatomy suggested European ancestry. Good bone quality and the presence of desiccated soft tissue indicated a PMI of less than five years.

I saw no evidence of antemortem or perimortem disease or trauma. At least nothing that had left its mark on the skeleton.

What I found shocking was the pattern of postmortem treatment.

Feathers. Glitter. Facial mutilation.

And the probability that one hand had been severed and taken elsewhere.

A pattern identical to the one I'd observed with Bear and the others.

I was recording my findings for entry into a computer file when the screech of the desk phone startled me. Stripping off and tossing a glove into a toe-tap flip-top container, I crossed to it.

"Dr. Brennan," I answered, noting as I picked up that the call was internal.

"A happy Tuesday to you." Chirpy as hell.

"And to you."

"I hope y'all had a lovely weekend."

"I did, Mrs. Flowers. Thanks for asking."

A hopeful pause.

When I didn't elaborate, "I'm sorry to interrupt, but Detective Slidell absolutely refuses to take no for an answer. That man can be most tenacious."

"Indeed, he can," I affirmed, not totally clear as to her meaning. "What does he want?"

"He says it's imperative that he talk with you, toot-sweet. I'm paraphrasing, of course."

"Of course."

"I explained that y'all are busy doing an autopsy, but—"

"Tell Detective Slidell that I'll call him back shortly."

"That won't be necessary."

Mrs. Flowers loved roping people into Q & A fencing matches. At that moment I wasn't in the mood for games.

"What does that mean?"

My brusqueness was met with a reproachful silence.

"I apologize. I didn't mean to snap."

"No offense taken."

"Could you please phone Detective Slidell and report that I have news for him?"

"As I said, that won't be necessary."

"Oh?" Voice neutral, masking my annoyance.

"The gentleman is waiting in your office. He said you suggested that would be best."

"Did he."

"He did."

"Fine." It wasn't. "Offer coffee and tell him I'll be there shortly."

It took less than ten minutes to secure MCME-741-25, wash up, and cross to my office. Enough time for Skinny to escalate from prickly into full-on belligerent.

"Sorry you had to wai—"

"I got a goddam job to do." Theatrically tapping his watch.

"Serve and protect." I circled to the chair behind my desk. "Such a thankless task."

"You're a regular Henny Youngman."

"Seriously? That's the most recent comic you can reference?"

"The guy was funny."

"Glad someone is. This creep tacking up carcasses isn't a load of laughs."

"I talked to your pal Kumar again." Slidell segued straight to his current pet theory. "She thinks the doer's a perv."

"You may be overstating her opinion."

"How's that?"

"She thinks the doer's behavior could *possibly* have a sexual component."

"Don't everything when you get right down to it? I mean, there's guys get their rocks off licking the labels on cans of baked beans."

I had no response to that, so I said nothing.

"Tell me about this latest batch of bliss," Slidell ordered.

I briefed him on the remains Devlin Finch had collected. Explained the human bones I'd found in the mix. The cut marks suggesting intentional removal of a hand.

"Just the one DOA?"

I nodded.

"Sonofabitch."

"Yeah," I agreed. "Sonofabitch."

"What else can you tell me about this Finch find? Give me more details."

Secretly appreciating Skinny's use of alliteration, I told him what I could.

He listened without interrupting, left ankle cocked over his right knee, one finger worrying some remnant of breakfast on his shirt, which, as usual, looked like it had been plucked from a department store discount bin.

"That's it?" he asked when I'd finished.

I nodded glumly. "One large segment of frontal bone survived. Patches of adherent tissue showed that the decedent's eyelids had been stretched wide and sewn in place. When viewed under magnification, the stitching indicated a skilled hand."

"Just like the others."

"Just like the others," I agreed.

"So we're talking about a guy who knows his way around a needle and thread. Maybe a professional seamstress or a tailor?"

"A surgeon or dentist?" I tossed out.

"Some kind of lab rat?"

"An acupuncturist? A pharmacist?"

"More likely just your run-of-the-mill low-life druggie."

"Maybe." I didn't think so.

"I don't give a rat's ass what this perv needs to make his whistle throb." Slidell sounded dangerous. "Animals is bad enough. But no one diddles with human corpses on my turf."

CHAPTER 12

Convinced that the displays were the result of some erotic fantasy, Slidell wanted to round up every registered sex offender in the state.

It took some doing to talk him down and redirect his energy.

After adamant arguing on my part, and much blustering on his, he stormed off on a two-prong mission.

First, he'd compile a list of open MP files—people who'd gone missing in the region over the past three years. Those data might prove useful with regard to the question of human corpse ID.

Then, he'd pull reports of unresolved pet disappearances and of animal mutilation cases spanning the same period. Those data might prove useful with regard to the question of perp ID.

I'd offered to go with Skinny. His response had been less than gracious.

Alone in my office, I forced myself to focus on Nguyen's hated case inventory. With minimal success. Feeling useless and antsy, I kept finding excuses to avoid the damn thing.

A coffee refill. A toilet break. A check of traffic congestion in the street below.

Slidell had been gone almost four hours when I'd had it. Unable to take the inactivity a second longer, I decided to contact Adina.

My call was answered on the first ring.

"Dr. Brennan," a voice I recognized as Adina's sang out. Her office phone must have had some sort of caller ID.

"You're working your own phone these days?" I asked.

"My receptionist is on vacation."

"Isn't the whole goddam world?"

"Whoa. What's up, girlfriend?"

"Sorry. Didn't mean to snap."

"I've put you on speaker. I can hear you pacing."

"You have excellent ears."

"Sit down."

I did.

"Have you eaten anything today?"

"No."

"You know that's unhealthy."

I said nothing.

"Hungry and angry. As you're aware, the hangry combo can be a trigger."

"What are you, my sponsor?"

"I'm your friend."

"Sorry." I was saying that a lot. "But I'm not thinking about alcohol."

"Good. Now tell me what's got you so anxious."

"Your prediction was spot-on." I picked up a pen and began rolling it across my knuckles.

"You'll have to do better than that."

"Remember I told you about a whack job nailing animal corpses to trees?"

"Yes."

"He's moved up to humans."

"I feared that might be the progression. How many people so far?"

"Just one."

"How did he get the remains?"

"No clue."

"Do they look fresh?"

"No. I'm seeing details that suggest they came from a coffin burial."

Brief pause as Adina digested what I'd told her.

"So, at this point there's only one set of human remains that you *know* of," she said.

"That makes me feel better."

"No charge for counseling services."

"As the duck said, put it on my bill."

"Are you implying I'm a quack?"

"We really have to stop this."

"Yes." Adina agreed. "Before it gets fowl."

I squelched every poultry pun that came to mind.

"Are you certain it's the same guy?" Adina asked after a brief pause.

"One missing body part. Similar paint, feathers, and glitter. The lab has everything, but I'll bet my grannie's goat the analysis shows a match."

"Your grannie has a goat?"

"Call the coroner." Eyes rolling. "I may die laughing."

That joke fell flat. After several beats, Adina asked,

"Could it be a copycat?"

"What's the fun there?"

"Take over someone else's fetish and up the stakes."

"I suppose anything's possible," I said, chewing on that. "Listen. Can I ask you a question?"

"Lay it on me."

"Slidell has totally embraced something you said to him. He's convinced these displays are erotic in nature and is drilling down on sex offenders to the exclusion of everyone else."

"The man has succumbed to monovision in the past."

"Nicely phrased."

"I have medical training."

"Based on what I've told you, is there anything else you can say about the doer?" I asked, hoping for a shred of a lead.

"Brief me again on the pattern."

I did, then waited out another, longer silence.

"As before, this is strictly off the record," Adina said at last.

"Understood."

"I'm guessing your guy is a homely little dude who gets very little sex. Perhaps none at all."

"So, Slidell's correct? It *is* about sex?"

"Only indirectly. I still think it's really about control. The guy has no power over women, or men, whichever side he plays. No control over people in general. But he *does* feel in charge when dealing with animals."

"Only now he's displaying human remains."

"At risk of repeating myself, that's troubling."

I heard heavy footsteps in the corridor.

"Gotta go. I believe Detective Dimwit is in the house."

"Enjoy."

"Right."

Slidell paused in the hall and kicked the door. Hard.

"Yo."

I got up, crossed my office, and opened it wide.

Skinny stood holding a cardboard box crammed with what appeared to be case files. A long roll of paper cut diagonally across the top stuck out behind his sweat-stained left pit.

"What's up?" I asked.

"You gonna let me in, or do I die of old age standing here?"

I stepped back.

Skinny entered and dumped his load on my desk.

"We're going old-school," he said, pulling out another laundry-challenged hanky to wipe his brow.

"Old-school," I repeated in way of a question.

"This joint got a bulletin board?"

"I think there's a portable somewhere in storage." Since the dawn of the digital age. I didn't add that.

"How 'bout you bring it to the conference room."

"Wouldn't it make more sense to upload all the data—"

"Just get the goddam thing."

Locating the goddam thing took longer than I thought.

By the time I pushed through the conference room door, the late-afternoon sun was hanging even lower in the sky. A soft tangerine glow lit the long mahogany table, interrupted by diagonal shadows cast by the Venetian blinds' slats.

Slidell was aglow, too, the orange tinge looking brash coming off his grease-slicked hair.

Skinny was laying out a series of plastic containers. Each held push-pins, one set with blue caps, one with green, one with yellow, one with red.

"Help me with this," he ordered, unfurling the scroll. Which turned out to be a map of North and South Carolina.

As I held each corner down, Slidell tacked it in place.

"We're gonna start by plotting every case of a missing pet that never turned up."

"Going how far back?"

"Three years."

Though skeptical, I went along with Skinny's plan. He mined the files—old-school, one spit-moistened finger running through the hard copy in each. As he called out names and locations, I worked the board.

Ninety minutes later, dozens of blue pins dotted the map.

"Now we're going to add calls involving animal mutilation."

"Hopefully there aren't many of those," I said.

"You'd be surprised."

Though fewer in number, the array of red pins was impressive. And showed one area of overlap with the blue spread.

Silence surrounded us as we both studied our handiwork.

"Looks like a Venn diagram," I said.

"Don't go getting all jargony," Slidell said.

I considered how I might explain the concept to a high schooler.

"A Venn diagram is an illustration that uses overlapping circles to show the logical relationship between two or more sets of items."

Frowny stare.

I dropped down to middle school.

"Think of it this way. Circles that overlap have a commonality. Circles that don't overlap share none of each other's traits."

Slidell's next question suggested he grasped the concept. Maybe.

"Can it do three?"

"You mean add another data set?"

"There you go again with the lingo."

"Yes."

"Let's plug in displays."

We used green pins to plot the locations at which decorated remains had been found.

Again, one pattern was obvious.

While there were outliers, the diagram showed a triangular area in which all three colors overlapped densely. Reports of missing pets. Reports of animal mutilation. Decorated displays.

"Looks like the jerkwad's liking Highway 74 these days," Slidell said. "Lately he's working a stretch northwest from Matthews."

I couldn't disagree.

"The hoods he's hitting are mostly residential, but there's also some areas with warehouses and depots."

"You're thinking he lives within that overlap area?"

"Maybe," Slidell mumbled, eyes never leaving the board. "Or maybe he keeps his nasty little hobby away from his crib."

"In an area he considers safe. One he knows well."

"The toad probably don't venture too far from his comfort zone."

I suspected Slidell was thinking aloud, not talking to me. Still, I tossed out,

"Perhaps he has a place he uses as his hunting ground."

"Yeah. Why piss off the neighbors by snatching their pets?"

"If that's true, he'd have to own a car. Or have access to one."

"He sure as shit ain't hauling dead animals by CATS." Slidell referred to the Charlotte Area Transit System.

"Or bicycle. Some of the dogs were fairly big."

Skinny seemed lost in thought. "When you gave me that fill-in on those human bones, you said maybe they came from an old burial."

"I did."

"From a graveyard?"

"Yes. You should check for recent reports of cemetery vandalism."

Slidell nodded.

I crossed to the map.

"I'd start with this one," I said, indicating a small green patch in the densest area of tri-color pin overlap. "Holy Comforter Cemetery."

"Who the hell came up with that name? Sounds like some kinda big blanket."

I'd had the same thought.

"Here." Slidell pulled a printout from one of his folders and handed it to me. "This is a list of female MPs going back three years. Let me know if there's a match to the stiff you got."

"I'm not sure the woman died that recently."

"Humor me."

Lumbering to his feet, Slidell strode toward the door.

"What's your next move?" I asked.

He turned. I knew the look on his face.

"You say this sonofabitch is a ghoul." A vein throbbed in the center of Slidell's sweat-slick forehead. "A ghoul and a pervert."

"I didn't—"

"A pervert making up for his limp dick by abusing animals."

I said nothing.

"I'll bet my left nut the guy's in the sex offender files."

With that, he was gone.

I turned to the list of names Slidell had provided. Six I could eliminate straight off based on their date of disappearance or on the bio-profile I'd constructed for the remains. Too young or too old. Too tall or too short. Wrong ancestry. History of a fracture or abnormality I hadn't observed on the bones.

That left me with three candidates.

Alice Anne Hunley Tumbler. Caucasian. DOB July 10, 1978. Reported missing eighteen months earlier by her son. Last seen walking her dog at Squirrel Lake Park near Matthews.

Corrina May Rummage. Caucasian. DOB February 4, 1992. Reported missing nine months earlier by her husband. Last seen leaving a Circle K on Sharon Road.

Laurel Jean Patel. Caucasian–Southeast Asian mix. DOB October 29, 2002. Reported missing thirty-six months earlier by her roommate. Last seen at a bus stop on Independence Boulevard.

I'd just finished my comparisons when Slidell returned.

He wasn't smiling. He wasn't frowning. But, framed in my doorway, his body language suggested he was wired for action.

"I've got him." Raising and waggling his phone.

"Sorry?"

"I've got the sick sonofabitch."

CHAPTER 13

"Forgive me. I'm not following."

"I've got the bastard what's been nailing up these freak-shows." Again, raising and waggling his phone.

I stared at Slidell.

He looked at me with what might or might not have been a smile.

"Jordan Allen Bright," he said. "Goes by Jax."

"Better than Jab."

"What?"

"Forget it." My mind had gone to Bright's initials.

I waited for Slidell to elaborate.

"Bright has a nasty habit of wagging his weinee at kids."

"So do dozens of other creeps. What makes you think—"

"*This* creep lives smack in the center of our rainbow overlap. And—you ready for this?"

Hating Slidell's guessing games, I circled a wrist.

"The guy's a vet tech."

"Which gives him access to animals."

"Bingo."

I considered the implications.

"You tell an owner that his dog or cat didn't make it, or that the animal has to be put down, then offer humane disposal of the remains," I said. "You return an urn full of ashes, keep the pet, and do what you want."

"Pretty cold, eh?"

"Glacial."

"You up for a surprise drop-in on this blight?"

I got to my feet and grabbed my purse.

Bright. Blight.

Not bad, Skinny.

The Cherry neighborhood, historically Black, lies about a mile southeast of Uptown. The area has caught on in recent years, like Elizabeth and Dilworth benefiting from its proximity to the city center.

Unfortunately, Bright's street hadn't hitched a ride on the gentrification train. Enormous elms lined both sides, keeping everything beneath them in perpetual shade. The homes were small and single-storied, some with detached garages, all fronted by tiny sun-challenged yards. Most were frame. A few were brick. All looked tired and discouraged.

Bright's house was a yellow bungalow whose foundation hosted thriving colonies of algae and mold. Dingy white trim. Gray door. Tiny front porch surrounded by wrought-iron railing painted to match the door.

Following Slidell up the mud-coated walkway, I heard music playing somewhere inside. Jazz piano. Maybe Thelonious Monk.

Slidell paused for a moment, then knocked.

A dog barked, high and frenzied.

No human responded.

Slidell knocked again, louder.

The music stopped but still no one appeared.

"CMPD, Mr. Bright. We need to talk to you."

Hearing Slidell's voice, the dog went batshit. Its paws made soft *thupping* sounds as it jumped up and dropped back to the floor.

"Easy, Millie." Though muted, I could tell that the voice was male.

Millie paid no attention and kept on yapping.

"Millie! Shut the freak up!"

Millie stopped in mid-yap with a sharp expulsion of breath. Locks snicked, and the door opened.

Bright was pale, baggy-eyed, and disheveled. His shorts were cutoff sweats. His dingy white tee was stretched to its full tensile capacity across a frame not yet obese but poised on the edge.

Millie eyed us from a position of safety tucked under Bright's right arm. I wouldn't say she was the ugliest dog I'd ever seen. But she was a contender. Her eyes were simultaneously beady and bulging, her snout unnaturally long and pointed. She may have come from a gene pool involving long-haired chihuahuas but could easily have passed as a rat.

Bright took in the scene with a slow five-second sweep. Slidell. Me. The Trailblazer parked on his drive.

"What's up, officer?"

"It's Detective. You Jordan Allen Bright?"

"Oh, my God. Here we go again."

"You Bright?"

"What? Did some child go missing in Outer Mongolia?" Then, to Millie, "Have the police nothing better to do than harass honest citizens who've paid their debt?"

"I'll bet you was *honest* with that kid you groped at the A&W."

"Oh, my freakin' lord. That was eight years ago." To Millie. "Eight years!"

Millie rendered no opinion.

"I know you're real busy these days squeezing puppy glands and all, but we're hoping you got a minute to do your civic duty."

"Actually, I was—"

"You got a minute." A statement, not a question.

"Of course." Bright stepped back, Millie squirming and whining in his grasp. "Please, come in."

We followed Bright through a foyer into a parlor, both floored in linoleum trying to look like oak. Gesturing us to a sofa draped with dog hair–coated red wool blankets, he dropped into a chair opposite.

I sat, already planning a trip to the dry cleaner. Slidell remained standing. Millie settled on her master's lap.

Propping his chin on one hand, Bright assumed an expression of bored tolerance.

Millie watched us warily, growling low in her throat.

"Don't bite the nice policemen," Bright said, stroking the dog's head. "We may need to cite them for harassment."

"You're a real cocky guy." Slidell's voice had that edge.

"I try. Look, *detective,* I get it. I'm registered. Give me the date of the current incident. I'll tell you where I was, and you can be on your way."

Cocky doesn't play well with Slidell. Seeing color blossoming in both his cheeks, I spoke up.

"We're looking into a series of pet disappearances." I left it at that.

"What in the world does that have to do with me?"

I explained the decorated remains. Bear's killing and beheading. The missing body parts. Kumar's suspicion that the displays had a sexual component. All the while watching for a reaction.

"Ghastly." Accompanied by a theatrical shudder. "But getting it on with dead animals is *not* my thing."

Either Bright was a world-class actor, or the man was genuinely not involved in what I'd described.

"The pattern fit the bill for any of your pals?" Slidell asked.

"I don't have 'pals,' detective." Digging into a pocket, Bright withdrew a treat and offered it to his dog.

Slidell cut me a sidelong glance. I knew the message. While he continued the interview, I looked around.

Saw nothing amiss.

Except the dreadful décor.

We'd just buckled our seat belts when Slidell's mobile buzzed. He pressed it to his ear, effectively muffling the caller's voice.

"Yo."

Skinny listened, face revealing nothing.

"How long ago?"

Pause.

"Which one?"

Longer pause.

"You've contacted next of kin?"

A few more exchanges, monosyllabic on Slidell's part, then he disconnected.

Perhaps to annoy me, perhaps digesting what he'd just learned, Slidell said nothing until we'd gone several blocks.

"That was your boss," Skinny finally piped up.

"Dr. Nguyen?"

"No. The head of MI5."

I bit back a snarky reply.

"She's got a possible ID on the remains dumped at the tree."

"Oh?"

"Eleanor Godric."

"What's the bio-profile?"

"White female, age forty-seven, short, maybe five-two."

"That fits."

Slidell turned from East 4th Street onto Queens Road.

"Cause of death?" I asked.

"Don't really matter."

"What? Why?"

"Godric died of natural causes. Something to do with her liver."

"When?" I queried. Jesus. I felt like I was playing twenty questions.

"Eighteen months ago."

I understood where this was going. "Her remains were stolen from a cemetery?" I ventured. I'd suspected as much when first eyeballing the corpse.

"Give the lady a—"

"Which one?" I asked. Just curious. The grave's location didn't really matter.

"I got people looking into that."

"How does someone pull that off? Don't graveyards have cameras?"

"Either our doer's real crafty, or their security is shit."

"Do you think—"

"I said I got someone working it."

Alrighty then.

I glanced at my phone, still on silent mode.

Four calls. All from Ruthie.

Digits on the screen indicated the time was five twenty-nine.

"Crap! I've got to pick up my niece."

"Don't streak your undies. The kid won't mind waiting a few minutes."

My ex, Janis "Pete" Petersons, still lives in the home we purchased early in our marriage, a two-story frame affair in an unrelentingly family-friendly hood in southeast Charlotte. Over the years, he hasn't done a thing to change the layout or appearance of the house. Same Williamsburg-themed siding, shutters, and front door. Same double-car garage. Same overgrown half acre of fenced backyard.

I find the setup an odd choice for an attractive, single man closing out half a century of life. But then my ex is an odd guy. Witty. Sexy. Generous. Pete is a rockstar father, but made a lousy husband. Too much of the "sexy" generously shared with others.

Pete claims he stays put because of his dog. Boyd is an enormous Chow with spikey red-brown fur, scary teeth, and the gentleness and patience of a Sunday school teacher.

Rush-hour traffic was brutal. It was going on six when I finally pulled onto Pete's drive.

Slidell was wrong. The kid *did* mind.

Ruthie was sitting on the front stoop, looking tense and on edge, thumbing the screen of her mobile with irritated jabs.

"You said you'd come as soon as I called," she said, chucking her shoulder bag onto the floor and herself into the passenger seat of my car. "Uncle Pete left thirty minutes ago."

"I'm sorry." There it was again.

"I rang you four times."

"I silence my phone while working."

"I was about to call an Uber."

Why didn't you?

I didn't say it.

"What would you like for dinner?" Big smile.

"Food."

Easy, Brennan.

"Does Greek sound good?"

"Whatever."

We rode the rest of the way in prickly non-conversation mode, Ruthie working her phone, me focusing on traffic.

A quick stop at the Mad Greek and we were home by seven.

I put the bag holding our gyros on the kitchen table, added plates, napkins, and utensils. Got two cans of LaCroix sparkling water from the fridge and set one at each place.

Ruthie's hunger overrode her inclination to pout.

We were eating in relatively amiable silence when my iPhone rang. Retrieving the device form the counter, and noticing Slidell's number displayed on the screen, I clicked on.

"You somewhere you can talk?"

"Hold on."

Mouthing "sorry," I pushed through the swinging door into the dining room.

Ruthie glanced up at me but didn't respond.

"Okay," I said.

"Timeless Peace," Slidell said.

It took me a moment to make the mental bridge.

"The cemetery from which Godric's body was snatched."

"Yeah."

"That's the one on Central Avenue?"

"Yeah."

"Is Timeless Peace one of those operated by the city?"

"Negative. It's private."

"When do the owners think the body was taken?"

"Sometime last week."

"Did they report it?"

"They were unaware of the situation until yesterday. Like I suspected, their security is shit."

We spoke a few more moments, then disconnected.

I returned to the kitchen.

Looked around in shock.

Ruthie was gone.

CHAPTER 14

The back door stood wide open. Beyond the screen, I could hear the usual pre-twilight symphony of crickets and frogs. The rhythmic *tic-tic-tic* of a neighbor's sprinkler. The distant hum of traffic on Queens Road.

Hurrying across the room, I slipped outside.

The evening was early September warm and muggy, the air heavy with the scents of overripe peonies, damp earth, and mown grass. Of water that had passed through a spigot and hose. And of something else, sweet and earthy.

A substance rich with terpenes.

Ruthie was a dark cutout against a sunset slowly yielding its color to the woolly gray of dusk. She sat atop my garden table, slumped, back toward me, arms hanging between splayed knees.

As I watched, she raised a hand to her face. A small oval glowed orange, lighting her features and carving soft valleys around them. A moment, then smoke paler than the deepening twilight coned from her mouth.

"Hey, lady," I said.

Her head whipped around.

"You startled me."

"Didn't mean to." There. I didn't say sorry.

"I guess the cat's out of the bag." Raising the joint, which was squeezed between her right index finger and thumb.

"You do know that weed can alter your judgment," I said, only half joking.

"Kind of like political ads."

"Good point." The kid really was funny.

"I don't smoke often. Honest. And I only do it when and where I know I'll be safe."

"Grass isn't legal recreationally in North Carolina." Christ. I sounded like a hundred-year-old granny.

"I know."

"If you plan to apply to colleges soon, a drug bust on your record could complicate things."

She shrugged.

"I hope you never smoke and drive."

"Do I look like a moron?"

"Of course not."

"Besides, I have no wheels. I am forced to depend on the kindness of strangers." Doing a passable Blanche Dubois imitation.

"Are your parents aware—"

"God, no. Mom would kill me." Her eyes went wide. "Are you going to rat me out?"

"Your secret is safe with me," I said, "unless I feel that you're endangering yourself." How I'd make that determination was better left for another day.

"Thank you, Aunt Tempe. You're the best."

"May I ask where you got the grass?"

"Remember I went on that visit to UNCC?" Her eyes gave a varsity-level roll. "It was my mother's idea. She insisted and wouldn't take no for an answer even though I've made myself absolutely clear that I've maxed out on the sitting-in-class thing."

"But you digress."

"Right. Our group's guide was a grad student—in psych, I think. A totally rad dude."

"And?"

"After the tour he asked me to join him for coffee."

"He hit on you."

"It wasn't like that."

"What was it like?"

"He introduced me to some of his friends. They have this sort of club, I guess. I don't know."

"What was his name?"

"Lester."

I raised both brows in question.

"Lester Malloy. Or Malory. Or something like that."

"Lester hooked you up with the marijuana?" Making a mental note to run this guy down through university channels.

She nodded.

"How old is Lester?"

"Seriously?" Angry, two-handed hair tuck behind both her ears. "That's exactly where my mother would go."

I waited.

"Shit. I don't know. *Grad student* age."

I just looked at her.

"Jesus, Aunt Tempe. I'm not planning to marry the guy." Full-on petulant. "Maybe in his midtwenties?"

"Ruthie, I know this little chat means you no longer view me as cool. But you're staying in my house, so I feel responsible for your safety."

Ruthie's eyes were doing the granddaddy of rolls when my mobile gave forth with the *Kill Bill* whistling clip currently programmed as a ringtone. Ruthie cocked a brow but made no comment.

Again, Slidell's number filled the screen, so I answered.

"Hold on."

Pressing the phone to my chest, I asked my niece, "Do you need anything, sweetie?"

"I'm totally cool."

"Do you have plans for tonight?"

"Hang here, watch some Tube, turn in early."

Perfect.

"Are we good?" I asked, pointing at her, then at myself.

"Totally," she said.

"What's new?" I asked Slidell as I reentered the kitchen.

"The squirrel alibied out."

"Which squirrel?"

"Bright. *Jax*"—with a mocking lilt—"claims he went to Orlando on vacation. Says he was there for two weeks, got back yesterday. Who the hell goes to Orlando for fun?"

Knowing the question was rhetorical, I said nothing.

"Anyway, I checked out his story. One credit card told the tale. Gas receipts. Tolls. A charge at the Magic Manse Motel in Kissimmee. A one-week pass to the Magic fucking Kingdom."

"World."

"What?"

"It's Disney World."

"Don't matter if it's Disney freakin' Universe. I got another possible."

"Another sex offender?"

"Eeyuh."

"I think you may be reading more into Dr. Kum—"

"I'll be interviewing this dirtbag before he has time to take a morning shit."

"When? Where?"

He told me.

"I'll be ready," I said.

Slidell was twenty minutes late. But he'd stopped at a Starbucks for morning coffee, so I couldn't be too cross.

As I sipped, burning my tongue on liquid registering at least a thousand degrees, Slidell briefed me on our target.

"Hugh Norwitz, white, age forty-four. Busted in 2012 on a 14.190.9."

"I know you'll tell me what that is."

"Indecent exposure. The prick whipped out Mr. Happy at the Manor Theater during a matinee of *The Dark Knight Rises*. Meaningful, eh?"

"Deeply."

"Norwitz was over eighteen, a couple of the *exposee*s were under sixteen. That made the act a class H felony."

"He did time?"

"Not much. But the incident got him registered as a sex offender. During a pop-in visit in 2018, a social worker spotted child porn. Then investigators found the mother lode of naughty kiddy pics on his laptop."

"He was busted for possession of child pornography."

"Am I not making myself clear?"

Santa Claus with a bad dye job and an even worse shave. That unlikely combo of descriptors popped to mind when I first laid eyes on Hugh Norwitz.

The man looked older than I expected. His neck skin hung loose, his jawline and cheekbones hunkered indistinct beneath layers of fat. A profusion of burst capillaries reddened both his cheeks. To say the Morticia-black dye job looked amateur would be excessively kind.

As anticipated, Norwitz was less than thrilled by our early-morning ding-a-ling at his artsier than Carmel-by-the-Sea Fourth Ward home. Dressed in a silk bathrobe and sherpa-style wool-lined slippers, he ordered us off his porch with an imperious flick of one wrist.

Slidell flashed his badge and laid the usual cop prose on him. Drawing himself up, Norwitz wrapped each of our palms in a weak spiritless grip, and invited us in.

The air in Norwitz's home felt Torrid Zone warm and humid. I guessed that thermostatic choice was for the benefit of the enormous, vining philodendron spreading across two of his living room walls. A carefully placed pair of blue spots illuminated the somewhat unsettling plant.

But the mongo flora was the least bizarre of the artifacts filling Norwitz's home. Taking a seat in the dining room as directed, I looked around. Saw dead animals everywhere, most stuffed and posed in poorly executed attempts at simulating their natural behaviors. A red fox, head lowered, one forepaw lifted and curled. A copperhead, body coiled, fangs bared. A Canadian goose, wings spread, a fish in its half-open beak.

Those weren't the items I found most disturbing. A stuffed cat occupied the top level of a set of shelving opposite the table, tiny patent leather boots on its hind legs, a miniature whip grasped in one raised paw. A squirrel wore a tutu and fishnet stockings on its shaved hind limbs. Two rabbits, each tuxedo attired, hugged in a bipedal cottontail embrace.

Every animal had the same beady glass eyes. The same crude stitching defacing its fur or feathers or scales.

"What the fucking fuck?" Slidell mumbled, taking in the array.

"Please sit down, sir. I've harmed no one."

"Yeah?" Jabbing a beefy forefinger in the direction of the dancing bunnies. "Tell it to those two."

"It's what I do to relax."

Still standing, Slidell whipped around to face Norwitz. "And what the galloping Christ *is* it you do?"

"Taxidermy."

"You kill animals so's you can yank out their innards and stuff them?"

"I kill nothing. I collect carcasses."

"You disembowel carrion and shove sawdust up their butts."

"That makes it sound crude."

"Ain't it?"

Affronted, Norwitz skirted Slidell's question. "An interest in taxidermy isn't that strange. I was just at a conference attended by hundreds of practitioners, some hobbyists, some professionals."

"So, this is your hobby, eh? Taxidermy with a little S&M twist?"

"My art is a unique blend of life and death."

"Art?" Slidell's eyes were now crimped with disgust. "And where is it you get 'supplies'"—hooking air quotes—"for this art? It sure as shit ain't Michaels."

"I scout rural areas. Roadsides. State and county parks."

The spots threw the same aquamarine light across Norwitz's face that they cast on the wall behind him. I couldn't help but think that the illumination made him look ghoulish.

Slidell hit Norwitz with the usual rundown of cop questions. Where were you when the remains appeared on the Frog Pond tree? On the day Bear disappeared? At the time Eleanor Godric's grave was disturbed?

Norwitz was unsure of his whereabouts but promised to consult his calendar. Which was at his place of business. Which was a two-person accounting firm.

Uncertain what Slidell's motives might be—perhaps to shock and pry loose info—I watched as he pulled a printout from his pocket and held it in front of Norwitz's face.

From my angle I could see that it was a photo taken during the Godric autopsy.

Norwitz glanced at the image. Quickly away.

"Terrible," he said, swallowing hard.

"You know anything about that?" Slidell asked, eyes narrow.

Norwitz answered with a slow shake of the head.

"You sure on that?"

"One hundred percent. That's not a sight I would ever forget."

CHAPTER 15

"That sonofabitch is so dirty I can smell the stink coming off his skin," Slidell said as we crossed the lawn outside.

"Guilty of what?"

"For starters, doodling dead animals."

"Taxidermy does not equate to bestiality."

I waited for Slidell to unlock the Trailblazer's doors.

"That ain't what I'm saying," he continued, sliding behind the wheel.

"What are you saying?"

"I'm saying the guy ain't right."

"That's harsh."

"Killing helpless animals is harsh."

It seemed pointless to pursue the conversation, so I let it go.

"Now what?" I asked, buckling my belt, then lowering my window to encourage the circulation of air already smelling of Skinny.

Slidell considered, left hand on the wheel, right index finger corkscrewing in his right ear.

"Now we talk to the NOK."

Next of kin? "Haven't we already done that?" I asked, thinking he meant Bear.

Inspecting, then flicking something I didn't want to imagine, Skinny yanked his mobile from his belt and, employing the same digit he'd used to mine the aural intruder, jabbed at the screen. After eyeballing the address proposed in response, he programmed the vehicle's navigation system.

Directions were delivered by what sounded like a chirpy robot. Slidell gunned the engine, and we set off.

"You plan to tell me whose next of kin we're about to assault?" I asked, a bit testy.

"Eleanor Godric."

"The lady stolen from her grave?"

"Eeyuh."

"Why?"

"You got a reason why not?"

I didn't.

Slidell explained that Eleanor Godric had only one living relative, a grandnephew named Harvard Boynton. Boynton, an unemployed art teacher, had lived on the outskirts of South Gastonia for the past two decades.

WAZE navigated us west on I-85 and south on HWY 321, then, after several miles, onto a two-lane cutting through cornfields that looked wilted from the relentless late-summer heat. Eventually, he rolled to a stop by a shingle-roofed wooden sign identifying the entrance to Brook Mountain Mobile Home Park. Looking around, I saw no sign of either of the natural phenomena described in the name.

Boynton's trailer was one of those silver affairs that look like sausages with the corners squared off. A spindly pine struggled to shade it. A Chevy pickup, probably new in the eighties, sat on a nearby patch of gravel.

Hand-painted in scrolly black-and-green lettering on the jerry-rigged enclosure surrounding the trailer's wheels were the words *Warning: Redneck in Residence.* A set of homemade wooden stairs connected a tiny landing with the ground.

Before Slidell and I were out of the SUV, the trailer's door opened, and a man stepped onto the stoop. He wasn't what I expected, given the message scrawled on the base of his home.

Standing about my height, the man exhibited a body mass that couldn't have exceeded mine. His skin was pale and seriously freckled, his ginger hair drawn into a meager bun atop his head.

His outfit was hard to describe. Or explain. Neon-yellow long-sleeved tee. Baggy beige cargo shorts held up by blue-and-orange silk fleur-de-lis suspenders. Striped green-and-red knee socks. Birkenstocks.

"Whatever you're peddling, I don't want it."

"Are you Harvard Boynton?" Slidell demanded, his gruffness probably triggered by distaste for the man's attire.

"I'm *warning* you," Mr. Suspenders said, with an attempt at bravado that didn't really land. "Leave now or I'll call the police."

"It's your lucky day." Slidell flashed his badge. "We are the police."

Mr. Suspenders scurried down the treads, Birkenstocks slapping at his colorful heels. "Let me see that."

Slidell extended his arm. Yanked the shield back when the man attempted to take it.

"Are you Harvard Boynton?" Slidell repeated.

"Maybe." With a sullen tilt of his head that threatened the integrity of the topknot.

"You got an Aunt Eleanor?"

"I did. She died."

"Auntie leave you a bundle so's you could buy this little palace?" Slidell cocked his chin at the mobile home.

"Eleanor didn't leave me a dime. What's this all about? Why are you here?"

Slidell ignored Boynton's questions. "Harvard. That's an odd name. Your mama have aspirations for you? Something that didn't involve trailer parks?"

Boynton said nothing.

Slidell did his quick segue thing, a trick intended to rattle an interviewee.

"You got pets, Harvard? Maybe a dog or a cat?"

"I have fur allergies, so I keep canaries."

"You eat a couple of those birds now and again?"

"Jesus. No. What kind of question—"

Slidell's phone buzzed in his shirt pocket. After checking caller ID, he strode off a few paces and turned one shoulder to us.

"Is he always like this?" Boynton murmured, half under his breath.

"Yes," I said.

"I have to go, or I'll be late for a job."

"What sort of job?"

"I perform as a clown at kids' parties."

I was about to comment but Slidell rejoined us.

"Let's go," he said to me. To Boynton, "Don't plan no European vacations. I ain't done with you."

Back in the Trailblazer, now truly a bake oven, Skinny explained why he'd cut short the interrogation.

"Nun found another one."

There was so much to unpack there, my brain struggled to organize questions.

"A nun?" The gray cells settled on that first.

"Sister Mary Adelbert," he replied, casting a sideways glance at me. "Real name Mariana Kowalski. She's at St. Peter's. You're a mackerel snapper, eh?"

"I was raised Catholic."

"Why is it nuns chuck the names their parents spent months thinking up for them?"

"Some do, some don't." Not wanting to engage in a theological debate, I left it at that. "The nun found another what?"

"Corpse. All dressed up for the show."

"A fresh body?"

"Not clear."

"Human?"

"Apparently."

"Same postmortem treatment? Eyelid stitching, feathers, glitter, one missing body part?"

"Eeyuh."

"Where?"

"Cordelia Park."

"Where's that?" I'd never heard of it.

"Northeast of Uptown."

I knew Skinny was amped when he dug a portable LED rooftop beacon from the center console and planted it on the SUV's roof.

"Buckle up!" he barked.

I did.

Strobing *red-blue-red-blue-red-blue*, we raced across town,

Skinny white-knuckling the wheel. *Moi* bracing two-handed against the dash.

A google search had shown Cordelia Park as a small patch of green space not far from the Little Sugar Creek Greenway. In less than twenty minutes we screamed into its tiny, paved parking area.

After the breakneck sprint through traffic, I needed a moment to bring my heart rate back down from the stratosphere. As the thumping settled, I scanned my surroundings.

Our Trailblazer shared the small, hedge-enclosed space with four patrol cars jammed at haphazard angles, doors flung wide, radios spitting. Beyond them was a late-model sedan, undoubtedly an unmarked CMPD vehicle.

Also present was a low, sleek number that might have been a Corvette. The sort of car you herniate yourself getting into and out of.

At the unsubtle sound of our arrival, two heads had popped up inside the Vette. Quickly dropped back down out of sight.

Young love, a sappy cluster of neurons had offered. Sweet.

At ten a.m. on a Wednesday? their more practical brethren had countered. With cop cars screaming in from all directions? More like horny desperation rudely interrupted.

The moment Slidell killed the engine we both fired out.

Cordelia Park was similar to the other sites favored by our doer. Same wood chip–blanketed playground. Same swing sets, merry-go-rounds, and slides. Same picnic tables sheltered by corrugated tin roofs. Only one grill here.

Chest-high chain-link fencing separated the park and playground from the adjacent woods. A patrolman stood guard at the gate. Slidell badged him and he waved us through.

We encountered another uniform a few yards into the trees, her face ashen beneath a sheen of sweat. She straightened on seeing us but said nothing.

There was no need.

The buzzing flies gave notice enough.

Behind the cop, a half-naked man hung upside down nailed to the trunk of a large live oak. His legs were spread, his bare feet pierced by what appeared to be railroad spikes.

The man's arms dangled limp beside his head, his right hand, purple and swollen, just a few inches short of the ground. His left hand, severed neatly at the wrist, was nowhere to be seen.

Swatting at *Diptera* annoyed by my presence, I stepped closer for a better look.

The man's eyelids were stretched wide and sewn above and below his orbits. His pupils, though dilated, fixed, and opaque, seemed to register surprise in death. Glitter winked sunlight off the man's hair and skin, and bundled feathers projected from each of his ears.

And this scene offered a macabre new twist.

Beside the human corpse, a dog's body was suspended by its hind legs. A small one, maybe twenty pounds, with a curly black coat and eyes that had been honey-brown in life.

A decorated corpse with a missing body part. Except for the canine, the pattern was all too familiar. And there was one other new element.

A pair of letters gaped raw and ugly on the man's forehead: *PE*. The eggs of energetic female flies were already whitening the borders of the incised flesh.

I shifted my focus to the dog, circling the carcass to take in a full three-sixty view. Its torso had been shaved to create a furless patch on one side. The same two letters were carved into the bluish-white rectangle of exposed skin: *PE*.

"What the fuck's *PE*?" came from behind me.

Slidell had gone so silent I'd almost forgotten he was there.

"Initials?" I tossed out.

"Hot damn. Chalk up the solve," Slidell said sarcastically.

"Physical education? Petroleum engineer? Pulmonary embolism?" Piqued by Slidell's sarcasm, I began voicing whatever popped to mind.

"Are you trying to piss me off?" Slidell sounded as irked as I felt.

"I don't hear *you* making any brilliant guesses," I said, wrist-wiping sweat from my face.

"This scumbag thinks he can screw with animals 'cause they don't count for nothing." Slidell was again thinking out loud. "Maybe rob a grave or two. Either play buys a slap on the wrist."

"He's not wrong on that."

"Yeah? He's wrong on one thing." Skinny's face had deepened to the color of a pickled beet. "No one messes with people's pets on my turf. No how. No way."

Ryan had commented on Skinny's protective attitude toward animals. A character trait my years of interaction with him had not revealed.

Slidell jabbed a thumb at the inverted man on the tree. "This vic look human to you?"

"Obviously."

"The body's still fresh?"

"The flies think it's fresh enough."

"That's it." Breathing hard, Skinny yanked his mobile from his belt. "This asshole's gone beyond sick pranks. Now he's looking at a murder-one charge."

Slidell was punching buttons when we heard the gate creak.

Startled, we both turned.

CHAPTER 16

The nun looked like an extra from a movie set in wartime Poland. Even before arthritis crooked her spine, she couldn't have claimed more than five feet in height. All other personal details—weight, figure, hair color—were hidden by the old-style black-and-white bandeau squaring off across her forehead and the veil and habit draping her body.

Trailing the ancient nun was a younger woman with mousy brown hair cut in no discernible style. Her face, though pallid and creased, was devoid of makeup. Her outfit of white blouse, gray skirt, ankle socks, and flats was as bland as attire can be and still qualify as clothing.

My spine suddenly straightened. Muscle memory resulting from years of admonishment concerning my posture. Noting a squaring of Slidell's shoulders, I wondered if he'd also been the victim of parochial schooling.

"It's the devil's work." The croaky proclamation was accompanied by the raising of one knobby, blue-veined hand.

Taken aback, I said nothing. Ditto Slidell.

The nun worked the familiar pattern on her forehead, sternum, and shoulders. Then she crossed her arms and shot her hands up under her sleeves.

Nun pose. The phrase floated back, forgotten for years.

As a kid I'd often pondered the secrets of those billowy recesses. I knew the sleeves served as temporary repositories for tissues, used and unused. But what else? An extra missal? A spare battery? A loaded Glock 19?

"I apologize," the younger woman said, proffering a hand. "I'm Sister Mona Bierhals."

"Temperance Brennan."

We shook. The woman's grip made me think of tapioca.

"Sister Adelbert has been quite unnerved since spotting that abomination in the tree."

"I understand," I said, before Skinny could open his mouth. "I'm sure the experience is upsetting for her."

I suspected both nuns remained in the park solely because the first responder cops had ordered them to.

"Gimme more kibble," Sister Adelbert demanded loud enough to be heard in Atlanta.

"Don't let the squirrels get too close," Mona warned, while producing a cellophane bag labeled *Backyard Buffet for Wildlife*. "I'll join you shortly."

The elderly nun took the feed and hobbled off.

"I'm not sure Sister Adelbert fully grasps the significance of what she's seen," Mona said.

"I understand," I said again.

"Sister Adelbert took her holy vows when she was only nineteen years old. She's now eighty-four. As you might guess from the woefully outdated habit she favors, the woman is quite set in her, well, habits."

"Cordelia is her favorite park?"

"By far. I bring her here often."

Sudden thought.

"On one of your outings, might you have crossed paths with the person who nailed the remains to the tree?"

"If so, I didn't notice. I'm too busy keeping an eye on my charge." Nodding toward the octogenarian nun now tossing kibble in a circle around her feet.

"Might she have noticed?"

Mona shrugged. "It's possible. Sister Adelbert's hearing is shot, but her vision seems fine."

"May I ask her a few questions?"

"Of course. But I'll warn you. Have a getaway plan. Once the old gal starts talking, it's hard to escape."

Mona beckoned to her companion.

Emptying the last remnants of corn and nuts onto the ground, the elderly nun shuffled over to join us.

I shot Slidell a "let me handle this" look, then greeted Adelbert and commented on one of the squirrels.

"That fat guy looks like the leader of the pack."

"She's a pesky one," Adelbert said in a voice much larger than expected for such a small person. "Actually, that little bugger yonder is alpha."

Adelbert indicated a smallish squirrel off to one side of the group. Seeing four sets of eyes pointed its way, the animal froze, bushy tail twitching like a night worker overdosed on caffeine.

"Did you know there are two hundred and eighty species of squirrels in the world?" Adelbert asked, rheumy eyes shifting between Slidell and me.

"I did not," I said.

"Ground squirrels, tree squirrels, flying squirrels. Did you know that chipmunks, prairie dogs, and groundhogs are also squirrels?"

"I wasn't aware of that, either."

"The eastern gray is the most common variety around here. That's what these fellas are."

A bit more squirrel talk, then I managed to maneuver to the topic that had brought us to the park.

"I understand it was you who noticed the remains nailed to the tree."

"Damn straight."

I looked at Mona, surprised. She shrugged.

"Detective Slidell"—I tipped my head toward said detective—"is trying to catch the person responsible for these grisly displays."

The nun looked at Skinny and me expectantly, perhaps curious about my use of the plural.

"I'm wondering," I continued. "Might you have gotten a look at the person responsible?"

"Of course I did. I may be old, but I'm not blind."

"How'd you know you was eyeballing the bastar—the person that nailed the thing up?" Slidell interjected far too sharply.

"He was walking away from the tree with a rope ladder slung over one shoulder and a leather bag hanging from the other. I told all this to one of the cops over there."

"Can you describe the man?" I asked.

"You a detective, too?" Adelbert eyed me with suspicion.

"No, sister."

"Figures. Because that's one big assumption you're making, young lady."

"I'm sorry?"

"You thinking right off that the culprit is male."

"Am I wrong?" I asked, embarrassed because she was right.

"No. But the guy wasn't huge. And he wasn't a real snappy dresser."

"What does that mean?"

"Keep in mind, I only caught a glimpse of him from a distance."

"Yes, sister."

"His shorts were tan and baggy. His shirt was blue and black. He hadn't bothered to tuck it in."

She paused, perhaps *tsk-tsk*ing inwardly at the flagrant affront to her dress code.

"Anything else?" I prodded.

"I remember his sneakers. They were such a bright lime green I thought my eyes might tear. And they had that black line on one side. Kind of like a long-tailed checkmark, I guess."

"A swoosh? The Nike logo."

"If you say so. It's beyond me what people wear these days."

"How old do you think this guy was?" Slidell spoke up again.

"Too old for such ridiculous footwear."

"Not a kid?" he pressed.

"Definitely not a kid."

"Did you notice anything else?"

"Like what?"

"Hair, skin, or eye color. Hair style? Height? Build?" Slidell's eyes were boring into the tiny woman.

The old nun shook her head. "I just saw him that once, and I was too far away."

"Did he get into a vehicle?"

"Seems so. Maybe. I'm not sure."

"What make?"

"I don't know much about cars."

"Can you describe it?" Slidell was, for Slidell, being very patient.

Sister Adelbert closed her eyes, going back in her mind to that day in the park. Opened them.

"It was small. And very dark blue. Maybe black."

"Did you catch the tag?"

Adelbert looked at me.

"The license plate," I clarified.

"No. One of those Amazon trucks was double-parked and blocking my view. But I wouldn't have been able to read a license plate from that distance anyway."

Slidell shifted his feet and cocked his chin. A signal that he was eager to move on.

"Thank you, sisters," I said. "You've been very helpful."

"You're most welcome," Mona said.

"I'll pray for you," Sister Adelbert said.

And crossed herself.

While Slidell returned to headquarters to follow up on our interview, I spent a couple of hours sorting through long-ignored correspondence at the MCME, then headed to the Annex to appease my niece, whose multiple calls I'd missed because my phone was again in silent mode.

Maybe it was low blood sugar, having eaten nothing all day. Maybe it was knowing my cupboards were bare. Maybe it was my conscience pointing out that the situation was due to my hatred of shopping. Maybe it was the friggin' heat. For some reason, my spirits had dropped into the cellar.

Coming through the back door, I called Ruthie's name. Got no response.

I saw zero sign of Birdie. Even the cat seemed to be keeping his distance.

Parking my keys and phone on the counter, I crossed to the refrigerator. Not optimistic, I opened the door and stood a moment, enjoying the *whoosh* of cool air.

In my absence, a miracle had taken place.

The shelves and drawers were crammed with a variety of healthy foods. Broccoli. Romaine and iceberg lettuce. Campari tomatoes. Carrots. Apples. Grapes. A dozen yogurts in a dozen flavors.

Choosing apricot, I grabbed a spoon and sat down at the table.

A note lay centered on one of the place mats.

> Got hungry. Called Instacart.
> Got bored. Called Uber.
> Meeting the UNCC group.
> See ya!

Kids today are more resourceful than you ever were, my naggy conscience piped up again. *You'd have binged on Coke and chips and waited for an adult to appear.*

Teens have cell phones now, I defended my adolescent self. And takeout options up the wazoo.

I ate the yogurt, hoping protein would improve my outlook.

Idly gazing out the window, I spotted something odd.

Having lived in the Annex a very long time, I know all my neighbors and their vehicles. A black sedan was parked in the spot reserved for the Woos, an elderly couple who didn't drive and had never owned a vehicle.

The CIA has nothing on the gossip network at Sharon Hall. Had the Woos purchased wheels, I'd have heard within days. They rarely had visitors. And no one ever parks in someone else's slot.

I knew the car didn't belong to the Woos. And I knew I'd never seen it before.

I scanned the vehicle, maybe a Honda. It was parked facing me, but sunlight glinting off the windshield masked its interior. I couldn't tell if anyone was in the front or back seat.

Had the car been there when I'd arrived home?

Had it followed me?

Retrieving my phone from the counter, I mimed dialing, then talking. Pretending to disconnect, I began snapping pics of the Honda.

Then, slipping the mobile into a pocket, I faked exiting the kitchen, squatted, and duck-walked back to the window. Hunkered down out of sight, I observed the Honda. Maybe Honda. If it remained parked where it was, that meant I was paranoid. If it left, that meant what? I wasn't sure.

I watched for maybe five minutes. Was about to call it quits when the driver started the engine, and the vehicle began rounding the circle drive toward my unit. Staying low, I raised my phone above my head and took more pictures.

When I was certain the Honda had passed my front window, I rose for a better view. Saw the car reach the bottom of the hill, turn right, and vanish.

Opening my laptop, I downloaded the pics so I could see them better.

The car was a four-door black Accord with a decal on the right side of the back window and a starburst pattern on each of the hubcaps.

I expanded and studied several shots, hoping for a fuller view of the license plate.

CHAPTER 17

Unlike Sister Adelbert with the vehicle at Cordelia Park, I was able to make out three characters: TL3. I entered the letter-number combo into my Notes app. Added: *black Honda Accord.*

Then I clomped upstairs, peeled off my sweat-soaked clothing, and took a quick shower. I was planning to treat Ruthie to dinner at a restaurant of her choice. Maybe it was the sight of all that refrigerated produce, but I was in the mood for lettuce roll ups and hoped she'd choose Baoding.

Point of information. My brain is an impulse buyer when it comes to cravings.

Before that outing happened, unbeknownst to me, it would be an AT&T evening. My mother was the first to call. She had no news to share, just wanted to chat. Then it was Harry, offering a heads-up that Mama thought I sounded tense. After disconnecting with my sister, I returned to the kitchen to feed Birdie. Still no sign of my niece.

To kill time, I booted my laptop, created a file, and uploaded the pics of the Honda that I'd taken with my phone. Belly full, the cat curled beside me and watched with disinterest.

Ansel Adams need never feel threatened by my photographic skills. Quickly snapped without benefit of a viewfinder, most of my shots were dark and blurry. I chose the four clearest and copied them into a photo editing app. Enlarged each until it verged on pixelation, then centered the license on the screen.

No matter how much I increased contrast or sharpened edges, the plate remained shadowy and largely unreadable.

Seven came and went.

Seven-thirty.

Still no Ruthie.

I tried her number but was rolled to voice mail.

Ryan was the night's third caller. He rang at seven-fifty.

"*Bonsoir, ma chérie*. How goeth your day?"

"I doubt that's a word."

"It's Old Saxon."

"Since when are you familiar with Old Saxon?

"I had to play one in junior high. I wanted slide trombone, but the kid with the pimples grabbed the last one."

"Did therapy help in overcoming your grief?"

"Mostly it was soccer. And dropping out of band. What's new?"

I briefed Ryan on developments since we'd last spoken. The identification of the stolen cemetery corpse as that of Eleanor Godric. Slidell's and my visit with Godric's grandnephew, Harvard Boynton. The interviews with Jeremy Dahmer, Jordan Bright, and Hugh Norwitz. The man and dog incised with the letters *PE* discovered in Cordelia Park. Sister Adelbert's description of the person she'd seen there.

"Bright and Norwitz are registered sex offenders," I added in closing.

"Slidell's still convinced the displays are erotic in nature?"

"Yes. I have to admit, Norwitz was one weird dude. The guy specializes in provocative taxidermy."

I described some of the items in Norwitz's collection.

"Nothing surprises me anymore," Ryan said. "I'll bet if you google sexy taxidermy, a zillion links will come up."

"I'll pass. Are you still planning to arrive on Sunday?" I asked.

"If the good lord's willing and the creeks don't flood."

"Rise," I corrected.

"What?"

"The saying goes, if the creeks don't rise."

"Like, unite to start a revolution?"

"Never mind," I said. "By the way, my niece may still be bunking in at the Annex."

"Awesome sauce."

"Your teen-ageese is worse than your Old Saxon."

"I'll work on it."

I debated mentioning the black Honda Accord. Decided against it. I had no proof that the driver had actually followed me.

"A word of warning, Tempe," Ryan said in closing.

"Yes?"

"Don't be offended if these taxidermists tell you to get stuffed."

We'd just disconnected when Ruthie arrived, clutching a flat, white box two-handed.

"Hey, girl," I said, probably sounding dorkier than Ryan ever would.

"Hey."

"You look like you're in a good mood."

"I've just had the most super-mega evening." Sliding the box onto the counter, she added, "I hope you like donuts. I didn't buy them. They were left over."

"You were with your UNCC pals?"

"Yeah. One of them—that guy I mentioned, Lester Meloy—gave me a hitch. Anyway, we went to this coffee shop near campus. It was fire."

"Mmm." Not sure if fire was good or bad.

"There are five of them. They're kind of a group."

"That's nice."

"Yeah, we totally gel. Except for this one chick I could do without."

"Why?"

"She's kinda salty."

My brows floated in question.

Ruthie gave a quick shrug of one shoulder. "I think she's an engineer or something. She's just, you know, extra."

I didn't know. But I let it go.

"You remember my friend Ryan," I asked, changing the subject.

"The tall dude with the Cumberbatch eyes."

"If that means blue, yes."

"Duh."

"Anyway, Ryan's coming for a visit."

"When?"

"Probably Sunday. But don't worry about him. I want you to stay as long as you like."

Ruthie said nothing.

"You know I love having you here, sweetie."

"Right," she said, her smile holding but her tone a few degrees cooler. "Until you don't."

With that somewhat cryptic remark, she turned and left the room.

The next caller was Slidell.

"I looked into this meeting Norwitz was talking about."

"What meeting?"

Paper rustled. I pictured Skinny running a finger through hand-scrawled notes.

"The NCTA."

A male voice sounded in the background.

"Hold on."

The line muffled as Skinny pressed the phone to his chest.

While waiting for him to reengage, I played a head game with the letters NCTA. The Northern Cypress Tinkers Association. The New Caledonia Turnpike Authority. The National Coalition of Turds and Assholes.

"The North Carolina Taxidermist's Association." Slidell picked up as though there'd been no interruption. They got a website."

"Don't tell me you went online."

"You want to hear this or not?"

"Go on."

"Norwitz was on the level. These toads got a society, and they hold an annual convention. I guess they compare notes on shoving sawdust up the butts—"

"There's one taking place soon?"

"As we speak. And right down the road in Clemmons. I'm thinking I'll drop by. Check these freaks—"

"I'm in."

Ruthie asked if we could eat at a restaurant called Red Rocks Cafe. A bit curious how she'd heard of the place, I happily agreed. The food is good, and the drive would take only fifteen minutes.

She also asked if this new friend of hers, Lester Meloy, could join us. I agreed to that request also, eager to see what Mr. Meloy was all about.

When we arrived at eight-thirty, the terrace was packed. It always is in good weather. Meloy was waiting behind a mug of beer at one of the outdoor tables, legs outstretched, ankles crossed, studying his phone.

Ruthie called out as we approached.

Meloy's head popped up. He smiled and rose, shirt glowing white in the dim lighting. With his neatly cropped hair and clean-shaven face, I couldn't help thinking the guy looked like a plebe at a military school. A tall one. I guessed his height at six feet plus.

Ruthie made introductions.

Meloy and I shook hands, then we all sat.

"It's such an honor to meet you, Dr. Brennan. Ruthie has told me so much about you. Please forgive me if I fanboy a bit."

"And it's nice to meet you," I said, surprised by Meloy's gushing enthusiasm. "I'm sure Ruthie has exaggerated—"

"Not at all. The work you do is so very important. You provide people with answers. With comfort in their time of grief. I truly admire you."

"Thank you."

"Can I get you something? A beer? A glass of wine? Are you hungry?"

"Starving."

In the past every item at Red Rocks was named for a local celebrity, some A-listers, the majority less alphabetically lofty. I missed that. Ordered the lemon herb chicken.

We made small talk while awaiting, then consuming our meals. As we were finishing, and the conversation began to lag, I asked Meloy about his graduate studies.

"I'm working on my master's thesis."

"In psych?" Thinking that's what Ruthie had said.

"Actually, my topic is interdisciplinary. Kind of a crossover between English Lit and psych, with a soupçon of philosophy tossed in for spice."

"Ah. The underappreciated 'soft sciences.'" I hooked air quotes.

"What do you mean?" Meloy's brows dipped.

"Don't get me wrong, much of anthropology falls into that category.

But at least biological anthro allows one to measure and weigh and photograph one's subjects. The scientific method. Hard data. That's why the subfield attracted me."

"One can formulate and test hypotheses with psychology."

"You're right. Maybe what I mean is one can't structure experiments and manipulate variables with humans the way one can with animals."

"I'm not sure I agree."

Not wanting the conversation to grow contentious, I shifted subjects. "Want to give me your two-minute elevator pitch?" I asked.

"Seriously?" The whole boyish face lit up. "You're really interested?"

"Of course." I wasn't. But the guy was so enthused I couldn't say no.

"I'm a Dante nut."

"Dante Alighieri, as in, *The Divine Comedy*?"

"Exactly. I'm fascinated by Dante's ranking of a society's view of evil. What's absolutely evil, what's fairly evil, what's maybe not so bad. And specifically, how those views change over time."

Seeing my expression, undoubtedly one of confusion, Meloy continued.

"The *Inferno*, the first book of the *Divine Comedy* was written in 1310. In it, Dante lays out his vision of hell. His Inferno. That vision was inspired by biblical references to the seven deadly sins."

"From the book of Proverbs," I said.

"Man, your aunt knows her stuff." The comment was directed to Ruthie, but Meloy's eyes held on me.

"Pride, envy, greed, sloth, lust, anger, and gluttony," Ruthie reeled off.

"You two are amazing," Meloy said flopping back in his chair.

"Credit all those Bible courses I was forced to endure as a kid," said Ruthie. She sounded a little miffed at the turn the conversation had taken.

"Have you begun writing?" I asked Meloy.

"Yes, ma'am."

"Fun times," I said.

"Oh, yeah." Rolling his eyes. Which were an odd dusky-gray flecked with olive.

We both laughed.

Meloy's mention of evil had taken me back to my recent conversation with Adina Kumar.

"I have a friend who studies evil," I said.

"Is he a psychologist?"

"She is."

"My research probably skews in a different direction than hers. I'm not concerned with defining evil. Or explaining its causes. Or preventing it. My focus is on the public perception of evil and how that perception changes over time. How does a society classify an act as evil? Based on what criteria? Does beating a helpless dog qualify? Sexually assaulting a nun? Imprisoning a child in some creepy underground chamber?"

"It's sooo hard to find creepy underground chambers these days." Ruthie's comment was delivered with a joking waggle of both hands.

"*Au contraire*," Meloy said. "Did you know there's a network of passageways under this city?"

"Really?"

"Yep. They're old mining tunnels."

"Can someone just, like, explore them?" Ruthie's tone suggested a mix of horror and excitement.

"Theoretically, yeah. Why? You thinking of taking a peek?"

"No way." With a head shake so vehement it bounced the braids sprouting from high on her scalp. "You know how psychologists say every person is afraid of something? My phobia is closed dark spaces. A subterranean tunnel would freak me out."

"It's a reasonable fear," Meloy said. "Bad things happen to people underground. That's why the city tries to keep the access locations hush-hush. But serious urban spelunkers know where they are."

"Urban spelunkers?"

"Some prefer the term building hackers. Or urbex. They're people who find and explore deserted sites."

"Sounds illegal." I was playing the naggy old granny again. "And dangerous."

"Right on both counts," Meloy agreed.

Ruthie continued her grilling as though I hadn't interrupted. "What kind of sites?"

"Could be anything. An abandoned amusement park, hospital, school, insane asylum."

"How do urbexers find these places?"

"Mostly online. Websites like Forbidden Places, for example."

"Definitely not for me, but this is too totally rad." Ruthie's eyes were Frisbees. "Have you explored any sites here in Charlotte?"

"Several."

"What was your fave?"

"An abandoned boys' prison out in Cabarrus County."

"No way."

Meloy nodded. "The Stonewall Jackson Manual Training and Industrial School. The facility opened in 1909 and was in use until not that long ago. The place is one grim mother."

As Ruthie started to ask another question, the waiter appeared with our check. Before I could dig out my wallet, Meloy produced a credit card and handed it to him.

"I'm happy to—" I said, trying to rush in.

"My treat, Dr. Brennan. It's a privilege to dine with you and your niece."

The three of us left the restaurant together. Wishing us a good evening, Meloy veered off toward the parking lot.

I offered Ruthie a ride home to Katy's house. Again. She refused, again, saying she was a big girl and could find her own way.

I waited until Ruthie's Uber arrived and she was safely inside. The driver made a U-turn, a right onto the street, then a left one block south.

Crossing to my Mazda, I noticed a vehicle leave the curb a few yards down from where we'd been standing. The silhouette behind the wheel wore a ball cap, so I couldn't tell if the driver was male or female. The car's head and taillights were off.

I followed Ball Cap's progress, hoping he or she would realize the vehicle was dark. When the car passed under a streetlamp, I could make out its color and model.

A black Honda Accord.

The Accord made a U-turn, a right onto the street, then a left one block south.

Was Ball Cap following Ruthie?

As a wave of uneasiness washed over me, I tried but failed to make out the plate.

Yanking my cell phone from my purse, I dialed my niece's number.

CHAPTER 18

Early the next day, Slidell and I set out to mingle with taxidermists.

Clemmons, a suburb of Winston-Salem, claims a population of twenty-two thousand residents and boasts more than five hundred holes available to golfers. The town's main point of pride is its proximity to Tanglewood Park, a recreational area offering tennis, horseback riding, gardens, campgrounds, and, of course, golf.

Members of the NCTA—the butt-stuffers, as Slidell had taken to calling them—were holding their annual conference at the Village Inn, just off I-40. At ten-thirty he swung his Trailblazer into the hotel's parking area and killed the engine.

We spent a moment assessing the setup. Saw a red-roofed overhang shielding a glass-walled lobby accessed via double glass doors. A low-rise wing shooting off to the left. The entrance to a place called The Crosby, presumably a bar, lit by neon signage halfway down the wing.

Wordlessly, Slidell and I got out and went in through the main entrance.

Inside, the place looked like every other convention hotel I've ever visited. Gleaming tile on the lobby floor. Globe pendants overhead. Patterned faux-wool carpeting on corridors leading to rooms in which marriages were celebrated, proms danced, business strategies hammered out.

I assumed meetings were in session, since the large open space was mostly deserted. A placard on a tripod listed options: educational seminars covering topics such as stitching and air brushing; a trade show with exhibitor demonstrations; a mounting competition.

A man and woman stood to the right of the reception desk, shoulders touching, but not talking. Both appeared to be well past sixty. Their red plaid shirts looked like variations on a theme.

Four women huddled in a scrum, discussing a pamphlet held by the tallest of the group. Raised voices and agitated gestures suggested sharp disagreement.

A priest sat in one of the upholstered armchairs, hands resting on the handle of a carved wooden cane. As with everyone that I'd encountered since arriving at the Inn, staff excepted, he wore a plastic-encased badge on a lanyard looping his neck.

"Yeah, baby."

The utterance brought my attention back to Slidell. The big man was already on the move, striding toward a beverage cart being rolled into position against the far wall.

Equally desperate for caffeine, I followed.

Wiggling free a Styrofoam cup, Slidell helped himself by thumbing the lever on the industrial-sized coffee maker. After adding three packets of sugar and the cream-like contents of two tiny plastic containers, he stirred, sipped, then winced.

"Jesus Christ, that's freakin' scalding." Touching a finger to his upper lip.

I pointed to a sign beside the urn. *Hot Coffee.*

"Yeah, but they don't gotta make the stuff like it's lava."

I said nothing.

Blowing across the offending liquid, Slidell started to share his take on the crowd.

"These yahoos look like they fell off a slow boat—"

"What is it you hope to accomplish here?" I asked curtly. I'd overdosed on Skinnyisms during the one-hour drive from Charlotte.

"I'm *hoping* someone knows something about the dickhead nailing corpses up on my turf. The *dickhead* now adding humans to his sick little game."

"Have you thought about what to say?"

Slidell swiveled to face me, brows V-ing down above the bridge of his nose.

"I'm thinking I'll open with something like, 'Excuse me, ma'am, any chance you know a sick fuck gets his jollies nailing up dead animals or robbing graves?'"

"I doubt that approach will prove productive."

"What are you, my dialogue coach?"

"I'm sure these people view themselves as colleagues. They've probably known each other for years," I added, drawing on my own experience as a member of the American Academy of Forensic Sciences, and my annual attendance at the AAFS conference.

"I could just badge 'em."

"Sure. The hard Johnny Law come-on always loosens tongues."

After some discussion, we decided to divide and conquer. Skinny would work the men while I interviewed the women. At my suggestion, we came up with a set of questions that, hopefully, would seem nonthreatening and yield cooperation.

I decided to start with the quartet bickering over the pamphlet. Quickly closing the gap between us, I called out in my friendliest voice.

"Having a good conference, ladies?" An inane question asked endlessly at AAFS meetings.

Four faces swiveled my way, their expressions varying. One seemed surprised, one annoyed. Two looked totally neutral.

"We are," one of the neutral pair responded, a woman with a bad red dye job wearing the entire line sold by some Target cosmetics counter. "And you?"

"I am."

"Excellent." Red Dye's badge gave her name as Cheri-Lynn Dirkus, her business as The Hunter's Friend Taxidermy in Pigeon Forge, Tennessee.

"Have you spotted any interesting sessions on the program?" I posed another standard small-talk meeting query.

The four exchanged glances far too mischievous for adult women. When Dirkus, who seemed to be the group's spokesperson, leaned toward me, I detected the sweet aroma of bourbon.

"This info is not for public consumption, but we're here because our employers paid to send us," Dirkus said. "We've become friends over the years, and we're less interested in the latest taxi methods than we are in spending time together."

"In the bar!" Chirped a woman with tight gray curls and a lopsided smile resembling the slash on an Amazon box.

"And meeting men!" Added another, younger woman with freckles covering every inch of her face. She was large but not fat, just thick-necked and broad chested.

"Any luck on that score?" I asked, glancing at her badge. Her name was obscured, but I could see that the employer was Sammy's Taxidermy and Tannery in Saluda, North Carolina.

"So far all clunkers, no keepers," Freckle Face said with a laugh.

"May I ask an odd question?" I kept my tone light.

All four nodded.

"Do any of you know a man named Hugh Norwitz?"

As before, the women's eyes met. This time the shared message seemed revulsion, not mischief.

"Is Norwitz a buddy of yours?" Dirkus asked.

"Not at all."

"Did he hit on you?"

"No."

"Why are you interested in him?"

Seeing no reason to hold back, I laid out the bare essentials of the situation involving Bear and the other animal displays. I did not name the main players: Crawford Joye, Bear's owner; Eleanor Godric, the corpse stolen from a cemetery; Adina Kumar, the psychologist who'd profiled the doer and predicted an escalation in behavior; Ralph Balodis, the retired veterinarian; Jordan Allen Bright, the sex offender turned vet tech. The man and dog hanging in Cordelia Park.

I concluded by saying that Hugh Norwitz's name had come up in a few interviews. I made no mention of Norwitz's old conviction for child pornography.

Three of the women listened attentively. The fourth might have. It was hard to tell since she made no eye contact but continuously scanned the lobby in the way convention-goers do, searching for more interesting or more prestigious conversation ops.

When I'd finished, Dirkus asked, "What's your role in all this?"

I explained my part in the investigation.

"And the oaf over there?" she asked, chin-cocking Slidell, who was bully-questioning a man with a salt-and-pepper beard reaching almost to his enormous belt buckle.

"He's a detective." I left it at that.

Again, Dirkus looked to her companions.

Again, they nodded in unison, like a trio of puppets worked with a single string.

"The four of us have been coming to these meetings for years," Dirkus said. "So has Hugh Norwitz. But I doubt any of us would claim to *know* him."

"Why not?" I asked.

"The guy's not exactly social," Freckle Face said.

"Let's be honest," the tall woman said. She was Larkie Oddle with Benny's Wild Game Taxidermy and Butcher Shop in Chapel Hill. "Norwitz is a creep."

"I'm down with that," Freckle Face agreed.

"A creep how?" I asked.

Freckle Face shrugged one polyester leopard-skin-clad shoulder. "Arrogant. Overbearing. Self-important."

"He's a bully used to getting his way," Dirkus added.

"Bingo." Oddle jabbed a finger of agreement at her companion.

"Do you think Norwitz is capable of committing the atrocities I just described?" Sweeping my gaze over four pairs of eyes.

"Do I think he could kill and behead a dog?" Oddle asked.

"Yes."

"Without missing a heartbeat."

The other three did their synchronized nodding thing.

A second to digest that, then I asked, "Does anyone else come to mind who might fit the profile?"

They gave that some thought. Or pretended to in order to make me happy. Then each shook her head.

A follow-up question was forming on my tongue when motion in my peripheral vision caught my attention. Turning, I noted that the lobby had grown significantly more crowded.

Through the press of bodies, I could see Slidell thumb-jabbing at me, then at the corridor through which we'd entered. The not-so-subtle gesture meant he was ready to move on.

I thanked Dirkus, Oddle, and the other two for their cooperation and assured them their comments would remain confidential.

"If you think of anything else, please give me a call," I encouraged, handing out my cards.

"Of course," Dirkus said.

I wove my way toward the hall to join Slidell. We didn't speak until we'd moved far enough away to be able to hear.

"Christ almighty, I feel like one of those fish packed asshole to armpit in a can."

"Sardines don't have arms."

"Always the know-it-all." Slidell's face was glossy, his cheeks flushed from the proximity of so much warm flesh. "You score anything useful?"

"Hugh Norwitz is a creep and an arrogant bully," I said.

"Yeah?"

"That was the take among the ladies."

"Well, ain't that a pisser. The guys I questioned thought he was the salt of the earth."

"Seriously?"

"One old geezer described him as courtly, whatever the hell that means." Slidell checked his watch. "I need grub."

The Crosby wasn't open for lunch. And Slidell had a "hankering" for pizza. So, we trudged through the heat to the SUV and drove a short distance to a place called Spaghetti Park. Seemed a reasonable choice given Skinny's craving.

Skinny ordered a build-your-own Sicilian pizzetta. I listened with dismay to the long list of toppings he wanted, including doubles on onions and garlic. Wondered if I should buy a full-face respirator mask for the trip home.

I chose the wild mushroom ravioli. Which turned out to be excellent.

Slidell and I spent the rest of the day interacting with conference attendees, making the same queries again and again. Many of those we questioned had met Norwitz, but none knew the man well enough to offer insight into his character.

When we asked if any other NCTA member might fit our doer's profile, one name came up twice. Ozmand "Ozzie" Key.

The last presentations concluded at five. Then the venues and corridors slowly emptied as people headed to their cars, to their rooms, or to The Crosby for drinks.

Slidell and I made one quick swing through the pub. Eyes focused on their Pinots and Manhattans, or on the parquet floor, the badge-wearing patrons were now cool to our presence. Realizing we were accomplishing nothing, we decided to call it a day.

Skinny drove like a madman, saying he was eager to run the name Ozmand Key. With his typical tunnel vision, he was certain the guy would come up on a sex offender list.

Though I suspected the lovely Ms. Lyric was the impetus for Skinny's lead foot, I said nothing. Buckled up, I leaned back, closed my eyes, and thought about my upcoming visit with Ryan.

Eager to distance myself from all things taxidermic.

CHAPTER 19

Traffic was heavy and moved like sludge through a clogged pipe. The drive to Charlotte took almost two hours.

Arriving home shortly before eight, I zapped a frozen dinner of P.F. Chang's Dan Dan noodles and ate while watching CNN with Birdie. The cat appeared to tense during coverage of the Middle East bombings but kept his opinion to himself.

After washing my utensils and wiping down the table and counter, I showered, then tried reading the Sandra Brown novel I was halfway through.

My eyelids grew heavier with each page. Not the fault of the book. A dinner of noodles will do that to my hypothalamus.

At ten I gave up and headed to bed.

Despite my postprandial drowsiness, sleep eluded me.

I spent hours tossing and turning, punching the pillow, kicking off, then retrieving the comforter. Checking and rechecking the time.

Midnight came and went.

Two a.m.

Three-thirty.

My mind scrolled through the possible causes. Maybe the day's outing with Slidell. Maybe the chemicals contained in frozen meals. The week's events looped ceaselessly in my overstimulated brain.

I pictured Bear and the other animals found nailed to trees, their faces painted and glittered, their features stretched into macabre expressions.

I saw Eleanor Godric, the cemetery burial. The mixed bag of bones from Steven's Creek Nature Preserve. The man and dog hanging in Cordelia Park.

I heard voices.

Ralph Balodis explaining the use of a scanner.

Adina Kumar predicting the doer's escalation.

Sister Adelbert describing a man wearing shorts.

Jordan Allen Bright telling his dog, Millie, not to bite Slidell.

Hugh Norwitz and what Slidell called his erotic taxidermy hobby.

Other players in my nocturnal operetta came from closer to home.

Slidell, still obstinately focused on sex offenders.

Katy, off to South Carolina to comfort a client.

Ryan, arriving on Sunday.

Ruthie, moody, but apparently happy here. Katy told me that Kit had phoned to report his daughter's desire to spend her senior year in Charlotte.

I rendered only one opinion on that, saying it was a big step. A decision that was up to Katy, Ruthie, and her father. Or was that two opinions?

Birdie lay silently curled at my side. I reached down to stroke his head. He didn't withdraw, nor did he crank up his usual low-pitched buzz.

The cat seemed unhappy with me. Or was I imagining censure where none existed?

My thoughts drifted back to Ruthie. To our Red Rocks meal with her UNCC friend Lester Meloy.

Meloy had been a charming and witty dinner companion. His enthusiasm for his—in my opinion somewhat esoteric—research was endearing.

Then why had the encounter with Meloy left me feeling uneasy? Was the guy's speech too glib? His charm too slick?

Or was I being overly critical because of Meloy's connection to my niece? Though a few years older than Ruthie—living the grad school versus the high school chapter of life—he seemed interested only in mentorship. Perhaps friendship.

The black rectangle that was my front-facing window unexpectedly oozed to gray.

I glanced at my bedside clock.

The glowing digits said 4:17.

What the hell?

Before I could cross the carpet for a peek outside, headlights slashed the darkness around me. Shadows elongated and veered sharply.

Then, as quickly as it had brightened, the room dimmed again.

I lay with my heart beating a wee bit faster.

Who would be mounting the circle drive at this hour? A doomsayer gaggle of brain cells demanded.

Not your business. A more rational cluster replied.

My neighbors' well-being is my business.

You're becoming that snoop that everyone hates.

The doomsayer neurons had no comeback to that.

Back in bed, I cleared my mind and gave free rein to my thoughts. Like a Sidewinder missile, they arrowed straight to Bear and the other animal displays.

Despite learning almost zilch at the NCTA conference, Slidell remained convinced that our doer was a psycho taxidermist. Maybe Hugh Norwitz. Maybe Ozzie Key.

I wasn't feeling it.

But what *was* I feeling? My subconscious kept teasing my higher centers, hinting at some tidbit just out of reach.

What tidbit? A piece I was failing to recognize? A pattern I was missing? What kind of pattern? A pattern suggestive of what?

Frustrated, I forced my attention to Ryan's upcoming visit and began a mental list of possible outings. The Whitewater Center. The NASCAR Hall of Fame. The Mint Museum.

Somewhere along the way I finally drifted off.

Ryan was hating the smell of sweaty bodies assaulting his nose. The taste of exhaust coating his tongue. The sun's heat scorching his shoulders and scalp.

Above all, he was hating the roar of the powerful V8 engines blasting his ears.

Bottom line. Ryan was loathing NASCAR.

Again, he complained about having to be at the Speedway.

Again, I told him why we were there.

My explanation had something to do with Slidell. And Birdie.

Ryan opened his mouth to respond.

Another car screamed past, drowning out his words.

Another.

Another.

Mind clawing to the surface from a very deep sleep, I opened my eyes.

The room was filled with that hazy half-light that presages the coming of dawn.

The clock now said 6:47.

The souped-up race car shrilled again.

No, it was the phone.

I lifted the device and clicked on.

"Yes."

"We may have us another one."

"Detective Slidell?" Over-enunciating as one does when trying to sound awake.

"No. It's room service ringing with your wake-up call."

It was too early, and I'd had no coffee. I said nothing.

"I just got off the phone with Harve Acorn," Slidell went on. "Acorn caught a call about a body at the McDowell Nature Preserve."

"Acorn's the tall gray-haired detective who walks with a limp?"

"Yeah. The guy's a real piece of work, thinks—"

"McDowell is down off York Road?" Suspecting where this was going, I was coming awake fast.

"Yeah. Acorn heard about the cases we're looking at. You know, through the cop shop grapevine, and he—"

A woman spoke in the background. I couldn't make out her words.

"Hold on," Slidell said.

The line muffled.

Birdie took advantage of my silence to head butt my arm. I stroked his head, which was not what he wanted. He was jonesing for breakfast.

Seconds passed, then Slidell was back.

"Acorn figured this new DOA sounded like our doer. Paint, glitter, face messed up, missing body parts."

Bird nudged me harder. This time, I ignored him.

"What's the plan?"

"I'm meeting Acorn at McDowell in sixty."

"I'll be ready in thirty."

Lake Wylie was created in 1904 when the Catawba Power Company built a dam and power plant between Charlotte, North Carolina, and Fort Mill, South Carolina. The thirteen-thousand-acre body of water straddles the border between the states like a giant meandering millipede.

Hugging a stretch of Wylie's shoreline is the McDowell Nature Preserve. Like the other locations in which animal remains were displayed, McDowell is composed mostly of undeveloped forest and grassland, but also contains picnic and recreational areas. Also like the other sites favored by our doer, McDowell is easily accessed via a major thoroughfare.

During the drive to the preserve, Slidell briefed me on the little he'd discovered about Ozzie Key.

Key, now in his forties, was a native Charlottean who'd dropped out of South Mecklenburg High School to enlist. Following his discharge from the army, he hadn't bothered to pursue a GED.

Currently, Key lived alone—no wife, no kids, no girlfriend, no roommate—in a small rental home off North Sharon Amity Road. He worked part-time as a Wendy's cook, part-time as the shampooer for a dog spa near the Southpark mall.

Slidell learned that Key had a sheet going back to his middle school years. Nothing major, nothing violent. Shoplifting. Petty larceny. One auto theft bust that landed him in the can for five years. Several DUIs.

All in all, Key's profile didn't read like that of a candidate for MENSA.

The day's outing unfolded as a reboot of our trip to Chantilly.

Until we connected with Harvey Acorn.

Harve the Nut, to his friends. Of whom there were few, according to hearsay.

My policy is to avoid gossip about the personal lives of others. That strategy often leaves me out of the loop. Truth be told, I'm happy that way.

So, here's what I knew about Harve the Nut.

Three years back, Acorn had left the NYPD to accept a much less prestigious job with the department in Charlotte. There was talk at the time, of course, with explanations varying.

One version had it that Acorn had appeared drunk at the workplace once too often. Another that he'd been caught *in flagrante delicto* with the captain's wife. Another that he'd been nailed taking a bribe.

Acorn's account of his southern migration relied on far less drama. He attributed the change of locale to his personal arrival at a tipping point regarding three issues: snow shoveling, commuting, and paying through the nose for his kids' private schools.

I'd met Acorn several times over the years. Folio briefings, strategy sessions, police charity events, that sort of thing. But I'd never worked with the guy.

That said, my limited exposure to Acorn had been enough to form an opinion. For once, I couldn't disagree with Skinny and the others.

Acorn was a pompous prick with a ninety-ton chip on one shoulder. A man with an elevated view of himself. A man who always insisted on having the last say.

Acorn's vehicle was part of the usual crime scene carnival in the McDowell parking lot to which Slidell had been directed. The MCME and CSU trucks. Several CMPD cruisers. An armada of unmarked cars. Cordelia Park all over again.

A pair of vans each bore the logo of a local TV affiliate, one for ABC and the other for CBS. A news crew sat inside one. A cameraman and an on-air reporter stood outside the other. Both looked annoyed at being denied access to the actual body recovery. Blood and gore boosts ratings, and they weren't getting the footage.

Like Slidell, Acorn drove an SUV. Unlike Skinny's, his was black.

Acorn was waiting behind the wheel, one hand clutching a YETI cup, the other hanging from an arm draped around the back of the passenger seat. A very long arm.

Slidell and I alighted. I hauled my recovery kit from the trunk, then we started toward the black SUV.

On recognizing Slidell, Acorn muscled himself out onto the pavement, long, skinny limbs working in oddly graceful concert. Yielding to the heat, he'd abandoned his jacket and wore only a short-sleeved blue shirt and khaki pants—size 36 giraffe. His tan leather shoes looked like the product of a factory in Verona.

The two men greeted each other when five feet apart.

"Detective."

"Detective."

"DOA's still here?" Slidell asked.

Acorn nodded. "The little lady ME's been and gone. Her recovery team is waiting until CSU clears the scene."

Little lady ME? I said nothing.

Acorn's gaze slid to me, then back to Slidell. His right eye was such a deep earthy brown it was impossible to distinguish iris from pupil. His left eye was the milky blue of over-washed denim.

"Doc Brennan's been working these animal cases," Skinny offered in justification for my presence. "I understand this new one's jazzed up like the others?"

"She's working them how?" Acorn asked, ignoring Slidell's question.

"She knows bones. Now, you gonna tell me what we got here?"

"It sure as hell ain't bones."

Crossing his arms and spreading his feet, Slidell drilled Acorn with a laser stare.

"Okay, genius. It ain't bones. How about you tell us what the fuck it *is*."

"I think it's best you see for yourself."

CHAPTER 20

Adina was right. The doer was escalating.

That was my first horrified reaction.

Acorn had led us through the woods to a ten-foot square marked off with yellow police tape. The enclosed area had been cleared of all low-hanging vines and ground creepers, vegetation which now lay in a heap to one side.

A pair of uniforms stood guard, feet spread, thumbs hooked into their Sam Browne belts. Both sported dark Aviator Ray-Bans, making their eyes impossible to read.

The two CSU techs wore white, hooded, front-zippered coveralls. One was dictating notes into his phone as the other shot video.

The two-person MCME team waited off to one side. A folded body bag lay at their feet.

All but the videographer turned as the three of us emerged from the trees.

Greetings were exchanged. Names.

The cops were Hayes and Z something with a lot of syllables. And an abundance of dark hair knotted at the nape of her neck.

I'd done one recovery with Hayes. A putrefied body jammed in a culvert. He'd been competent and professional. I'd never met Z.

The MCME crew was composed of an old-timer and a newbie. Joe Hawkins and I had worked dozens of cases together over the years. He looked his usual glum, cadaverous self.

Hawkins's younger partner introduced himself as Winslow. He was in his twenties with thin, sandy hair, pale splotchy skin, and thick glasses with weird pinkish-orange frames. I wasn't sure if Winslow was the guy's first or last name.

"What's happened so far?" I asked no one in particular.

"CSU processed the scene, but we were told not to touch the DOA until you arrived," Hawkins said.

"Pain in the ass," Acorn said. "We could be done and out of here by now."

Ignoring that rather rude comment, I addressed Hayes.

"Did you recover anything of interest?"

"Candy wrappers, a Bud can, and a shit ton of condoms."

"Party hardy." Acorn twirled one finger in the air.

"No one's disturbed the remains?" I clarified.

"One ballsy squirrel," Hayes said.

"I discouraged him," Acorn said, grinning.

Wondering what "discouraged" meant, not really wanting to know, I scanned the scene.

The deceased was seated below a towering loblolly pine, legs straight out, arms twisted backward and nailed to the trunk. The head was hanging low, the neck vertebrae jutting sharp as the dorsal fins on a shark.

My mind flashed to the corpse discovered by Sister Adelbert in Cordelia Park. To the unearthed cemetery burial that was Eleanor Godric. The similarities were striking.

I logged details.

As with those bodies, this one was human and wore a ball cap. Blue paint and glitter had been applied to the head and face.

Below the cap, a red paisley bandanna covered the decedent's scalp, knotted low in back. A gold stud in the shape of a clenched fist pierced the left ear.

I noted skin the color of weak tea. Kinky black hair corkscrewing from the bandanna's edges.

The decedent's pants had slipped below a level ideal for decorum. The bared genitalia looked shriveled and bluish in the bright morning sun, but clearly proclaimed that the corpse was male.

On top, the man wore a gray sweatshirt with the sleeves cut off and one word scrolling the front: *Chanel.* His boxers were plaid. His feet were bare.

Like the Cordelia Park vic and unlike Godric, this person hadn't been dead long.

Rigor mortis refers to a stiffening of the body due to a decrease below critical levels of adenosine triphosphate, or ATP. Beginning in the facial muscles approximately two hours after death, the rigidity gradually progresses to the limbs. Completing at anywhere between six and eight hours postmortem, rigor can persist for up to two days.

Thanks to some merciful weather deity, there was a slight, though erratic breeze that morning. A fitful gust sent the man's fingers swaying like laundry on a line. The joint flexibility suggested that rigor had come and gone.

But how long ago had he died?

More logging.

Decomposition occurs in four stages: autolysis, bloat, active decay, and skeletonization. Early action features skin discoloration combined with the release of gases and fluids. Both changes were evidenced by an odor strong enough to trigger a gag reflex, a fetid mix reminiscent of putrefying meat and rotting vegetation.

Necrophagous insects—mostly flies at this point—had opened a dance hall on the decedent's face. This pattern was typical, with the *Calliphoridae, Sarcophagidae,* and *Muscidae* ladies arriving within minutes of death and favoring the eyes, mouth, and nasal openings, orifices ideal for sheltering their eggs.

But the dense concentration seemed excessive in comparison to the rest of the body. The man's face appeared to be moving, like a seething mass of miniature rice grains.

Pulling on latex gloves, I raised my mask and stepped closer. The flies rose in a buzzing, frenzied cloud.

Acorn's handiwork lay beside the corpse, the number of bullets in the small furry body suggesting overkill. Though disgusted, I made no comment.

Slidell said nothing.

Ditto the uniforms and CSU techs.

Clasping my hands behind my head, I lifted my hair, hoping the brief release of heat might help stave off the vomit. Holding my breath, I squatted beside the remains.

One look confirmed my suspicion.

Below the egg mass I could see grotesquely mutilated features. Empty orbits with the lids stretched wide. A flattened nose. Lips drawn back and fixed in a macabre death grin.

Incised into the forehead were the familiar letters: *PE*.

And there was something new that sent a chill down my spine.

Pulling my iPhone from my back pocket, I shot pics from several angles.

"You don't trust CSU?" Acorn asked, speaking through fingers covering his mouth.

"Never hurts to have backups," I said without turning around.

Swatting at the aerial kamikazes dive-bombing my eyes, I rose and circled the tree for a better view of the hands.

Hand.

The left one was missing. The truncated muscles and tendons of the wrist had turned black due to exposure to the elements. As with the disfigured face, a teeming mass of ova blanketed the raw stump.

"Can we move this along?" Acorn made no effort to hide his eagerness to be gone.

Stripping off my gloves, I swiveled to face him.

"Is there somewhere else you need to be, detective?"

"Always."

Ignoring that seemingly egotistical reply, I said, "As with the other corpses turning up, a hand has been taken."

"Meaning?"

"I believe a profiler would call it a signature."

Acorn eyed me with an expression I couldn't read.

"A mosquito is lunching on your cheek," I said following a long moment during which I'd debated not telling him.

Acorn slapped at his face, was eyeballing the squashed offender when his mobile buzzed. Flicking the bloody corpus, he wiped his hand on his pants, then yanked the phone from his belt. Without excusing himself, he stepped away and turned his back to me.

Taking Acorn's cue, I dialed the MCME. Following the obligatory pleasantries with Mrs. Flowers, Nguyen picked up.

The chief apologized for leaving before I'd arrived, said she'd received an urgent call about an infant drowning. Thanking me for going to the preserve, she requested an update.

I obliged, assuring her that the McDowell case was linked to the earlier animal displays. Cited specifics.

Repeating that she was sorry for needlessly interrupting my day, Nguyen said there was no need for me to remain on site. She promised to phone Hawkins to authorize transfer of the body to the morgue.

After disconnecting, I watched Acorn, still engaged in animated conversation. Wondered. Why wasn't he asking the usual cop questions about victim profile, body treatment, cause of death, PMI?

While I'd inspected and photographed the dead man, Slidell had walked over to talk to Winslow and Hawkins. Skinny rejoined us now.

"Doc," he said, nodding to me as he swiped a sweaty forearm across his sweaty brow.

"Detective."

"Harve," he said, wagging his chin at Acorn.

"Erskine."

Slidell looked back at me. "What's your take?" He produced a small notebook with a stub of pencil shoved into the spiral binding.

"You know anything I say now will be very—" I began.

"Yeah, yeah, yeah." Spit-thumbing pages and positioning the stub over one.

"The deceased appears to be male."

"No!" Skinny slapped the pad to his chest in faux shock.

"Do you want to hear this?"

Slidell circled an impatient wrist.

"Based on skin color and hair type I suspect he's of African ancestry."

"The guy's Black."

"Yes."

"Age?"

"There's some graying at his temples, some sag at the jawline and below the eyes, but his teeth look goo—"

"I don't need the whole frickin' medical file."

"Without X-rays and dissection this is very preliminary," I said, cool as glacial runoff. "But I'd estimate he's somewhere between forty and sixty."

Slidell's eyes rolled up, brows angled low.

"You're shitting me, right?" he said.

"At this point that's the best I can do."

"That age range includes half the planet."

"Hardly."

Slidell mumbled something I didn't catch.

"And there's one other thing." I paused, creating needless drama.

"Are you trying to annoy me?"

I was. Childish, but having to deal with both Acorn and Slidell and a maggoty corpse put my nerves on edge.

I described what I'd spotted within the folds of the red bandanna.

"I'll be goddammed," Slidell said.

"Nguyen and I will do a full analysis to verify."

"Sonofabitch," Slidell said.

"Well put," I agreed.

Acorn said nothing.

Slidell dropped me at the Annex. Before leaving the kitchen, I stripped off my smelly clothes, secured them in a plastic garbage bag, and set them out on the porch.

After showering and shampooing for a very long time, I dressed in clean jeans and a tee. A quick tuna sandwich, then I headed to the MCME.

Birdie wasn't pleased with my lightning strike dine and dash. But in our brief phone conversation, Nguyen had said she'd begin the postmortem as soon as the body arrived at the morgue.

The McDowell case wouldn't be assigned to me. The remains were sufficiently intact to allow a normal autopsy. So why my interest in this man?

Similarities between the McDowell scene and the earlier animal displays were undeniable. The ball cap. The blue paint. The glitter. The two-letter incision.

Driving uptown, I kept hearing Adina's words in my head. Kept seeing the recent series of corpses.

Small forest creatures.

Larger species.

A beloved pet.

A cemetery cadaver.

A man and dog hanging from a tree.

A recently deceased human with a bullet hole in his skull.

It was clear that Adina's prediction was coming true.

The doer had shifted from animals to people. Then from the long-dead to the recently deceased.

As I'd first realized at Cordelia Park, the bastard was escalating.

Had he or she shot the man in the bandanna found at the McDowell preserve?

Who was bandanna man?

What was the meaning of the cryptic message: *PE*?

Why the stolen hands?

And the big enchilada: How soon would the sick sonofabitch strike again?

CHAPTER 21

It was Friday afternoon, so I offered to assist Nguyen on the autopsy. Hawkins flashed me a look that said he was relieved. At least, I *think* that was what he was telegraphing. It's hard to tell given the perpetual frown. He was quickly out the door.

The McDowell remains were logged in as MCME-753-25. Nguyen did a full postmortem.

The paper bag, placed on the man's hand at the scene, was removed. His nails were scraped and clipped, his fingers inked and rolled for prints.

Following careful external observation and X-ray scanning, a Y-incision was cut. The rib cage and skull were sawed. The brain and internal organs were removed and sectioned. Tissue samples and ocular fluid were collected for possible toxicology and other testing.

The autopsy revealed no surprises.

Bandanna man was a Black male who'd weighed one hundred and seventy-two pounds and stood five feet nine inches tall. His bones were slightly porous but, given his age, not abnormally so. His joints showed some early arthritic remodeling.

Fractures in the man's jaw and eight right ribs attested to a long-ago auto or bike accident, maybe a fall. Every break had healed well.

There were no tattoos, surgical or traumatic scars, birthmarks, skin lesions, or other abnormalities.

Livor mortis, a purple discoloration due to the settling of blood on the corpse's downside, indicated that the body hadn't been moved after death.

The teeth totaled only fourteen in number. Yellowing and extensive decay suggested a lack of concern with dental hygiene.

Trace evidence collected from the man and his clothing, now drying on a rack, consisted of soil, pebbles, vegetation, six beetles, one spider, and a boatload of ants.

I'd harvested the right pubic symphysis and the medial end of one clavicle. Developmental changes on both pointed to an age of fifty, plus or minus ten years.

Sadly, the man carried nothing to help with an ID. No wallet. No driver's license. No insurance, Medicaid, Medicare, or Social Security card. No watch or amulet with a name engraved on the back. No initials penned onto the labels of his undies.

The State Bureau of Investigation is North Carolina's central repository for criminal history record information based on fingerprints. We started with the SBI's Computerized Criminal History File, the CCH. Got no hit.

The AFIS, or Automated Fingerprint Identification System, is primarily managed by the FBI under the name Integrated Automated Fingerprint Identification System, IAFIS. The database includes 185 million prints of individuals who have been arrested, undergone background checks for certain types of employment or licensing, and are known or suspected terrorists. We went there next. Again, bombed out.

By the time Nguyen and I finished, it was well past seven. Stripping off my scrubs, I took another quick shower, changed into street clothes, and headed out.

Walking from my car to the Annex, the air felt like a warm, moist blanket on my skin. The sun was low, tinting the grounds and buildings of Sharon Hall with a yellow-pink watercolor wash.

Approaching my unit, I heard voices singing "Volare." Both were soprano, one was off-key.

A tsunami of aromas engulfed me when I opened the kitchen door. Tomato. Oregano. Fresh baked bread.

Mental head slap.

I'd invited Katy and Ruthie for dinner. They'd accepted but insisted on doing the cooking. A subtle comment on my culinary skills?

"Hey, guys." Masking any surprise I was feeling.

Katy was at the sink, Ruthie at the stove. Both turned, my niece pantomiming a handheld mic with a large wooden spoon.

They sang in unison.

Volare oh, oh,
Cantare oh, oh . . .

"Bellissimo," I said, digging deep for any remnants of Italian still stored in my left hemisphere.

"È la notte degli spaghetti!" Katy announced, flourishing one hand.

"Splendida." I set my purse on the counter. "Are you finding everything you need?"

"Si."

"Can I do anything to help?"

"No, signora!" Katy feigned horror at the idea. "Please relax. The moment our final guest arrives, the chefs are ready to plate their creation."

Before I could query that unexpected response, I heard a vehicle pull up outside. The engine cut off, a car door slammed, then footsteps crunched on the walkway.

A quick rap on the side panel. The screen door opened, and Lester Meloy poked his head into the kitchen.

"Am I late?"

"Not at all," Katy assured him. "Come on in."

Meloy entered and handed Katy a bouquet wrapped in tissue stamped with the word *GreenWise.* Carnations, roses, and some flora tinted blue that shouldn't have been.

"Dr. Brennan." Meloy favored me with a big sunny grin. "Thank you for hosting."

"Like a bad coin, I keep turning up." I smiled back.

"More like a lucky penny." Impishly winking one olive-flecked eye.

Jesus. Was the guy mom-schmoozing me? Or was he this obsequious with everyone?

"Something smells good," Meloy said, glancing toward the stove.

"And it's ready to eat!" Katy chirped. "Please sit down. I'll put these lovely flowers in a vase while Ruthie serves."

Katy and Ruthie had gone all out. Bone China dinnerware. Crystal goblets. Linen napkins. Octagonal mirror place mats. Items I'd almost forgotten I own.

The pasta was tasty, though a bit salty. The wine looked sketchy, but I wasn't imbibing, so I didn't care.

As during our dinner at Red Rocks Cafe, conversation moved unfettered from topic to topic. Eventually—inevitably?—it meandered to questions about interesting cases I'd encountered throughout my career.

As is my policy, I tried to dodge.

Meloy pressed. More brownnosing? Or was the guy genuinely interested in my work?

I talked about the exhumation of a lady buried in a casket with a squirrel and a parrot. All three had been embalmed. I described how a cadaver's missing teeth were found woven into a chickadee's nest.

Meloy asked a million questions about each case.

When I tried to change the subject, he queried what I'd been doing that very day. I sidestepped with a cursory comment about an old man found in the woods. Taking the hint, Meloy shifted to talking about the recent Panthers game.

Katy and Ruthie had purchased raspberry and lemon sorbets for dessert. A perfect closing act.

As Meloy reached for the bowl Katy was offering, his shirt collar shifted, exposing four dark letters on the side of his neck. While appearing not to, I tried to read them.

Apparently, I wasn't cagey enough.

"You've noticed my tattoo," Meloy said, eyes not exactly twinkling but showing amusement.

My cheeks burned.

"Don't be embarrassed." Thumb and finger pinching the collar, Meloy yanked the fabric farther sideways.

"*LIVE.*" Interpreting the word as an adjective, I pronounced it with a long "I."

"Or is it live?" Ruthie asked coyly.

"Ah. Life advice," Katy said. "But live how?"

"Freely? Wisely? Joyfully?" Meloy offered. His smile had gone Orinoco wide.

"It's actually a group," Ruthie said.

Katy and I looked a question at her.

"Lester can explain it better than I can."

"We are absolutely nothing unique or interesting. Quite the opposite. We are the embodiment of the world's oldest cliché." Meloy chuckled. "Students searching for the meaning of life."

"The universe, and everything," Ruthie chirruped, pleased with herself.

All eyes now shifted to her.

"You know, *Monty Python*? Never mind."

"I get it," I said, surprised that my niece was a fan of the irreverent humor I loved.

"So how *is* it pronounced?" Katy pressed.

"However you like," Meloy replied.

"What's the group's focus?"

"I'm afraid we're rather *unfocused*," Meloy said. "We're not political. We don't back a sports team. We don't support a cause, like saving the wombat."

"What *do* you do?"

"Not much."

"Do you have a clubhouse? A secret handshake?"

"No."

"Do you meet regularly? Connect online?"

"Not really."

"What's the mutual interest?"

"Sorry?"

"What attracts group members to each other?"

"Not to sound self-serving, but I think the attraction is me."

I noticed a narrowing of Katy's eyes. Knew that she was about to have a field day with that rather egotistical statement.

"Would anyone like more sorbet?" I asked, hoping to avoid confrontation.

Katy ignored me.

"Do your groupies wear tees with your image on the front? Special pins known only to each other?"

"With all respect," said Meloy, his lips rising in another of his mile-wide grins, "I'm afraid you've misinterpreted my meaning."

A beat, then Katy leaned back in her chair.

"Perhaps I have," she said, matching Meloy tooth for tooth. "Perhaps I have."

Meloy left at nine, saying he'd be happy to drive Ruthie home. Katy stayed to help with cleanup.

While scraping and rinsing, Katy asked about Ryan. I told her he was due to arrive on Sunday. She made some ribald recommendations I was glad Ruthie wasn't present to hear.

Mostly, we critiqued our departed dinner guest.

Katy had found him amusing and "wicked" smart.

For me the jury was out. While I sensed a gargantuan ego hovering below the surface, the man was pleasant enough company, witty, and well-mannered. And he'd brought flowers.

We'd just wedged the last plate into the dishwasher when my mobile sounded. I'd switched the ringtone to "Hello!" from *The Book of Mormon*.

"Jesus, Mom. Who'd be calling this late?"

"Probably spam," I said.

Katy snatched the phone from the counter.

"Unknown caller."

"My hands are soapy. Can you hit ignore?"

She thumbed a key, then framed me up in the viewfinder.

"Say cheese."

"Katy." With a warning note to my voice.

"I want proof that the great Temperance Brennan washes dishes just like the rest of us."

"Very funny."

"Smile."

"I'm not looking my best."

"That's the point."

Knowing my daughter would not be dissuaded, and that I could delete the shot later, I made a goofy face.

"This beauty's definitely going to the *Charlotte Observer*," she said, keying in a command to forward the image to herself.

"I'm sure if you did send it to the paper there'd be a seismic spike in subscriptions."

Katy didn't laugh. Her eyes remained glued to my mobile, brows now crimped in confusion.

A beat, then she held the device up, screen now pointed at me.

"Holy shit, Mom."

"What?" From across the room, I couldn't see the pic that had caused her puzzlement.

"Why do you have this image on here?" she asked.

Grabbing a hand towel, I crossed to her.

Now I was the one to look baffled.

CHAPTER 22

"I know this man," said Katy.

I could only stare at her.

"Why do you have his picture on your phone?"

"Who is he?" I asked, sidestepping her question.

"Why is this guy's pic on your phone?" she repeated.

A brief stare down ensued. I cracked first.

"That's a photo of the body found at the McDowell Nature Preserve, the case I mentioned briefly at dinner. I'm so sorry if he was a friend of yours."

"How did he die?"

"He was shot."

Katy flinched as though slapped.

"Who is he?" I asked gently.

"Quaashi Brown. Everyone called him Quash."

"How do you know him?"

"I don't really *know* him. I saw him now and then at the shelter."

"Can you tell me where he lived?"

"Tent City, until the heartless bastards shut that down."

Katy referred to a homeless encampment that grew up inconveniently close to Uptown. Upsetting to the more sensitive—the less compassionate?—among my fellow Charlotteans, the hodgepodge of makeshift shelters had eventually been demolished, the unhoused forced into facilities or back onto the streets.

"After that?"

"Rumor was he had one of those tents near the Clanton Road exit off I-77."

"Are you sure it's Quash?"

"Oh, yeah. I recognize the earring."

"What's his story?"

Katy shrugged both shoulders. "He was an old geezer who occasionally dropped into the shelter for a meal."

"I believe the man was still in his *fifties*," I noted with an eye roll.

"I'm just saying. The guy wasn't planning a spring break in Daytona."

"Do you know anyone who might have wanted Quash dead?"

Shaking her head glumly, Katy handed back my phone.

"Any idea what the letters 'PE' might mean?" I ventured.

"Price to earnings ratio?"

"I sincerely doubt that."

At ten-thirty, Mama rang to say she had squirrels in her attic. Not a euphemism. She had a legit rodent problem. Lots of scratching and scurrying paws overhead. I helped her search the internet for a pest control service that promised to trap and release.

We'd barely disconnected when Ryan phoned to provide his flight information.

Again, he offered to call an Uber.

Again, I said I'd pick him up at the airport.

When I was finally in bed and had turned off the light and silenced my phone, the ol' gray cells dived straight into dissecting the evening's dinner conversations.

Meloy had asked endless questions about forensic anthropology. My educational pathway. My position with the MCME. My role at a crime scene.

Standard queries for those interested in the processing of death. Tedious, but nothing surprising.

Having seen a brief online article in the *Observer* about a body found at the McDowell Nature Preserve—note to self to determine how that little gem had come to be—he asked if I was involved in the case. I admitted that I was and outlined the basics.

Talk rambled on through various topics. The pros and cons of Ozempic and other GLP-1 receptor drugs. A horrific accident at the Charlotte Motor Speedway. The potential benefits and threats of AI.

My last conscious thought before drifting off:

Meloy hadn't posed a single follow-up about the McDowell case—what I now knew to be the Brown case.

Mildly surprising.

Birdie nudged me to consciousness from a jumbled dream about flowers and chipmunks. Or maybe they were Mama's squirrels.

Forcing my eyes open, I squinted at the bedside clock. The digits indicated it was just past six.

I drew Birdie close and stroked his head, hoping for a few more hours of shut-eye. Unaware that the day would spiral from disappointing to depressing to truly horrendous.

Cuddles were not what the cat had in mind. Wriggling free, he positioned himself to chew on my hair.

"Fine," I said, throwing back the covers. "But we're not going to make this breakfast at dawn thing a habit."

Birdie looked at me with round, yellow eyes. Questioning my inappropriate reference to eating at sunrise?

I descended to the kitchen, planning to throw some kibble into a bowl, then hurry back up to bed.

My brain had other ideas.

Ideas that did not involve additional sleep.

I should have known they wouldn't.

After tossing about for a good twenty minutes, I propped myself up and grabbed my mobile.

No voice mails.

Three texts.

The first was an ad from a spa about a skin care sale.

The next was a notice that my car was overdue for an oil change.

The final message was from Nguyen about fragmentary skeletal remains unearthed at a construction site in Fourth Ward. Nothing urgent. The bones were at the morgue, and she was fairly confident the deceased was an animal.

I'm a person who can't rest if there's a task to complete. I've always been that way. I was one of those kids who finished the science project or wrote the English essay well in advance of the due date. Annoying, granted, but that's how I'm wired.

Even though it was the weekend, I decided to pop in at the lab. I could confirm that the newly arrived DOA was nonhuman. And I could plug away at Nguyen's damn case inventory.

I know. Get a life.

The MCME was quiet in the way institutional buildings are when largely deserted. No gurneys rattling. No doors whooshing. No elevators bonging.

A weekend crew was there, of course. Including the new guy, Winslow, of undetermined surname.

By nine-thirty, I'd changed into scrubs and Winslow had rolled the remains, now designated MCME-766-25, to autopsy room four. Just habit, not due to concerns about odor.

I was unzipping the small black pouch when my mobile sounded. Holding my gloved hands away from my body, I crossed to the counter to check the screen.

Crap.

A moment of hesitation, then I answered.

"Brennan." Knowing that formal greeting would probably draw censure.

"We got us another one." Background noise told me Slidell was calling from his car.

"Another one?"

"Jesus. I'm working homicide here. Whadaya think I'm talking about?"

"A body?" Fervently hoping for a negative response.

"With all the trimmings."

"Where?"

"A Girl Scout campground called Pod Village. Apparently, the little ladies will be needing some serious therapy."

My empathy with the scouts, I refused to acknowledge the wisecrack.

"But this round the perv added a new twist," Slidell continued.

"What?"

"Better you see for yourself."

"Wait. Why do you need me?"

"Two reasons. First off, I ain't good with kids."

"The girls are still there?"

"No. We flew them all to Paris so's they could jamboree."

Easy, Brennan.

"And the second reason?"

"I'm told the stiff ain't exactly pristine."

"Fine." It was so far from fine, a high-precision GPS system couldn't measure the distance.

"Give me the address," I said resignedly, reaching for a pen.

"I'll pick you up in thirty."

"At the Annex."

Yep, I thought again. *Groundhog Day.*

Peering through the windshield of the Trailblazer, I gave silent thanks for small favors. Unlike the recovery at the McDowell Nature Preserve, this one wouldn't require a hike through vegetation infested with man-eating mosquitoes.

Less than half an hour after leaving the Annex, Slidell's navigation announced that we'd arrived at our destination. We were on Idlewild Road in southeast Charlotte. A sign on a freestanding brick wall announced that the property belonged to the *Girl Scouts Hornets' Nest Council.*

The usual three-ring circus was already clogging the street. I noted a pair of white sedans with the blue CMPD logo, a coroner's van, a CSU truck, a couple of unmarked cars, probably belonging to detectives.

A white Sprinter bore the logo of WSOC-TV, Charlotte's ABC

affiliate. So far, no other media had picked up on the radio transmissions concerning the body. Or they'd deemed the situation non-newsworthy.

A Nissan Pathfinder sat at the front of the line of parked vehicles, three silhouettes visible through its open rear hatch. Small ones. I assumed these were the scouts who'd spotted the body.

Slidell pulled to the curb and we both got out. Cruisers flashing *red-blue-red-blue-red-blue* blocked each end of a circle drive sweeping up through an acre of lawn. A uniformed officer stood beside each cruiser, feet spread, arms crossed in identical poses.

Slidell strode toward the cop on the left. I followed. Seeing us approach, the woman straightened and dropped her arms, keeping her right elbow slightly cocked.

Drawing close, Slidell badged the woman. She glanced at his shield, then stepped to one side and waved us through.

"Body's how far back from the building?" Slidell asked.

"About ten yards. The scene's taped off and a detective is on site. CSU's doing their magic. You can't miss it."

Slidell hot-assed it up the drive toward a modern redbrick structure devoid of any whimsy or caprice. I followed, again surprised that Skinny could move that fast. We were halfway there when my mobile sounded.

Digging the phone from my pocket, I checked the screen, then clicked on.

"Hey," I said, failing to suppress a big goofy grin.

"Bonjour, ma chère."

I knew from Ryan's tone that something was wrong.

"What's up?" We rounded the building and cut diagonally across a stretch of mown grass toward a cluster of trees.

"A ferret."

"Sorry?" When I entered the shadows, the temperature dropped a good ten degrees.

"This could be an aviation first."

"There's a problem with your plane?"

"The plane's just dandy. Except for Elton John, who's disappeared into its bowels."

"You're going to have to explain that."

"We'd just boarded when a lady opened her pet carrier to calm her ferret. Availing himself of the unexpected portal to freedom, Elton John—that's the ferret, not the lady—bolted."

"You're kidding, right?"

"*Je suis sérieux.* We passengers, now disembarked, are cooling our heels at the gate while a squad of ferret busters searches for the escapee."

"How long might that delay you?"

"Ferrets are slippery little buggers."

"Can't the crew go ahead and take off and wait for the thing to show itself?"

"Apparently not. What are you doing?"

I told him about the remains I was out to collect.

"We'll laugh about this later," he said, not sounding amused.

"Keep me posted," I said.

Disconnecting, I heard Slidell address someone, then a wheezy exclamation.

"Well, I'll be goddammed."

Stashing the phone, I hurried toward him.

CHAPTER 23

The cop hadn't been kidding.

The scene had been processed to hell and back. Vegetation had been stripped. Tape had been strung. Surfaces had been dusted. Pics had been taken.

Acorn stood to one side. On seeing us, he nodded but said nothing.

Thanks to orders from Nguyen, the corpse had been left in place. It lay belly-up, facing away from the path. Though dappled with shadows cast by the thick overhead canopy, its skin looked ghostly pale against the dark substrate upon which it lay.

Necrophagous insects had arrived and begun their recycling act. When I stepped closer, they rose in their usual buzzing cloud.

The person had died wearing a teal polo, blue plaid Bermudas, and sandals. The shorts had been pulled, or had worked their way down to knee level, making it evident that the deceased was male. A khaki bucket hat—the kind favored by fishermen—sat askew on the man's head, blocking a view of his features from where I stood.

Brown paper bags covered the man's hands and feet. Evidence markers circled him, each small yellow triangle indicating the location of an item that might or might not prove meaningful later.

Signs of scavenging were limited to the right arm and ear. I suspected neighborhood dogs, excited by the scent of death, but not hungry enough or feral enough to really go at it. Purpling on the man's back and buttocks suggested he'd died where he lay.

"Sonofabitch."

Pushing past Acorn, Slidell continued into the clearing and rounded the vic. His expression, more than his exclamation, caused something to grip my insides.

Skinny is a veteran of hundreds of murder investigations. He's seen women stabbed so many times they appeared to have gone through shredders. Newborns wrapped in trash sacks and tossed into dumpsters. Transgender teens castrated, beaten, and strangled. Rarely does he emote at a scene.

Slidell's face had gone tight with a mixture of feelings I couldn't read. Disgust? Anger? Pain?

I glanced at Acorn, who'd paused at the trailhead.

No giveaways there.

A long second, then Acorn said, "I'm going to check that CSU collected everything and got all the pics they need. No reason those guys have to hang around."

I stepped sideways as far as I could.

Acorn eased past me and disappeared back the way we'd come.

Moving forward, I circled the body and drew up next to Slidell.

One quick scan and the gut-grip tightened.

The cockeyed blue cap rested on enormous "what-me-worry?" ears. Mousy brown hair curled from below its band. The familiar letters gaped raw on the forehead beneath its visor. *PE.*

"Jesus."

"Yeah," Slidell agreed. "That's why my ass is here."

Appalled at what I was seeing, I said nothing.

"The asshole who used this spot for a body dump knew the area."

"Agreed." I spoke knowing Slidell was in "think aloud" mode. "Before CSU did their thing, that path was probably impossible to see."

"It's that vet, yeah?" This time Slidell did address me, oblivious to the fact I was fighting back tears.

I nodded.

"What's his name?"

"Balodis," I managed. "Ralph Balodis."

"Any idea who might have offed him?"

I shook my head slowly.

"Any idea how long he's been dead?"

I forced myself to appraise objectively.

"Not long," I said, not up to sharing details about livor and rigor and decomp and flies.

"Can you be more specific?" Slidell's voice was taking on that edge.

"Given this damn freaking heat, I'd say less than forty-eight hours."

Slidell's brows floated up at my sharpness.

"But that's only a prelim—"

"Yeah, yeah. You seen enough so's your boss'll be happy?"

I nodded. Slapped a mosquito on my neck.

"I'm green-lighting a body bag to get this stiff gone." Yanking his mobile from his belt. "If those girls are still here, how about you keep 'em distracted."

"Has someone called their parents?"

"How the bloody hell would I know?"

Inwardly cursing Slidell's boorishness, I turned and walked back toward the scout headquarters building.

To say the girls were eager to discuss their discovery would be the understatement of the century. Even though they'd already given two accounts—one for the MCME transport crew, one for the cops—they were on fire to retell their most excellent adventure. I had to keep reminding them to speak one at a time.

There were three in all. Elodie Timmons. Georgia French. Rivka Steiner. I guessed they were all about fourteen. Couldn't help thinking the trio looked like a Benetton ad.

Timmons's skin was cocoa, her cornrows parted with surgical precision. She was every bit my height.

French had short, curly carroty hair. Nervous, she kept picking at cheeks scattershot with acne.

Steiner was a study in contrasts with wintery pale skin and very dark hair. Her hazel eyes were magnified by lenses attesting to lousy eyesight.

Knowing I should wait until a parent was present, I approached them.

"Hey," I started out.

"Hey," they mumbled in unison.

"Rough morning?"

"Beyondo rando," Timmons said.

"Care to talk about it?"

"It was grody to the max." French wrinkled her nose, compressing its scatter of freckles into one brown splotch.

"Flies were, like, totally crawling up the bro's nose!" Steiner's eyes were saucers behind the thick glasses.

"I thought it was cool." Timmons was the only one whose adrenaline level might have been close to normal. "You know, like *CSI* or *Bones* or something."

"You watch too much television," French said.

"And you don't?"

"I'm not, like, addicted."

"Really? Every time—"

"I'm sorry you had to see what you did," I said, interrupting the squabbling.

"My cat died last summer. By the time we found her body she looked as disgusting as that dude back there." Steiner jabbed a thumb over one shoulder.

"Eww," French said.

"Bite it," Steiner snapped. "She was a great cat."

"Can you describe what you saw?" I tried another approach.

"We already told the cops everything we know." Did Steiner now sound guarded? Or simply teenage bored?

"I understand. But you three are the only *actual* eyewitnesses." I looked at Timmons, hoping her TV crime drama habit might work in my favor. "We need to keep asking questions until we're satisfied that we've covered every possible base. It's routine."

"Who's 'we'?" Eyes narrowed, Timmons hooked air quotes around the pronoun I'd used. I had to admire the kid. She was no dummy.

Using middle school language, I explained who I was and what I do.

"Sick," French said.

"Gross," Steiner said.

"Whatever," Timmons said. "But, like we told the cops, we don't know shitzo."

Fifteen minutes later, I had to agree. Except for one important detail.

According to Timmons, she and her friends were working on some sort of Girl Scout merit badge requiring a minimum of three hikes. When they'd gone on their first trek late Thursday afternoon, Balodis's body hadn't been under the tree. When they'd set out early today, it had.

That timeline corroborated my preliminary PMI estimate of less than forty-eight hours. Balodis had probably been killed sometime Friday.

"Did you get a look at the man's face?" I asked gently.

Three solemn nods.

"Do you know him?"

Three violent head shakes.

I was about to pose a follow-up when footsteps sounded on the path at our backs. We all turned.

In seconds, a very sweaty Slidell emerged from the trees.

Raising a thumb and finger to his lips, Skinny whistled loud enough to be heard in Nairobi.

The MCME techs, again Hawkins and Winslow, were butt-leaning on the front panel of their truck. Startled, both looked his way.

Slidell circled a hand in the air. Showtime!

Winslow opened the truck's rear doors, withdrew a gurney, popped the legs down, and began wheeling it toward Slidell. With a nod in my direction, Hawkins followed.

Alert to the possibility of grisly, ratings-boosting footage, the occupants of the WSOC van flew into action. One was male, the other female. Both looked to be fresh out of junior high.

The man, dressed in jeans and a black tee, pulled a camera-mic combo from the van's rear and positioned it with the building as a backdrop. The woman, wearing a blue silk blouse and tan pants, took a moment to fluff her hair and apply lipstick using a compact mirror. I recognized her as a journalist who often did on-scene reports.

Wanting no part of the media hoopla, and knowing I might be a target, I beelined to Slidell's Trailblazer. Slumped low in the passenger seat, I phoned Nguyen. As expected, I got the MCME's messaging service.

I reported that the Idlewild Road remains would soon be in transit to the morgue. That the DOA was an adult male with multiple gunshot wounds and one missing hand. That the body appeared sufficiently intact to allow a normal autopsy.

I finished with an unenthusiastic offer to be present if needed.

Then I waited.

Slidell didn't join me for another forty minutes.

We were almost to the Annex when my mobile rang. Seeing Katy's name, I answered.

"Hey, sweetie."

"Hey." Her smiling face filled the screen.

"What's up?" I asked.

"Are you in a car?"

"Yes."

"Where are you going?"

"Home."

"What have you been doing?"

"A recovery."

"Oh." The smile faltered a little, but she seemed curious. "Anything exciting?"

"No."

"How long have you been out?"

"Since early morning. Why?"

"So Ruthie's not with you?"

"No."

A slight pause, then, "I'm not sure where she is."

"Is that a problem?"

"No. I suppose not. Who knows?"

"That answer covers a range of possibilities."

"Ruthie has agreed to keep me looped in on her plans. Mainly so I have intel if Aunt Harry calls."

"Why doesn't Harry phone Ruthie's cell and talk to her directly?"

"She does. If Ruthie doesn't answer, I'm up next."

A typical MO for my baby sister. If Harry wants a conversation, she wants it on demand. *Her* demand.

"Are you worried?" I asked.

"Not really. It's just that Ruthie usually leaves me a note. Today, nothing."

"Was she home last night?"

"I think so. I got delayed at the center until after eleven. When I got here her door was closed and her light was out. I didn't want to wake her, so I didn't look in."

"Was her bed slept in?"

"She always makes it in the morning, so that tells me nothing."

"Do you think she's with her UNCC pals?"

"Probably." Now with the smile gone.

"Do you have an issue with them?"

"I've met some of that group. Once, briefly, when they came to pick Ruthie up."

"And?"

"Mostly they seemed geeky, but harmless."

"Mostly? Sensing there was something Katy wasn't saying.

"I don't know. I got a weird vibe from a couple of them."

Before I could poke at that, she added,

"I know Ruthie's precocious and funny and smarter than fuck. But these guys are grad students. Why would they hang with a seventeen-year-old kid?"

CHAPTER 24

Ruthie was buried in sand, mouth agape, gulping for air. Slidell was wobbling toward her on a bike he couldn't control. Ryan was crouched low, coaxing a rabbit from beneath a boulder.

"It's too late." Ryan rose to full upright, eyes blue lasers, body a black cutout against a burning white sun. *"We have to—"*

My eyes flew open.

My heart was skipping hard, and I didn't know why.

Sunlight streamed through the blinds covering my bedroom windows, throwing bright diagonal slashes onto the carpet.

Birdie was pressed tight to my back.

I reached around to stroke his head.

The cat stretched and purred, then curled into a ball.

I lay a moment, trying to uncork this new dream and let it breathe.

Typically, my nighttime visitations are straightforward remixes of recent events. Nothing particularly enigmatic or creative. But my id had gone the extra mile with this one.

I gave the analysis a good five minutes.

My forebrain refused to interpret for my hindbrain.

Whatever.

I checked the clock.

Eight-forty-one.

Momentary alarm was followed by pleasant realization.

It was Sunday.

I had no class to teach. No lecture to present. No urgent case awaiting my attention at the morgue.

Ryan's flight had been canceled, so I wasn't certain when he'd arrive.

Little flip in my southern parts thinking about that.

I got up, threw on shorts and a tee, brushed my teeth, and knotted my hair in a topknot. Birdie watched my sketchy toilette, miffed that his breakfast hadn't come first.

I'd just filled the cat's bowl when my mobile sounded.

"Wow," I said. "Two calls in two days."

"Very funny." Katy wasn't laughing and her voice sounded strained.

"Are we grumpy?" A word my daughter had used to described herself at age three. An expression I still employ, much to her annoyance.

"I'm calling to let you know that Ruthie is here."

"What time did she get home?"

"Two-seventeen. I know because I couldn't sleep until I heard her come in."

"Mmm."

The irony made me smile. Katy had been a hellcat as a teen. Her difficulty with Ruthie was mirroring my experience raising her.

"What's that supposed to mean?" she asked.

"Just mmm."

A brief pause. Then,

"She wants to go up to Boone later this week with these UNCC students who seem to have adopted her. I don't think it's a good idea."

"Why not?"

"She's seventeen, they're in their twenties. I know what college road trips are like."

"When did you go on a college road trip?" A rebel like Ruthie, Katy hadn't started at the local university until she was older.

"I saw *Animal House*."

"Belushi was hilarious in that."

"Jesus, Mom. I didn't call for a movie review."

"What does Kit say?" Ignoring the prickly rebuke, I queried my nephew's take on the issue.

"Ruthie's doting Papá is currently at a camp outside Yemassee, South Carolina, fishing for drum. The place is so remote there's no cell signal.

I think that's part of the appeal. While he's off the grid I'm supposed to direct any questions about Ruthie to her grandmother."

"Okay. What does Harry say?"

"She's cool with it. But your loosey-goosey sister would be cool with flying to Pamplona to run with the bulls. No offense intended."

"None taken." Katy was right. Harry wasn't the best judge of what was adolescent appropriate.

"Besides Lester Meloy, have you talked with others in that group?" I asked.

"Just a woman named Danielle Hall. And only to exchange greetings when she came to pick up Ruthie."

"What is it you'd like me to do?"

"I've invited Meloy and Hall to join Ruthie and me for a picnic dinner at Freedom Park. I want you to come."

"When?"

"Tonight."

"Ryan's flight has been delayed and I'm not sure when he'll arrive." Read: I'd rather not.

"No problem. You'll actually be closer to the airport."

"Katy, I—"

"I'll see you at seven."

Dead air.

Less than an hour later, Ryan called.

"Hey."

"Allô, mon amour."

"What's the latest?" Reading his tone, I knew the news wouldn't be good.

"I just spent forty minutes on the freaking phone with freaking American Airlines."

"You spoke to an actual human being?" I was astounded he'd accomplished this given that every passenger from the ferret trip was trying to rebook.

"Her name was Ardeth. Don't ask how I managed the miracle of live contact."

I didn't.

"According to Ardeth, every flight into Charlotte is sold out until tomorrow afternoon.

"Did you try the website?"

"That's where I started."

I said nothing.

"The lovely Ardeth was very sorry."

"I'm sure she was."

"It's probably just as well." Ryan tried to put a good spin on the situation. "I should do some winterizing."

"Winterizing."

"You know, change to snow tires, check my supply of warm socks, hunt down the electric blanket—"

"I'll see you tomorrow, then."

Katy brought fried chicken, green beans, and mashed potatoes. Baklava cheesecake for dessert. Every dish was excellent. Because the meal came from Barrington's, one of my favorite restaurants.

God bless takeout.

Meloy was as charming as he'd been the first time we met.

Danielle Hall was . . . what?

A lot.

While I had no idea what to expect, I certainly wasn't prepared for the woman who showed up.

For starters, Hall was six foot two with a physique that suggested hours in a gym. Probably years. Her skin was so devoid of pigment it made me think of the troglofauna living deep in caves. Her hair was dyed an unfortunate baboon's butt red. A gold ring pierced her right brow.

As we spread our blanket, then ate, I kept sneaking glances at the intricate tattoos showing dark against Hall's pale skin. The most striking featured a black snake with one orange eye. The serpent's head wrapped Hall's right thumb and its body spiraled her wrist. When we'd shaken hands following Katy's introduction, the creature had appeared to lunge for my face.

Despite the startling first impression, Hall turned out to be excellent company. She'd traveled extensively, liked many of my favorite authors, and was passionate about animal rights.

When it came up that Hall was working on an advanced degree in engineering and employed part-time by the city, Ruthie asked her about the passageways underlying Charlotte. Apparently, my niece had been intrigued since our earlier discussion of the subterranean network.

"Would you like to visit sometime?" Hall asked.

"You've gone down there?" As before, Ruthie sounded breathy with awe. Maybe trepidation.

"Many times," Hall said. "I'd be happy to take you on a tour."

"Pass."

"It's dark and dank, but perfectly safe if I'm guiding you," Hall said.

"Call it a phobia, or whatever. Gloomy, underground tunnels are not my thing."

"Let me know if you change your mind."

"Never gonna happen."

Conversation then shifted to the topic of phobias. At one point, Ruthie insisted we go around the group with each person naming the thing they feared most.

Hall mentioned spiders.

Katy went with heights.

Ruthie stuck with small dark spaces.

I said mine was losing people I love.

Meloy admitted to anxiety when around dogs.

"No way," Ruthie said, with one of her snorts.

"I was attacked by rottweilers when I was a kid."

Meloy rolled up his left sleeve, revealing a scar running from his wrist to the soft, veined triangle of his inner elbow. Sinuous and shiny, the pale swath looked like a worm crawling his flesh.

"Oh, wow," Ruthie said.

"How did you escape?" Katy asked.

"A neighbor heard the commotion and turned a hose on the pack."

"Your hero. You must have loved that guy," Ruthie said.

"He was the owner who never properly contained the beasts."

"That's messed up," Ruthie said.

"Damn straight." Color rose to Meloy's cheeks. "Excuse the language."

"You call that language?" Ruthie guffawed.

"Don't get me wrong." Meloy scanned the faces around him. "I don't hate dogs. I have two myself. A collie and a retriever. Poppy and Red. Well, I *had* two."

"One died?" Ruthie's question was honeyed with sympathy.

"Last week."

"Ohmygod. I'm so sorry. Losing a pet really sucks."

"I had to shoot Poppy."

"She'd grown too old to enjoy a good quality of life?" Ruthie asked.

"She was around fourteen months."

"Jesus," Ruthie gasped. "That's still a puppy."

Meloy shrugged.

"Why?" Ruthie said in a tone that sounded like a challenge.

"The dog was untrainable."

"What the hell does that mean?"

Reading the escalating indignation in my niece's tone, I jumped in.

"Has anyone seen the latest exhibition at the Mint Museum?"

"It means I wasted six months trying to teach the dog a few very basic skills. With zero success."

"So you *killed* her!?"

"It features costumes from TV series going back to the fifties," I said brightly, doing my best imitation of a smile.

"Everyone did love Lucy," Katy said.

Ruthie fired to her feet, every cell of her being radiating contempt.

"I can't stand it. You're all fucking heartless."

Slinging her purse strap over one shoulder, she stormed off in the direction of the park entrance.

CHAPTER 25

Was Ruthie out of line? Or just being a normal, temperamental teen?

Was her response to Meloy's admission justified? Or an overreaction triggered by hormones and worry?

Worry about what?

Those were my thoughts as I drove to work the next morning.

When I'd left the Annex, the temperature was already nudging into the eighties, and the humidity was thick enough to float small boats. But the radio meteorologist had tiptoed around the possibility of rain. Dark shadowing along the horizon hinted that the odds could be better than she'd implied.

Mrs. Flowers was at her effervescent best. I endured a brief chat about her nephew's role in his high school play before I managed to escape.

Entering my office, I dropped my case on the desk and shrugged into the sweater I keep in one of its drawers. Though it was Tropic of Cancer outside, Nguyen could be counted on to keep the facility in a state of arctic freeze.

I'd barely settled in my chair when my mobile rang.

After checking caller ID, I answered.

"Hey."

"Hey," Adina said, echoing my greeting. "What's up in the world of corpses?"

"Maggots and decomp."

"How is it you always have all the fun?"

"Not to mention the glamour." I smiled for the first time that day.

"Nothing says elegant like blood spatter on a lab coat."

"Amen to that," I agreed.

"Listen, I'm calling to ask if you want to go to a concert week after next."

"To see who?" *Whom*, Ryan might have corrected. I smiled more broadly, thinking of him.

"Dirt Monkey."

"I'm not familiar with the group. What are they—heavy metal? Doesn't sound like a jazz quartet."

"Or a trio of harpists. Actually, my younger colleague who gave me his tickets seemed totally bummed that he'd developed a conflict and couldn't make it. Apparently, they've got quite the following."

"Can I get back to you on that?" I asked, thinking about the last concert I'd attended a couple years prior. A seventies band on their third "farewell tour." An older couple in front of Ryan and me had seemed determined to smoke up the bountiful supply of weed they'd brought along. By the band's second set the fumes they'd created were so pungent that Ryan and I decided to pack it in.

"Sure."

Sudden thought.

"While I have you on the phone, may I pick your psychologist brain?"

"Sparse pickings, but shoot."

"My niece is acting moody."

"Ruthie, right?"

"Yes."

"She's sixteen?"

"Seventeen."

"Is it whiny I'm-going-to-die-of-boredom moody? Get-out-of-my room moody? Buzz-off-you're-the-dumbest-person-on-the-planet moody?"

"I doubt kids say 'buzz off' these days."

"You know what I mean."

I did.

"We were having a picnic yesterday when the subject of dogs came up."

"Who's 'we'?"

"Katy, Ruthie, a guy named Lester Meloy, an engineering grad student, and myself."

"What grad student?"

"Danielle Hall. She also works for the city."

"The gorilla with the funky hair and eyebrow ring?"

"That's unkind."

"She chooses that look."

I could think of no rejoinder, so I offered none.

"Do you know Hall through UNCC?" Adina asked.

"I don't really know her."

"Then how did this little gathering of odd fellows come to be?"

"Hall is Meloy's friend. They both belong to a campus club called Live. Maybe Live." I pronounced the name both ways. "The group has taken Ruthie under their wing." Its wing? Jesus. Why was my brain so concerned with grammar?

"You're a big, bad professor," Adina said. "Investigate the group through school channels."

"I did."

"And?"

"I learned zip."

"How can that be?"

"It's not an officially recognized organization."

"Back up. How did Ruthie meet these people?"

"She did one of those tours meant for prospective students and parents. Meloy was the guide."

"O-kaay." Intonation suggesting maybe it wasn't.

"You're an excellent judge of character, right?" I asked.

"Ted Bundy is permanently off my Christmas card list."

"I'm serious."

"Sorry."

"Meloy kind of sets off alarms," I said.

"What sort of alarms?"

"What do you mean?" *Where was she going with this?*

"Christ, Tempe. Goose-bumpy skin? Warbly echoes deep in your id? Or are you saying the guy literally smashes the glass on little wall-mounted boxes and pulls down the levers?"

"Of course he doesn't do that. At least not that I know of."

Impatient breathing riffed across the line.

"I don't know, Adi. He's just too . . ." I groped for a word. "Nice."

"Holy shitbuckets, girlfriend. You should have said so right off. Hang up and I'll call the crisis helpline."

"There is such a thing?"

"Yes. I think you dial nine eight eight."

I stashed that tidbit for potential use with my sister, Harry.

Then I took a moment to gather my thoughts on Meloy. To review mental images and replay conversations.

"What I mean is, the guy's almost *too* witty, *too* charming."

"He's slick? Shallow? Phony?"

"Hell, I don't know."

"You're saying that a lot."

"I am."

"Maybe try a concrete example?"

I told her about Meloy's retriever, Poppy. Described how he'd shown no remorse over shooting the dog.

"That does seem cold. But it doesn't mean he's evil."

"Right." A beat, then, "Just a minute ago you mentioned Ted Bundy."

"Scratched from my holiday card and invitation list. What about him?"

"Bundy was handsome. He used his good looks when trolling for victims."

"I've dated a lot of guys like that."

"One of Bundy's tricks was to wear a sling and pretend his arm was broken. He'd stand outside a store with a bag of groceries and ask a young woman to help him load the bundle into his car. Once she got far enough into the passenger seat, he'd snap the lock on her side, then drive to some remote place to rape and kill her. Later, he'd feel zero remorse."

"You suspect Meloy of being a serial killer?" Adina sounded simultaneously shocked, alarmed, and dubious.

"Of course not. It's just, I keep thinking about those behaviors you mentioned, along with others I've read about: glib speech, superficial charm, manipulativeness, callousness, failure to accept responsibility for one's actions."

"Sounds like a personality profile for a psychopath. And I also add narcissism, impulsivity, sexual promiscuity, poor behavioral control, and a parasitic lifestyle. Does Meloy exhibit any of those traits?"

"He has a high opinion of himself."

"He's a man."

"You think I'm nuts, right?"

A pause as Adina chose her words carefully.

"I think you're uncomfortable with Ruthie hanging with an older crowd. And that you may be overly judgmental when it comes to Meloy."

"Do you think I should ask her to stay away from them?"

"Would that do any good?"

Remembering myself as a teen, I doubted it would. "Not likely," I said.

"She's a smart girl, Tempe. Trust the kid."

"You're probably right," I said, not sure that she was.

"Or not."

"Or not."

We both laughed.

"Whatever happened with the nut job ornamenting trees with glittered-up animal corpses?"

"Nothing."

"The creep is still out there?"

"As far as I know," I said. "But I think you nailed it."

"No pun intended."

"Sharp point."

"It's too early." Adina groaned at my pun. "You win."

"Anyway, he—"

"Or she."

"The doer is upping his or her game."

"How so?"

I described the latest in the string of decorated remains.

I could almost hear Adina's brain working through the series. Then,

"He's gone from small forest creatures to larger animals, to pets, to cemetery remains, to live human victims." All levity was gone from her voice.

"The man in Cordelia Park. Quaashi Brown. Ralph Balodis."

"From total strangers to people you actually know."

"What are you suggesting?"

"I was right. The prick is escalating."

I said nothing.

"The next target could be someone close to you. Or, God forbid, it could be you."

"Let's not get overly dramatic."

"I'm glad Ryan will be there with you for a while."

"Are you saying I need a man's protection?"

"I'm saying I'm glad you won't be alone."

A *beep* announced an incoming call.

I tipped the phone to read the screen.

Unknown Number.

Normally I wouldn't answer an anonymous call. But Ryan was on his way, and I feared another travel misadventure.

"Gotta go, Adi. Thanks for listening to my angsty ramblings." Wanting to end on a positive note.

"Anytime, girlfriend. Let me know about the Dirt Monkey concert."

"Will do."

"Ciao."

"Ciao."

I disconnected and hit the button to accept the incoming call.

"Temperance Brennan."

No one responded to my greeting.

"Hello?"

Hollow background noise.

"Is someone there?"

Nothing.

"Dickhead." Jabbing an irritated thumb.

A case arrived at noon, bones found in a cardboard box marked *Peony* in the basement of a Baptist church off Beatties Ford Road. Dry, discolored, and odorless, one look told me they were the remains of a long-dead pig.

When I phoned, the pastor, an elderly gentleman named John-David Nellie, agreed to collect and inter the deceased in the property's small burial ground.

RIP Peony.

At two, I headed out.

A not-so-quick stop at Whole Foods, then I spent an hour making space in the fridge and pantry for all the impulse purchases I'd made. Frosted pretzels. Organic red cherries. Fuji apples. Avocados. Baby Bella mushrooms. Boston lettuce. Bok choy. Sliced prosciutto and honey maple turkey breast. Five different cheeses. Butter croissants, with and without chocolate chips. Pecan pie. Two New York strips large enough to feed Croatia. You get the picture.

At four, I showered, then spritzed myself with the Jo Malone London Rose & White Musk Absolu body spray Ryan had gifted me on my last birthday. Applying it in the only correct way, according to Harry. Pointing the nozzle into the air, then stepping into the cascading mist.

Birthday suit, birthday spray, some cluster of neurons chirruped as the tiny droplets settled on my skin.

I know what you're thinking. But it had been weeks since Ryan and I had been together. My mind was as bubbly as newly uncorked champagne.

When Ryan phoned at quarter past five, I set out for the airport.

I'd just turned onto Woodlawn when I noticed a black Honda in the rearview mirror.

Other images flashed. A black Honda Accord on the circle drive outside the Annex. Another leaving the Red Rocks Cafe.

Something had bothered me at the time of the second sighting. Was it coincidence? The same vehicle? If so, did it mean anything?

Having caught part of the plate, I'd done some half-hearted research but learned nothing. Deciding that I was being overly suspicious, I'd forgotten all about it.

You're acting paranoid again, Brennan.

Without thinking, I hung a right.

The Accord hung a right.

I made a left.

The Accord made a left.

Heart skipping a little faster, I sped up.

The Accord stayed with me.

CHAPTER 26

Ryan's plane arrived ahead of schedule. A gate was available.
An aviation miracle.

Le monsieur came down the ramp wearing jeans and a blue-plaid flannel shirt. Except for the bare ankles and Hokas, he looked like he'd dressed for timbering in Belarus.

I had to smile. And inwardly shake my head. No matter how often Ryan visits the Carolinas, it seems he's unable to retain a picture of summer in Dixie. Or maybe his Quebecois soul rejects the concept of intense and prolonged heat and humidity.

Ryan and I aren't prone to public displays of affection. PDAs, as Katy would say. Still, we greeted each other warmly.

Though the flight had landed early, the checked baggage took forty minutes to hit the belt. Ryan's duffel was not among those that did.

By the time Ryan made his way up the queue and filed a lost luggage report, it was going on seven. I was no longer in the mood to cook. Or, being honest, to watch Ryan cook.

He wanted tacos, so we stopped at Azteca, my favorite of Charlotte's many Mexican restaurants. And one that was directly on the way home.

I chose the chicken enchiladas. I always do. Ryan ordered Chile Verde extra spicy. Complained when the peppery sauce burned his mouth.

As we ate—Ryan sweating and pounding Dos Equis across the table from me—I filled him in on developments in my life. Katy. Ruthie. My recent cases at the MCME.

Ryan told me about his current investigations. One involved money laundering. Another insider trading. Yet another identity theft.

I smiled and nodded encouragingly, but only half listened. I find the subject of finance boring as hell.

The briefings were, well, brief in both directions. It hadn't been forty-eight hours since our last phone conversation.

We'd just begun our usual battle-for-the-bill ritual when my mobile buzzed.

The screen showed a number at the MCME.

"I'd better—"

"Of course," Ryan said.

"I'm sorry to bother you after hours," Nguyen said, not sounding at all contrite. "I hope I'm not interrupting anything."

"No, no." Yes. Yes.

Taking advantage of the distraction, Ryan snatched up the check and crossed to the cashier station by the front entrance.

"You asked that I keep you informed concerning MCME-753-25."

That took a moment of mental triage.

"The male DOA from the McDowell Nature Preserve," I said.

"I've scheduled the autopsy for early tomorrow. I'll be doing it myself."

"Do you want me to attend?"

"That's up to you."

I knew that tone.

"What time?"

"I plan to begin at eight."

"I'll be there."

I disconnected, feeling, what? Resignation? Disappointment? Irritation?

Definitely irritation.

Watching Ryan cross back to the booth, an autopsy was the last thing on my mind.

The next morning dawned dreary and gray, making it hard to get out of bed. That, and the fact that Ryan and I hadn't fallen asleep until well past one a.m. I'll leave it at that.

Ryan assured me he'd be happy on his own while I worked at the lab and asked if he might use my bike. I was good with that. Since his missing bag had yet to show up, he wanted to purchase a few toiletries. Then he'd buy provisions for a mysterious feast he intended to prepare. I was *very* good with that.

When I arrived at the MCME, Mrs. Flowers told me Nguyen was already suited up and cutting in the main autopsy room, with Joe Hawkins assisting.

The red message light on my desk phone indicated missed calls. Ignoring its somewhat frenzied flashing, I went directly to the women's locker room to change into scrubs. Suitably attired, I hurried down the hall to join the chief and Joe.

People think an autopsy is conducted in an atmosphere of hushed quiet. Some are. At large facilities, most are not.

Instruments clanged. Water pounded in a stainless-steel sink. An old Stones tune blasted from a boom box: "Paint It Black."

An elderly woman was under the knife on the closest of the three tables. Her scalp had been swirl-cut, her face peeled down below her chin. A pathologist was instructing his autopsy tech in a loud voice. The tech was buzzing through the woman's skull with a handheld saw, sending the smell of hot metal and bone dust into the air.

The McDowell corpse, now unofficially identified by Katy as Quaashi Brown, was stretched naked and supine on the farthest of the tables. An unzipped body bag lay abandoned on a gurney snugged to the wall behind it. X-rays glowed gray-and-white on a screen off to one side.

Nguyen was wrapping up dictation of her preliminary observations. Hawkins was shooting pics. Both were dressed in autopsy chic: blue-green scrubs and caps, paper aprons, and booties.

I crossed to them.

Up close, I noted that the overheads—their collective wattage sufficient to illuminate several airport runways—turned the man's toffee skin a sickly turd brown. The hair escaping his bandanna was smashed into wormlike squiggles against his cheeks and forehead. The letters beneath the forehead squiggles looked dark and raw. *PE.*

My first reaction. Brown looked like a prop for a B-grade zombie movie. *Maybe* Brown. I decided to wait before sharing Katy's information with Nguyen.

Joe directed a question to Nguyen by raising two dark caterpillar brows. Nguyen nodded.

With one deft maneuver, Joe inserted both hands into the open cranial cavity, teased the brain free, and placed it on a corkboard positioned beside the table.

I watched as Nguyen weighed, observed, and sectioned the brain. As she took samples and dropped each into a vial filled with preservative. As Hawkins sealed and marked the vials with identifying information.

At Nguyen's signal, Hawkins used a scalpel to make the proverbial Y-incision, slicing Maybe Brown's torso horizontally from shoulder to shoulder, then vertically down the center of his chest. That done, he went back to the oscillating saw to cut through and remove the sternum and the ventral portion of the rib cage.

One by one, Nguyen examined and snipped tissue from each of the internal organs. Lungs. Heart. Liver. Kidneys. Stomach. Pancreas. Spleen. Gall bladder. Intestines. Bladder.

On gross examination everything looked normal. No tumors, lesions, congenital abnormalities, or indications of past trauma or disease.

Setting the brain and entrails aside, Nguyen began her examination of the disemboweled body. Her face remained neutral—the part visible above her blue polypropylene mask—until she probed the man's anus.

"Palpate here," she said to Hawkins, indicating the location of the anomaly that had caught her attention.

Joe explored the area with the tip of one finger.

"Eyeh." Bushy brows going into full furrow. "Something hinky there."

The three of us gathered at the computer terminal to reexamine the lower abdominal X-rays.

It took a full minute until I noticed a subtle opacity maybe four inches up the anal canal, a white cloudiness obscured by an overlying organ.

"Look." I finger-tapped the white blob.

"What the frick?" Nguyen murmured, reengaging her scalpel.

Minutes later an object lay oozing blood and decomp fluids onto a folded towel on the instrument tray. Silver and flat, the thing measured two inches long by half an inch wide.

Needing no direction, Hawkins prepared an ABFO ruler to serve as scale and case identifier, shot pics, then took the object to the sink for additional cleaning. As the dark outer coating washed down the drain, a hairline crack appeared circling one end.

"It's a thumb drive," I said.

"Appears so," Hawkins said.

"Oh, my," Nguyen said.

I extended a gloved palm.

Hawkins placed the device on it.

Grasping what I suspected was a removable cap, I tugged gently with my index finger and thumb. The cap came off revealing a USB connector.

"You called it," Hawkins said.

"How odd," Nguyen said.

"Why would a data storage device be shoved up a vagrant's butt?" I asked, eyes moving from the thing on my palm to the man on the table.

Mild disapproval came my way from the others.

"Am I allowed to view the contents?" Nguyen may have been posing that question to herself.

"I've no clue where the law stands on ass drives," I said in response.

More disapproval.

"The contents might help with a positive ID," Hawkins said.

"True," I agreed.

"Do you think the data will still be readable?" Nguyen sounded dubious.

"Even if it is, access will be password protected," Hawkins predicted with his usual glum pessimism.

"Maybe. Maybe not." Though I suspected Joe was right. "Only one way to find out."

"Disinfect thoroughly." Nguyen's directive was coated with cringe at the thought that one of her terminals might be polluted.

While I cleaned the device with an alcohol swab, Nguyen logged into the MCME system. When she'd made a successful connection, I inserted the business end of the drive into the terminal's USB port.

An icon appeared on the screen. A key, with the label *USB DISK* beneath it.

I double-clicked on the key.

A new screen appeared. On it was a single blue folder.

The hairs on my neck rose to full upright.

The folder was labeled with one word: *Evil.*

My gaze met Nguyen's.

Eyes giving away nothing, she offered another of her go-ahead nods.

I opened the folder.

All my synapses fired straight to anxiety mode.

Superimposed on a background that looked like a scene from the underground horror movie *Creep,* two letters crawled slowly from left to right: *PE.*

I watched the cryptic message inch sideways, unable to look away.

Reaching the right edge of the screen, the letters disappeared, and the monitor went black.

I sat back, a million questions elbowing for recognition, some relevant, some ridiculously immaterial.

Who shot the video?

Why?

When?

What did it mean?

Was it a prank? A warning? A threat?

If a threat, directed toward whom?

Me? Nguyen?

Toward Brown?

Why?

Was Brown alive when the device was introduced into his anus? Had he placed it there himself? Or was he already dead and the insertion performed postmortem? If so, by whom?

Why?

Over and over, my brain kept circling to one central question.

How had the video file ended up on a flash drive inside the rectum of a homeless man? A homeless man found dead of gunshot wounds in a county nature preserve?

Nguyen's voice sliced into my consciousness.

"Detective Slidell is working this case, correct?"

"He is."

"I must contact him."

"Yes," I agreed.

My ears registered the rhythmic swish of Nguyen's retreating shoe covers. The rattle of a gurney. The *whoosh* of a cooler door.

Easy, Brennan.

I forced myself to draw a series of deep, calming breaths.

Ryan and I often discussed our cases. I debated. Should I share this bizarre story with him?

Except for knowing Slidell and a few others, Ryan was unfamiliar with the Charlotte scene. Looping him in would require reams of backstory. Given that our time together was so limited, I hated to waste any of it on tales of corpses with missing hands and oddly placed storage devices.

Still. If the device was meant as a threat, he had a right to know.

I was formulating a condensed version of events for Ryan's consumption when the issue of the thumb drive yielded to a new concern.

A much more terrifying one.

CHAPTER 27

"Ruthie's missing."

A simple declarative sentence. Two words.

But something in Katy's delivery chilled me.

"What do you mean?"

"Jesus Christ, Mom."

"Calm down."

"I am calm. Where are you?"

"I'm at work."

"Of course you are."

I didn't touch that.

"When did you last see Ruthie?" I asked.

"She went out around four yesterday afternoon and never came home." Katy's voice sounded unnaturally tight, her vowels too clipped, her consonants too hard.

"I thought you didn't worr—"

"She left a note saying she'd be back by nine."

"Where was she heading?"

"I don't know."

"Was she meeting Lester Meloy and that crowd?"

"I don't know."

"Did someone pick her up?"

"I don't know."

"Did she go on foot? Call an Uber?"

"Are you listening to me?" I could feel us drifting into that zone of tension that makes every utterance seem confrontational.

"She probably spent the night with friends, right?" Even as the words left my mouth, they sounded lame.

"Probably. But Ruthie's been good about letting me know her plans. It's the deal I have with Kit."

I almost laughed. As if my nephew would be at all diligent concerning his daughter's whereabouts.

"Did your Ring doorbell catch footage of Ruthie leaving?"

"The battery is dead."

Biting back the obvious response to that, I asked, "Do you know how to contact Meloy?"

"Yes. But I don't want to look like I'm helicoptering the kid. I mean, Ruthie *is* seventeen."

"Exactly. She's only seventeen."

"I'll give it a bit longer," Katy said. "If I don't hear from her soon, I'll contact Meloy."

I made a quick phone call, then grabbed my car keys and hurried out.

While Charlotte's neighborhoods may be village cozy, its Uptown is schizophrenically all about business and good times. Restaurants. Theaters. Stone-and-glass high-rise office towers. The Charlotte-Mecklenburg Police Department is housed at the heart of the beast, in the Law Enforcement Center, an enormous concrete structure looming over the intersection of Fourth and McDowell.

The LEC was my destination that weekday afternoon during a heat wave that seemed to be lasting forever. My car's AC system normally would have kept the oven temps at bay, but today it was either overwhelmed or disinterested in its calling.

Mercifully, traffic was light. Fifteen minutes after leaving the MCME I pulled into the visitors' lot at the LEC. Sliding from behind the wheel, I crossed asphalt that had to be close to the melting point.

The CMPD employs almost two thousand officers, so a steady flow of cops, each clad in deep blue and displaying a hornet's nest patch on one shoulder, was entering and exiting the building. Long story on the bug theme, one involving resistance during the Revolutionary War and a disparaging remark by General Cornwallis. Look it up. Or ask any local.

The CMPD maintains its own crime lab, directed by a man named Ron Gillman. After showing ID, I rode an elevator to the fourth floor, then walked a long and very shiny corridor to his corner office.

Gillman was perusing a file spread out on his blotter. He looked up when I knocked on the open door.

As a tall, silver-haired man with a body suggesting basketball or tennis, the only thing marring Gillman's leading-man good looks is a Lauren Hutton space between his upper central incisors. A big one. Or maybe that dental quirk contributes to his charm.

"Tempe." Big gap-toothed smile.

"Ron."

"Broiler out there, eh?" Perhaps noticing my sweat-soaked bangs and tee.

"It is."

"Take a load off."

I dropped into one of two chairs facing his desk.

"What can I do you for?" he asked.

Gillman listened without interrupting as I told him about the series of animal and human displays and the man from the McDowell Nature Preserve with the oddly placed storage device.

"I'm not sure I have a good response for that, except . . . wow," he said when I'd finished.

"Exactly. I'm wondering if there's info your guys can tease from the drive that I missed just eyeballing it."

"You said the man who had the device had been shot?"

"Yes."

"Actually, I just heard about this. His death is being treated as a homicide?"

"A possible homicide."

"Who's on the case?" Gillman asked.

"Slidell."

"Congrats."

"Thanks."

"Let's see what you've got." Gillman popped forward in his chair to hold out a hand.

"It's been disinfected," I said, placing the drive on his palm.

"Bless you for that." The lifting of one corner of his mouth left me unsure if the comment was teasing or literally meant.

Slipping on horn-rimmed glasses, Gillman studied the object in his hand. Then he picked up the phone and spoke to someone in the IT section.

"Things move faster if the request originates here," he said, replacing the receiver.

"That's why I came to you," I said.

"How did you get involved in all this?" Gillman asked, leaning back again and slowly swiveling his chair.

I'd just finished answering when a man appeared in the doorway, the name *Koster* embroidered above the pocket of his lab coat. He had a strong-boned, deeply lined face and a head of platinum hair anchored by ebony roots. I guessed his height at five three, his age at midforties.

Gillman introduced the man as Orson Koster, a new hire in the IT section.

I rose and we shook hands, me smiling, Koster not.

Gillman handed Koster the thumb drive and explained what I wanted.

"There's a long queue, so it may take a whi—"

"Could you do it now?" Gillman asked, not asking.

"On it." Koster turned to exit the office.

"May I watch?" Hiding my surprise at the man's brusqueness.

"Of course you may," Gillman said, ignoring Koster's frown.

I followed Mr. Sunshine down another polished corridor to a room containing an array of computers, lighting rigs, backdrop screens, and microscopes. Positioning two chairs in front of a terminal, my reluctant guide gestured for me to sit.

I sat.

After logging on, Koster inserted the thumb drive into the appropriate port. When the familiar home screen appeared, he double-clicked the key icon.

As expected, nothing happened.

"Okay, smart guy," Koster mumbled under his breath. "Let's have at it."

Koster worked the keyboard with lightning-fast fingers.

More nothing.

"Not bad, buddy boy." As before, Koster spoke to himself. "But not good enough."

I watched without comment.

Forty minutes and a million keystrokes later, the screen changed color and a rotating box appeared.

"Fucking A!" Koster hooted, air-pumping one arm.

I would have joined in the victory theatrics were I not frozen in shock, eyes glued to the monitor.

A video had launched, showing a setting as recognizable as my own face. The Annex with its ancient pine in the side yard, my Mazda parked on the driveway below.

A wavery transition morphed to a different but equally familiar tableau. One far more disturbing in its intimacy. In the intrusion it implied.

Footage of my bedroom filled the screen, recorded through the open door leading in from the hall. The lights were off, the walls and furnishings cast in an eerie blue-gray.

Koster must have picked up on my altered body language.

"You know the place?" he asked without turning.

"It's my home," I said, masking the white-hot anger sparking below my sternum.

"Yeah?" Whipping to face me.

I nodded, too shaken to reply.

"You cool to who shot this?" he asked, thumb-jabbing the screen.

"I've no idea."

"That's some heavy shit."

I said nothing.

"Want to view it again?"

"Yes."

We did.

And again.

The third time through, with the playing speed slowed, we both spotted a previously overlooked detail. A flick of purple-and-black entering the edge of the frame as the camera made its sweep of the room.

"Did you see that?" Koster asked.

I had.

"Go back," I said, twirling a finger.

Koster rewound and hit play.

"Freeze there!" I snapped when the purple-and-black flash reappeared.

He hit pause.

"I think that's a pocket," I said, squinting hard. "Holding some sort of paper."

Koster didn't agree or disagree.

"Can you zoom in?"

"Yes, ma'am."

Koster enlarged the area to the point of pixelation, adjusted and readjusted, finally landed at a setting that provided reasonably clean detail.

I'd guessed correctly. A folded document peeked from the side pocket of a jacket or shirt. A jacket or shirt worn by the person filming inside my home.

The anger flamed hotter.

Focus, Brennan.

I squinted at the front-facing portion of the document. Saw print and tried to make out the words. Got nowhere.

"Can you read that?" I asked, thinking Koster's vision was probably better than mine.

"Not a chance," he said.

"Would it help to rotate the image?" I suggested, hoping proper positioning might improve legibility.

It didn't.

"How about I try a little more cleanup?" he asked.

"Please."

Koster performed more of his cyber magic, expanding and sharpening the print. Another million keystrokes, and the boldest letters topping the document grudgingly crystalized.

. . . network of tunnels running beneath Charlotte's streets . . .

"Looks like a photocopy," he said.

"It does."

"What the hell does it mean?" Koster asked.

I provided a quick explanation. He'd heard of the tunnels, but always thought the stories were myth.

"Want hard copy?" he asked.

"Please."

Koster printed the screenshot.

I took the page, thanked him, and left.

Unaware that those very real tunnels would soon upend my life.

CHAPTER 28

As a precaution, I'd texted Slidell, briefly describing the contents of the thumb drive. I received no reply. Which did little to allay my concern.

I also heard nothing further from Katy. Hoped that meant all was calm on the Ruthie front.

The next morning, I woke jumpy as hell and unsure why. Noticing my agitation, Ryan suggested an outing involving physical activity. Despite the heat, we spent the day biking the Blue Line Rail Trail through the city.

Every couple of hours I stopped to give Katy a call. Got no answer and assumed she and Ruthie had gone off on one of their adventures.

That evening, exhausted from pedaling the eleven-mile route, Ryan and I opted for takeout sushi at home followed by an old black-and-white film.

It was Ryan's turn to pick and, predictably, he chose a western, *My Darling Clementine*. Though the genre isn't my favorite, Henry Fonda as Wyatt Earp was proving worth the watch.

A watch that was constantly interrupted.

The opening credits had barely faded when Katy phoned to ask if Ruthie was with me. Or if I'd heard from her.

My response was a double no.

She called again at nine. At nine-thirty.

I gave the same answer both times, with growing unease in my voice. Katy assured me that all was copacetic, probably just a crossing of wires.

Earp was heading for the big shoot-out at the corral when Katy rang again, now obviously distressed. Ruthie remained whereabouts unknown. She hadn't called and wasn't answering her mobile. Her voice mailbox was full and accepting no messages.

Seriously worried now, I advised my daughter to check Ruthie's room for contact information, then use what she found to phone the kid's friends. Katy was appalled at the idea of such an invasion of privacy.

Twenty minutes later she reported that the only numbers she'd scored were for Lester Meloy and Danielle Hall. She'd tried both. Neither had answered.

By midnight Katy was distraught and wanted to alert the cops. Her uncharacteristic anxiety goosed my apprehension to the level of real fear. I kept thinking about the thumb drive. About the home intrusion. About Ruthie being only seventeen.

About a serial killer on the loose.

Picking up on my vibe, not to mention all the phone calls, Ryan insisted on a full explanation. Which I belatedly provided.

When I finished, he chastised me for not confiding in him from the outset. Big surprise. Then he suggested we offer to search the neighborhood around the Annex on the odd chance Ruthie had headed our way. Katy accepted, with far too much emotion. Said she was working the streets near her town house.

Praying that we were all overreacting, I dug two flashlights from the pantry and checked that their batteries and bulbs were functioning. One lit up bright and eager. The other came on but looked a bit iffy.

Handing the good flash to Ryan, I grabbed my keys from the kitchen counter and we left the Annex. Birdie watched, astounded at the unusual wee-hours departure. Maybe.

Outside on the driveway, Ryan proposed we split up to double our impact. I could cruise in my car while he searched on foot.

Searched for what? A dropped purse? A lost shoe? A body?

Surely not that.

I agreed to Ryan's plan, but with the roles reversed. He rejected that idea. I argued that I was familiar with the sidewalks and yards in my hood and could better spot anything that seemed amiss. Reluctantly, he conceded the logic in that.

The night was velvety soft, the air alive with the efforts of millions of crickets. From far off on Queens Road, muted traffic sounds added to the closing-days-of-summer sonata.

Trudging down the circle drive, I was hyperaware of the total blackness enveloping the grounds of Sharon Hall. While the aesthetic parts of my brain are all in for quiet and quaint, the more practical portions question the wisdom of an HOA ban on any exterior light having more wattage than a smartwatch face.

I'd gone only a few yards when I heard an engine turn over at my back. Seconds later, headlights sliced through the darkness surrounding me.

Moving to the edge of the drive, I watched Ryan pass, then slowly descend. A brief pause at the bottom of the slope, then he turned right and disappeared up the street.

For a few minutes I peered into clumps of bushes and beneath leafy trees, shining my feeble light into crevices that revealed nothing. Wandering farther into the adjacent lot, I'd taken no more than a couple steps downhill when pain exploded in my lower back, just above my right kidney.

My arms flew up and my stride lengthened as I struggled to regain my balance.

A futile effort.

Three wild steps, then I lost control and went down. Hard.

Air exploded from my lungs as fire from the kidney strike shot up my spine and into my neck and chest. A bomb detonated in my skull when I hit the ground.

An eternity passed as I lay motionless, willing my spasming lungs to relax. More likely, it was half a minute.

When finally able to breathe, I placed trembling palms on the pavement and pushed up onto my elbows. I was still gathering my wits, simultaneously sweating and shivering, when I heard a soft, staccato scraping in the distance. Almost imperceptible at first, the muffled sounds slowly grew louder.

Closer.

Faster.

"Sacrebleu!" Ryan's disembodied expletive came out of the darkness.

Then he was squatting beside me.

"T'es-tu fait mal?"

When stressed, Ryan often reverts to the language of his childhood. As usual, he was unaware that he was doing so now.

"I'm fine," I said, not totally sure that I was.

"Qu'est-ce qui s'est passé?"

Clueless myself what had happened, I offered no explanation.

"Can you walk?"

"One way to find out."

Ryan reached down toward me. Rolling to my back, I gripped his hands, drew my feet to my butt, and gingerly sat up.

"Did you trip?" Ryan asked.

"I . . . I'm not sure." I didn't think so.

"You've done a spectacular job on your jeans."

I looked myself over. He was right. Even in the dark I could see that the denim was shredded at both knees. Raw skin showed pale and bloody beneath each gaping hole.

To say I felt stupid would be like saying the Decca execs regretted choosing another band over The Beatles.

"I'm missing a sandal," I said, hiding my humiliation.

I heard a joint pop as Ryan rose to his feet. Gravel crunched as he searched the drive.

Then, from a few yards uphill, "Bingo."

Seconds later Ryan handed me the flyaway footwear. Useless now, since the left ankle strap had been ripped from the sole.

"Do you want to try standing?" Ryan asked.

"Sure," I said with more confidence than I felt.

The same pair of strong hands gripped me under my pits. One minor stumble, and I was upright. Seconds later we were trudging uphill, me brushing dirt and grass from my belly and butt, Ryan arm-draping my back for support.

Once inside the Annex, I phoned Katy. She'd had no word from Ruthie.

"I'm going to call it a night," she said with an exasperated, perhaps exhausted, sigh.

"Oh?"

"Before Ruthie came to Charlotte her dad warned me that she'd pulled this kind of shit before."

"Taking off without leaving word?"

"Yes."

"Not cool."

"Not cool at all," she agreed.

"Now what?"

"I'm out of ideas."

What could I say? While it may have been wishful thinking—a part of me didn't dare contemplate otherwise—I assured Katy that all would be well and promised to take action in the morning if Ruthie hadn't appeared. Wanting no fuss, I didn't mention my tumble.

Then I hurried upstairs to shower. Insisting that I leave the door ajar, Ryan stripped to his jockeys, got into bed, and clicked on the TV.

While the hot water pounded my body and stung my abraded elbows and knees, and the muted sound of baseball play-by-play rose and fell in the next room, I ran through the incident again and again.

What the hell had just happened?

Had I simply face-planted?

That seemed unlikely. I'd been proceeding very carefully, aware of the slope.

Had I tripped, as Ryan suggested?

Again, unlikely. I'd scanned the ground as he and I returned to the Annex. Seen nothing larger than a twig.

I recalled the sense of a sudden spasm in my lower back.

A muscle cramp?

A thrust?

Was it possible I'd been pushed?

If so, by whom?

If I'd been pushed, had it been random, a case of my being in the wrong place at the wrong time? Had I crossed paths with an intruder? With a kid caught doing something he shouldn't? With a startled animal?

A gut-clenching alternative capered into the mix. One that had arisen cold and ugly as I lay on the ground.

Might the doer be the creep nailing decorated corpses to trees?

Might this sicko be so incensed at the disruption I'd caused to his hobby that he'd kidnapped my niece?

Realizing such musings were pointless, I turned off the spigot, got out, and wrapped myself in a towel. Minutes later, hair de-tangled, face moisturized, teeth brushed, I joined Ryan in bed.

"You good?" he asked, face crimped with concern.

"Just a banged knee," I said.

"Should I buy you a helmet?"

"Hilarious," I said.

"You smell good," he murmured, drawing me close.

"Thanks."

"I'm crushed. The Bird wants no part of me."

"That's odd." It was. My cat adores Ryan.

I called Birdie's name.

No cat appeared.

"Birdcat," I tried again.

Nothing.

"I didn't forget him outside, did I?"

"You did take a hit to the noggin."

Throwing back the comforter, I got up and checked the other upstairs rooms. Finding no cat, I hurried downstairs, repeatedly calling his name.

Nothing.

I probed the shadows of the hallway with moment-long sweeps. The parlor.

Entering the dining room, I noticed that the swinging door to the kitchen was closed.

Had Ryan done that? I always left it open.

Tiptoeing to it, I pressed my ear to the wood.

Heard only silence beyond.

I know the Annex as well as I know the lines on my face. The creeks and groans of her worn floorboards. The hum of air blowing through her old-fashioned vents. The clicks and taps of her outdated pipes.

My gut tightened.

The silence beyond the old door was wrong.

CHAPTER 29

I hesitated.

Enlist backup?

No way. I'd had enough drama for one day. Besides, I wanted no damsel in distress dynamic with Ryan.

Easing the door open, I peered through the crack.

Moonlight oozed in from the window, sparking the stainless-steel appliances and brightening the porcelain sink. Digits on the stove glowed neon orange.

The kitchen looked normal.

Until my gaze reached the back door.

Then my heart threw in a few extra beats.

A black swath bordered the jamb. The gap wasn't wide. Just big enough to accommodate a cat.

Shit! I may have cursed out aloud.

Had Birdie followed the call of the wild and ventured forth?

I hurried outside, whisper-calling his name to avoid disturbing the neighbors.

"Birdie?"

No cat.

I tried again, louder.

Louder.

I kept at it for several minutes before giving up. The night was warm. The grounds were reasonably safe. It wouldn't be the first time the cat had overnighted outside.

Moments later, back in bed, I couldn't help but wonder.

How *had* Birdie made his escape? Had I left the back door ajar when I'd returned from searching for Ruthie? Had Ryan? Had a breeze blown it open?

Had someone entered my house?

How?

Who?

The killer?

My upstairs toilet drips. It always has.

The next morning, after another lecture about locking my doors, arming my security system, and watching my six—which I assumed meant staying aware of what was happening behind me—Ryan said that something called a flapper needed replacing. At nine, he set off in search of the part.

When he'd gone, I made another loop of the grounds. Spotted no sign of Birdie.

Returning to the Annex, I phoned Katy.

Got voice mail. Guessing she'd already gone to the center, I left a message asking if Ruthie had turned up.

After brewing coffee, I booted my laptop, determined to make a dent in the dozens of emails I'd been ignoring over the past several days. Weeks?

Focus eluded me. My mind kept going to Ruthie and Birdie.

At ten, the hated task only partially complete, I took a break to give another shoutout to the errant feline. He remained AWOL.

I tried Katy again. Still no answer.

Ruthie. Same result.

Wondering if Slidell had made any progress finding Quaashi Brown's killer, I dialed his mobile.

Strike three.

I was out.

Disconnecting with an irritated thumb jab, I winged my mobile onto the counter.

Seriously, Brennan? You're acting like Harry.

To distract myself, I turned my attention to overdue paperwork owed to Nguyen.

The ploy succeeded. When I next glanced at the wall clock, both hands were pointing straight up.

Le monsieur still hadn't returned.

Ditto Birdie.

Assuming Ryan was intrigued by all the wondrous gizmos and gadgets, or whatever it is that appeals to men's brains in hardware stores, I decided to take a quick jog. Exercise would relax me, and I could look for Birdie. Changing to shorts, a tank, and running shoes, I headed out.

From that point, my memory grows hazy.

Sharon Hall has a small body of water at the back of the property. We call it a lake, though it hardly qualifies as such.

The lake's inhabitants tend toward the small and unexciting—darters and shad in the water, salamanders and frogs on the banks. Surrounded by pickleweed and corkscrew rushes, except for the landscaping stones rimming its perimeter, the feature is an archetypically Carolina pond. Uninteresting to anyone but aquatic biologists.

And my cat.

Knowing Birdie would beeline for the water, I headed in that direction.

One advantage to a white pet is its visibility. Except in blizzards.

I spotted no cat on the thin strip of shoreline. No snowy tail protruding from the surrounding vegetation.

Torn between worried and irked, I scrambled up a mound of algae-coated rocks near the water's edge. At the top, maybe ten feet off the ground, I braced my feet, hand-shielded my eyes, and did a three-sixty scan.

Saw nada.

I was beginning my descent, ass first, blindly testing for footing, when I heard movement behind me.

I froze, surprised by the adrenaline suddenly firing through me.

Then embarrassed.

Jesus, Brennan. You've been bellowing for the cat. Don't scare him off.

Then, before I could turn my head, something long and sinuous wrapped my right ankle. Startled, I loosened my grip to explore my leg. Bad move. Gravity and the slimy flora colluded to send me slide-banging downward.

I don't remember what I thought as I fell.

I didn't scream. No time.

I recall my already raw elbows and knees yielding more skin.

A sharp crack to my head.

". . . you okay, Dr. Brennan?"

Someone was crouching beside me, hands on thighs, sweaty face close to mine.

Did I recognize the features?

No name emerged from my fog-muddled brain.

"Are you hurt?"

Faux red hair. Gold ring. Gorilloid build.

Ruthie's UNCC friend Danielle Hall.

Hall offered a hand to help me rise.

"I slipped while climbing the rocks to look for my cat," I managed, feeling foolish.

"Algae can be a mean mother. You sure you're okay? Maybe I should take you to a hospital?"

Reflexively unwilling to admit that I'm ever anything less than ship-shape, I immediately protested. "No, no, I'm fine. Just klutzy. Never met a rock I couldn't trip over," I said, trying to affect nonchalance at having scraped skin off my limbs twice in the past twenty-four hours. *Jesus, Brennan, get your act together.*

We stood a moment, the noon sun sparking the hoop riding Hall's brow.

"You're probably wondering what I'm doing here." Hall broke the awkward silence.

"Whatever the reason," I said, wondering exactly that, "your presence was certainly serendipitous for me."

Hall regarded me blankly.

"Lucky timing," I clarified. Then a sudden thought occurred to me. "I don't suppose you've seen Ruthie in the last couple of days?"

"I'm sorry. I haven't."

"Would you happen to have contact info for Lester Meloy?"

"I do on my phone. But I don't have it with me."

"Right," I said, hiding my disbelief. These days, it seemed like everyone under thirty had their phone with them 24/7.

A moment, then, "Ruthie probably didn't tell you about my hobby."

"She did not."

"I mean, why would she?"

I said nothing, anxious to get inside and out of the heat.

"I paint landscapes. Most are crap, I know. But I like working with oils. Ruthie said your pond was bussin, so I wanted to get a few pics."

I assumed "bussin" was a positive thing.

"I suggest you shoot from the bottom, not the top of the rocks," I said.

"Smart," said Hall, winking and pointing a very large finger at me.

"Thanks again," I said.

"No biggie."

"Have at it." My attempt at a smile hurt the scrape on my cheek.

Hall gave a double thumbs-up.

I moved off toward the Annex, eyes doing one last visual sweep for the cat. An Amazon delivery truck parked on the circle drive blocked much of my view of the front lawn. Noting spiderweb cracking on the rearview mirror, I wondered briefly about the company's upkeep regs.

I was at my door when Hall yelled at my back.

"What does he look like?"

I turned, unsure her meaning. "Sorry?"

"The cat. Describe him."

"He's all white," I shouted. "And should be looking guilty as hell."

Hall gave yet another double thumbs-up.

The woman must have liked doing that.

I'm not an alarmist. But by late afternoon I was growing concerned.

Ryan hadn't returned.

Katy hadn't heard from Ruthie. She'd phoned Meloy but only gotten voice mail and left a message.

No cat.

I tried calling the two who were carrying phones.

Neither answered.

Though the temperature had risen into the midnineties, I decided to go out for another brief hunt for Birdie.

I'd done a quick spin around the property and was rounding my neighbor's hedge, hot, sweaty, and peeved as hell, when footsteps sounded behind me.

As I turned, I felt something sting my left arm.

A moment of dizziness.

Then the world went black.

CHAPTER 30

I awakened to total darkness.

A foul odor.

A wet, gritty hardness beneath me.

My frontal lobe throbbed.

My rib cage screamed.

Had I suffered a concussion? A skull or rib fracture?

Was I badly hurt?

I tried lifting my head.

Lightning forked across both retinas.

Queasiness roiled in my chest and bile flooded my mouth.

I swallowed.

The nausea refused to back down.

I swallowed again, mentally ordering my gut to settle. After a few moments I felt a wave of relief that seemed less than fully committed.

Inching trembling fingers up to my face, I felt the edge of a blindfold. Warm dampness on my right temple and cheek.

Blood?

I reoriented the same hand to explore my surroundings and encountered shallow water atop concrete.

The movement triggered pressure on my ankles.

I tried lifting a foot.

Felt a pull at my wrists.

Dear God!

I was trussed like a pig, my limbs bound and tied to each other!

Twisting and hyper-flexing one wrist downward, I tested again with my fingertips.

Ropes! Triple-wrapped and knotted!

Panicky, I tugged with both arms and both legs as much as the bindings allowed.

Water sloshed.

The putrid stink intensified.

Nausea threatened anew.

I settled back, panting and struggling for recall.

My brain was incapable of forming a meaningful synapse.

Lying motionless to thwart the vomit, I shifted my focus to sensory input.

My nose took in funk, mud, and damp cement.

My ears registered an echoey hollowness suggesting an enclosed space.

Was I in a basement? A cave? A vault?

A crypt?

My heartbeat ratcheted up at the thought.

My thoughts skittered like free radicals in my battered skull.

Tears threatened. I fought them down.

Think!

Slowly, memory bytes began to assemble.

The missing cat. The oppressive heat. The hedge. Danielle Hall.

How much time had passed since that conversation?

Was I still at the Annex?

If I was elsewhere, how had I gotten here?

Where was *here*?

Had I fallen again? Been pushed?

Flashback image.

The earlier tumble from the rocks by the lake.

Hall had been nearby then.

A stroke of good luck, I'd said.

But had her presence been other than serendipitous?

Had that spill been the result of a deliberate attack? Had this one?

What of the sting on my arm? A bee? A wasp?

A needle?

Had I been injected with a knock-out drug?

Had Hall been the attacker?

If so, why?

Had she tied me up and transported me?

Imprisoned me?

Why?

And again. Where was I?

The mental probing produced zilch.

I called out for help.

My cries echoed and bounced back on themselves.

I screamed until my throat was raw.

Maybe it was the fall, or a blow to my head, or a pharmaceutical cocktail polluting my blood, but consciousness came and went. Each time upon waking, I had no way of knowing how long I'd been out. Hours. Days? Surely not days.

I was wearing only the shorts and tank I'd donned to go jogging. They were soaked. My skin was goose bumped, my body shivering uncontrollably.

My gut rumbled with hunger.

The tomb-like darkness and silence played games with my mind.

One definition of crazy is the repetition of an action regardless of consistently negative results. I went through the same loops again and again. The futile wrenching and yanking. The useless questioning.

Was I going crazy?

Following each bout of frenzied thrashing, I'd lower my lids, hoping to heighten my awareness of other sensory stimuli. Unnecessary, since my optic nerves were inputting zilch.

It was to no avail.

There was nothing I could do but lie there in the muck and impenetrable darkness. Willing my eyes to see something when they were open. *Anything.* A thin trickle of light above or below the edge of the blindfold.

Despite the chill and damp, I must have fallen deeply asleep, for I woke with a start, my heart banging like a kettle drum in my chest.

Had my ears detected movement?

Every muscle tensed as I strained to listen.

Eventually, far off, a muffled sound tickled the stillness.

My breath froze.

The sound grew louder, fractured into rhythmic gritty sloshing.

Footsteps?

Whose?

Pay attention! one functioning portion of my forebrain screamed.

I twisted my head to face in the direction of the footfalls.

Moments, heartbeats, then the darkness along the lower edge of the blindfold eased almost imperceptibly.

Tipping my head backward at an excruciating angle, I could see shadowy contours in the gloom around me. I was in a long, narrow space. A dark cutout suggested an entrance point.

The footsteps grew closer.

The cutout brightened.

A figure appeared in the opening, flashlight in one hand, pointed at the ground. All I could tell was that the person was wearing a jacket with the hood raised. Otherwise, he—or she—was a featureless silhouette.

The figure cocked an elbow and a bright light hit me.

A hand flew up to cover my eyes. A reflexive but futile response. My arm could move only inches. And my orbits were tightly swathed in fabric.

The figure approached.

Since I could see little, I counted steps.

Two. Five. Seven.

The footsteps stopped beside me.

In my fingernail sliver of vision, I saw two shapes that had to be feet. Noted that the feet were wearing leather boots with yellow laces.

New odors rode the dank air. Sweat. Cigarette smoke. And something else. Not unpleasant. A blend of cedar and oil.

The owner of the boots didn't speak for what seemed an eternity. Then,

"Thanks for coming."

The voice was male. Young.

I answered without thinking, my attention focused on taking in data.

"Hardly my choice," I said.

"Good point."

"What do you want?"

"I'll do the questioning." Midwestern accent. But with an odd robotic lilt.

"Fire away," I said, sounding far more confident than I felt.

"Are you enjoying the accommodations?"

I felt my skin crawl. The voice was now high and warbly, like that of an elderly female. Had two people entered?

"I've had worse," I managed, steady, though adrenaline was pumping full blast.

The response was a macabre high giggle.

"You find this funny?" I asked, largely to keep him talking. Her? Them?

"I do."

"People will be looking for me."

"Sadly, they won't find you."

"You're fooling yourself."

"Am I, Dr. Brennan?"

My name! I wasn't a random victim!

"So." The boots widened their stance. "Do you think this little experiment is *evil* enough?" Giving a savage twist to the word.

"What little experiment?" I shot back.

"I suppose we could call it phobia games."

My mind scrabbled to connect dots. Experiment. Evil. Phobia. Where had that discussion taken place? With whom?

"Oh. Wait. I have that wrong." Now delivered in a baby voice that sent a slam of electricity straight to my breastbone. "Enclosed spaces is *Ruthie's* worst fear. You're frightened of losing people you love."

I said nothing.

"Or. We could call this an experiment in terror."

"Is that why you kill and decorate animals? To get off on their terror?" Anything to keep him or her talking. To buy time.

"I couldn't care less about animals. My interest is in the humans who happen upon my work."

"You skulk like a sewer rat waiting for some poor chump to find your displays?"

"You disappoint me, doc." Tone undisturbed by any whisper of warmth or disappointment. "Ever hear of GoPro cameras? The little beauties are so small even your CSU brain trust misses them."

"You're sick."

"Perhaps."

"What you do is risky."

"I don't mind risk."

"Your demented little game will end with you in jail." Unable to keep the revulsion from my voice.

"I doubt it."

"Why target me?" I asked after an unnerving stretch of silence.

"Why not."

"That isn't an answer."

"Because I can." Snapped with an alarming ferocity.

I said nothing, refusing to play further into the bastard's vile narrative.

"But. Onward and upward. Or perhaps I should say downward. I'll soon have the others. I won't bring them here, of course. That would be foolish."

Before I could unravel that cryptic statement, nylon whispered. Then an object dinged concrete, skip-splashed through water, and came to rest by my head.

The boots pivoted.

As the sloshing faded to silence, I began desperately groping the perimeter around me. Found nothing in the small space I was able to reach.

Flexing and extending my elbows and knees as much as my bindings grudgingly allowed, I inched to my right and searched that area. Still came up empty.

I scooched again and again until the ropes, now deeply embedded in my flesh, refused to grant a millimeter of additional slack. Then I rolled and repeated the maneuver.

On my second soggy thrust left, my trembling fingers contacted something small and hard. Breath frozen in my throat, I grasped and drew the object toward me.

Braille-reading details, I was stunned to realize my captor's toss-away was a pocketknife. With the nail of one semi-numb thumb, I teased the thing open, braced it where a slight rise in the floor met the wall above the water, and started running the ropes back and forth across the cutting edge.

Progress was unbearably slow. The blade was dull, and I had to move carefully to avoid slicing my skin.

Sweating and panting, I sawed until my arm muscles cramped, my captor's words skittering in my head.

. . . evil enough . . .

. . . experiment . . .

Snippets from earlier conversations percolated up to join the mix.

. . . classify an act as evil . . .

. . . manipulate variables with humans . . .

Where had that exchange taken place?

Red Rocks Cafe.

Lester Meloy had been present on that occasion, too.

Dear God! Was the UNCC student my captor?

I pictured Meloy. The boyish face. The neatly cropped hair.

The tattooed neck.

Quick as a muzzle flash, the inked letters reversed themselves in my mind's eye.

LIVE
EVIL

The realization sent a sharp warning twist through my gut.

With all the force I could muster, I continued working to sever my bindings.

I'd been at it for what seemed hours when the last sodden fibers finally gave way.

With clumsy fingers, I freed my wrists, then my ankles and struggled to my feet. My legs were numb. My entire right side felt weak.

Drawn by what I thought was the distant hum of traffic, I slogged through the pitch-black tunnel. Palm-feeling my way along a wall, I eventually reached the entrance.

A barred gate covered the opening top to bottom. On the right, a padlock secured the gate to a heavy metal hasp embedded in concrete.

Again, I almost cried.

You've got this!

Heat sparked in my chest.

Feeling the jolt animals get when smelling a predator, I lunged.

To my surprise, the gate swung on its rusty hinges with a grating creak. The padlock was either broken or had not been properly engaged. Or it might have been purposely left open.

I didn't have the focus to sort through the alternatives. Heart pumping, I shot through the opening.

The outside air smelled as sweet as any I'd ever breathed.

I drew two deep lungfuls.

Then I ran.

CHAPTER 31

I'd emerged into a gully of some sort.

It was night.

A steady rain was falling.

A lone sodium-vapor streetlamp high on one bank bathed the depression around me in sparkly peach tones.

Crickets did their cricket thing, undisturbed by the falling drops or by my sudden and less-than-graceful appearance. Now and then, something larger added a throaty croak to the rhythmic cheeping.

High above at street level, a lone horn honked.

My stint underground had pre-adapted my eyes to the darkness. A quick scan revealed a hairline path winding upward on the gully's far end. Backhanding moisture from my face, I jogged that way and followed the graveled trail up the embankment.

The path ended on a slight promontory. The city spread below like an ill-formed amoeba, windows glowing yellow, neon signs twinkling multicolored like the lights in a child's toy village.

I took a moment to get my bearings.

Off to my right, in the far distance, loomed the cavernous concrete shell that was the Bank of America Stadium. Beyond the stadium, the Truist Center, the BofA Corporate Center, the monolith on South Tryon whose name I didn't know.

My hair was winging medusa wild around my head. My tank and shorts were sodden and filthy and molded to my goose-bumped skin.

I felt myself simultaneously trembling and perspiring. Fever? Shock?

Either way, I needed help. Fast.

I had no phone.

No money.

No way to secure an Uber.

Looking around, I spotted a thin strip of gravel off to my left. Guessed it was another trail and that I was in a park of some sort. With no other option, I followed it, running as fast as I dared.

For what seemed forever, I pounded blindly through the dark, breath burning in my chest, feet splashing through invisible puddles dotting the path. Ignoring the drops pummeling my face and the twigs and vegetation clawing my limbs.

When I could run no farther, I dropped back to a panting jog, lungs in spasm and muscles burning, then to a limping walk.

Eventually, I came upon benches. All empty.

Of course they were empty. A fingernail moon peeking fitfully through the bloated clouds suggested an hour hovering around midnight.

A brief panting break, then I resumed running.

Within minutes I spotted, and heard, a couple coming toward me on the path. Arm-draping each other and belting out "Margaritaville," the pair appeared to be in their twenties. And quite drunk.

I waved and shouted, adrenaline still charging like a locomotive through my body.

"Yo! Yo!"

"Ohmygod!" Startled, the woman grabbed the man's arm.

"What the fuck, bro?" The man drew his girlfriend close.

"Don't be alarmed," I said, in the least alarming voice I could muster.

"I'm warning you! Stay back!"

Suspecting the guy was packing—isn't everyone in America?—I stopped and raised both hands high above my head.

"I had an accident. I've lost my phone."

"That isn't our problem, lady."

"Of course not. But it would be helpful if I could use your phone to make one quick call."

"Right. I lend you my cell and you haul ass."

"It's not a scam. I need help."

"How do I know you won't bolt with it?"

"Fair enough." I tried another tactic. "Will you place a call for me? Tell my friends where I am?"

"Why the fu—"

"Do it," the woman said, her face invisible beneath the raised hood of her Windbreaker.

"Seriously?"

"My gut says she's on the level, Arty."

"Your gut. That's—"

"Don't be a dick."

Muttering words not meant to reassure a stranger, Arty asked me, "What's the number?"

I told him that and my first name.

After punching digits, he brusquely informed the person on the other end of the line where they could collect me.

Slidell arrived with siren screaming, lights blazing. Ryan was riding shotgun.

Any energy I still possessed was spent on resisting their efforts to take me to a hospital. On insisting that they instead check on Katy.

When I shared my captor's comment about my fear of losing loved ones, they eagerly agreed to locate my daughter. The ER issue was a two-on-one battle, with Ryan and Slidell united in their opinion that I needed medical attention.

I repeatedly assured them that I was fine. At Ryan's insistence, I passed a pupil check and performed a straight-line walk. Tests I felt were more appropriate for a suspected DUI than a concussion.

In the end, I won. After I promised to file an official report the next day, Slidell drove me home.

Now I didn't care that Skinny and Ryan were waiting in my parlor. Though relieved that the cat had returned home safely, I ignored Birdie's scratching at the bathroom door. I showered until the water turned cold.

Then, head towel-wrapped and wearing sweats, I barefooted downstairs.

One of the two had made a Starbucks run. A collection of plastic-lidded cups covered the coffee table, each featuring the green siren logo. Each a size Grande. All but one empty.

Great. In addition to Skinny's normal hair-trigger temper, I'd be dealing with two guys wired on caffeine.

Though hardly in the mood, and committed to giving a full statement the next day, I'd provided a summary before heading upstairs, including everything I felt could possibly be germane. The bee sting. The tunnels. The constantly changing voice during the strange underground conversation with my captor. My sprint through the rain. Arty and his grudging phone call.

"Any idea who might have snatched you and why?" Slidell had asked when I'd finished.

While lying helpless underground I'd given these questions serious thought. Twisted and turned them and considered every possible explanation. My probing had yielded only two oddities in the recent past that seemed remotely relevant.

The first was Lester Meloy's dinnertime comment on the use of humans as test subjects. Had I been a player in one of his sick experiments?

The second was Danielle Hall's familiarity with the city's infrastructure. Had she used her knowledge of the underground network of storm tunnels to imprison me?

"It could be a huge coincidence," I'd said. "But Meloy and Hall?"

I mentioned both names, concluding with the strange fact that my captor had tossed me the knife.

Slidell had taken it all in, face reddening to the point I feared a cardiac episode. Then, predictably, he'd stormed out the door and roared off in his Trailblazer.

In his typical hotheaded fashion, Skinny ordered the arrest of Meloy and Hall. I'd barely finished my soap-and-suds cathartic when he was back at the Annex with news that both were en route to Mecklenburg County Jail Central.

"Charged with what?" I asked.

"We're working on that," Slidell said.

"Did you speak to Katy or Ruthie?"

"Not yet."

"I've tried twice but neither answers her phone."

"I'll send a unit by the kid's town house," Slidell said.

For a moment no one spoke.

"Can you positively ID Hall or Meloy as the person who took you down into the tunnels?" Ryan asked, a variation on the question Slidell had posed before racing off in his Trailblazer earlier.

"No." I'd thought about it. A lot.

"Shit," Slidell said. Again. With feeling.

"Try to remember," Ryan said gently. "Even the smallest detail could be helpful."

"You think I don't know that?"

Recognizing that my response was rhetorical, its sharpness born of my recent ordeal, neither man answered the question.

"He or she was probably a smoker," I said after a full minute of internal probing. "When we were close, I smelled cigarettes."

"Yeah?" Perking up at that minimally useful tidbit, Slidell dug a pencil stub and small spiral tablet from a shirt pocket. "What else?"

"He or she wore boots."

"What kind of boots?"

"Leather. With rubber soles and laces."

Slidell scribbled, then looked at me, brows raised.

"The laces were yellow. And there was some sort of logo burned into the heel."

"What sort of logo?"

"It was too dark to make out detail."

"What else?"

"That's it."

"That's *it*?" he asked in a tone suggesting frustration.

"I *was* drugged and unconscious," I said with a defensive edge.

"They probably jabbed you with a hypodermic full of Rohypnol," Ryan said after shooting Skinny a warning glance.

"The date-rape drug." I recalled the burning sensation in my upper arm. My assumption that I'd been stung by a bee.

"Yeah." Skinny did that snorty thing he does with his nose. "Only the bastard wasn't lookin' to score no nukkie at the movies. Any idea who mighta done it?" Intentionally or unintentionally Skinny repeated himself.

"I already answered that."

"Okay. Any idea *why*?"

"If I knew why, wouldn't I most likely know who?" Curt.

Ryan gave Slidell a look. "Detective, how long does the law allow you to hold these two?"

"Forty-eight hours. Then it's charge 'em or kick 'em."

I had a sudden thought.

"Could this have to do with the Quaashi Brown murder investigation? Could abducting me be a warning to back off?"

"I heard you was working that." Slidell's response wasn't exactly an answer.

"I identified the remains," I added. "But that makes no sense. Why send me the thumb drive with the video if you want me to disengage?"

Slidell said nothing.

"Did you question Meloy and Hall about Brown?" I asked Skinny.

"Eeyuh."

"And?" I pressed, a bit too sharply.

"Neither knows nothing about you being snatched or Brown being capped."

"What's your plan going forward?" Ryan asked.

"A night behind bars to allow Meloy and Hall enough time for some real dark thoughts. Then a couple of cozy chats at dawn."

"Play the lady and gent off against each other." Ryan knew the drill.

"Fuckin' A."

"Suppose neither cracks?" I asked.

"They always crack. But in the meantime, no more of your goddam middle of the night walkabouts."

Ryan got a call on his mobile at eight the next morning. He listened, replied with a series of brusque *ouis*, then agreed to something. His face told me that the something was not to his liking.

I asked no questions, allowing him to share at his preferred pace.

He imparted some details while at the stove cooking us breakfast. Omelets made of ingredients miraculously dredged from my fridge.

"Do you remember Pierre Giguère?" he began.

I had to think a moment.

"Your last boss before you retired from the SQ. Nice guy, bad toupee. Right?"

"It looks okay when he wears a hat."

No, I thought. It doesn't.

"That was Giguère on the phone earlier?" I asked.

"Yes."

"I didn't know you were pals."

"We're not, really."

I didn't pose the obvious question.

"Pierre only calls in a professional capacity," Ryan said.

I felt a prickle of unease, suspecting where this was going.

Ryan plated the omelets and put one on each of the mats I'd set out. Circled the table and took the chair opposite mine.

"This smells delicious," I said. Wanting to delay the inevitable?

"I went heavy with the olives and capers."

I had olives and capers in the house?

We ate in silence for several seconds. A silence strained by the knowledge of bad news in the offing.

Ryan broke it.

"I'll give you the condensed version of Giguère's message. In the last two months there have been three stabbing deaths in the southern part of the city, two in Petite-Bourgogne, one in Saint-Henri. The vics were all men in their twenties. Yesterday, there was another in Ville-Émard."

"That's awful. Same perp?"

"Maybe, maybe not."

"Gang related?"

"Two were patched in. The other two were known hang-arounds."

I made the unwelcome link.

"You worked the gang unit for years."

"I did."

"You know the players."

"Most."

"They want your help shutting it down."

"They do."

"What's the word on the street?"

"Surprisingly, there is none."

"Could the assailant be a lone wolf?"

"Nothing's off the table."

I thought about that. "You say this is the fourth murder in two months. Why come to you now?"

"The latest vic was fifteen years old."

"Sonofabitch."

"Well put."

"Giguère wants you back in Montreal," I guessed.

"He does."

"When?"

"He's booked me on a flight through Philly this evening."

Shit.

"More coffee?" I asked, trusting that those simple words wouldn't reveal my disappointment.

"Please."

I got up, refilled our mugs, and sat back down.

Ryan took my hand, intertwined his fingers with mine, and leaned close.

"Say the word and I won't go."

"Of course you should go."

"I wouldn't consider leaving if I thought you might still be in danger."

"I'm a big girl, Ryan. Besides, Meloy and Hall are in jail and Berkowitz's latest parole request was denied."

Ryan just looked at me.

"David Berkowitz? Son of Sam?" My laugh cracked into something too loud and too sharp. "Never mind. It was a joke."

"I can fly back to Charlotte in a few days."

"Of course. It's probably for the best. Slidell wants me to spend the next week eyeballing every mug shot ever taken in the tri-state area. And listening to a billion audio recordings to try to ID the mastermind of this unfortunate little incident." Trying to keep it light.

"Unfortunate little incident? Christ, you were kidnapped."

"And released unharmed."

"Some lunatic sent you video proof that he'd broken into your home. You need to take this *unfortunate little incident* more serious—"

"I'll be fine. I have Nguyen's overdue reports to keep me busy, which means I probably won't leave the Annex. Slidell has ordered surveillance, so it's likely a unit will pass by every five seconds," I added, wanting to lighten the mood.

Knowing further discussion was pointless, Ryan shook his head slowly while exhaling through his nose.

"I'll make it up to you," he said.

"Not necessary." I smiled, hoping to mask my frustration.

"Still. We have all day today," said Ryan, flicking his brows, Groucho style.

I flicked mine back.

My stomach performed its wee somersault act.

CHAPTER 32

After dropping Ryan at the airport, I went directly to the LEC to begin the tedious search that I'd described to him. I returned home late that day, and the next, back aching and eyes burning from plowing through thousands of mug shots and voice recordings.

The countless negative updates I gave to Slidell only served to irritate him.

In other words, I accomplished zip.

Ruthie phoned to say she was in Boone, having left for the mountains with friends. I didn't ask but assumed that negotiations between Harry and Katy had resulted in their green-lighting the trip. Given that Meloy and Hall were in jail, I did wonder briefly who these new mountaineering buddies might be.

I dialed Katy several times but she failed to answer her phone. I left messages, saying I was sorry for my recent unavailability and requesting a call back.

When I was finally free to return to the MCME, two new forensic anthropology requests had landed in my inbox.

The first case was easy. A hunk of pelvis, unearthed by a farmer plowing the north forty, was that of an elderly horse or cow.

The second case required a more detailed analysis. Dried and discolored bones had been found by a railroad worker in a wooden crate stashed in the far corner of an empty freight car. The skeleton, undoubtedly human, appeared to be old.

At six that evening, too beat to write a report on the remains of the long-dead traveler, I tried Katy again. This time she answered, apologizing for being incommunicado and explaining that she'd had a technology mishap. Forgotten in a back pocket, her cell phone had dropped into a toilet, thus necessitating a drying-out session in rice.

She was just leaving work. Since Ruthie was out of town, she hadn't made a grocery run. Still, she invited me to join her for dinner.

Dinner that I would purchase on my way to her house.

In the mood for Vietnamese, I swung by Lang Van and picked up double helpings of sweet and sour soup and chicken lemongrass curry, thinking those were Katy's favorites.

Making a left onto my daughter's street, I belatedly remembered that the actual dish Katy always ordered was a spicy concoction involving noodles.

Whatever. I'd tried.

Turned out my menu choices wouldn't matter.

For emergencies, I have a key to Katy's home. Out of courtesy, I always ring before entering.

I did so then.

No one came to the door.

I rang again.

Same result.

Thinking Katy might be outside on the rooftop terrace, I let myself in.

The place was cemetery quiet.

I checked the living and dining rooms, then called up the stairs.

Nothing.

Had I misunderstood?

Digging my mobile from my shoulder bag, I thumbed an entry on my list of family numbers. Somewhere in the rear, a rooster crowed.

Finding that strange, since Katy owned no poultry, I followed the sound to the kitchen.

The *cock-a-doodle-doo*-ing was coming from a mobile lying on a countertop by the back door. Crossing to it, I saw my number filling the screen. The digits disappeared as the crowing stopped.

Puzzled, I disconnected, pocketed my cell, and looked around. A crusted fry pan sat on the stovetop. Dirty dishes formed a wobbly stack in the sink.

Odd. Though somewhat disorganized in her day-to-day dealings, my daughter keeps an uncharacteristically tidy house. She claims that disorder in her personal space makes her itchy.

Returning to the front hall, I hollered up the stairs again.

"Katy?" Louder than before.

Crickets.

Feeling the first stirrings of unease, I climbed to the second floor and checked each of the bedrooms. Ditto the third floor, then the terrace.

The town house was deserted.

I stood silently for a moment, a listless breeze halfheartedly teasing my bangs. Four floors down, rush-hour drivers impatiently accelerated and braked, irked with the same jam-up they faced every day.

My emotions ping-ponged, unsure whether to land on anxious or angry.

Had some unexpected issue arisen after my conversation with Katy? We'd spoken less than an hour ago, so that seemed doubtful. And, were that the case, surely my daughter would have texted or phoned.

Perhaps left a note?

Seeing that possibility as likely, I double-stepped down to the first floor.

The sideboard by the front door was empty. Ditto the dining room and kitchen tables. The counters. I spotted no scribbled message taped to a mirror or wall.

Peering out through the kitchen window, I checked the backyard but noted nothing amiss. Through the row of small glass squares on the garage door I saw a dark silhouette I knew to be Katy's Volvo.

Baffled, I stood with my hand on the sill, unsure of my next move.

Wait?

Leave the food and go?

Stepping back from the sink, I unpocketed my mobile and, somewhat nonsensically, tried Katy's number again.

With the same result as before. More *cockle-doodle-doo*-ing from the phone on the countertop.

I was standing with my mobile pressed to my chest, undecided, when the thing shrilled in my hand.

I tilted and glanced at the screen.

Unknown number.

Nevertheless, certain that the caller was Katy, I clicked on.

"Hey."

My greeting failed to elicit the usual reciprocal "hey."

"I've arrived bearing chow."

A hollow silence hummed across the line.

"Katy?"

More silence.

"Where are you?" I asked, voice more sharply edged than normal. "Are you okay?"

Click.

Dead air.

What the hell?

My mind fired scenarios, each more horrendous than its predecessor.

I held a moment, heart hammering.

Screw it.

I punched a number on my speed dial list.

"Yo. Lemme guess. You figured out it's Clarabelle you got in your lab."

"What?" Totally focused on Katy, I missed Slidell's reference.

"The cow bone? That farmer's big score?"

"Katy's missing," I said.

"Whadaya mean, missing?" I could hear the cadence of male banter in the background, the murmur of a crowd. Figured Slidell was watching baseball.

"She invited me to dinner at her place," I said. "I'm here but she's not."

"That don't seem—"

"She didn't text or phone to cancel."

Slidell said nothing.

"To take off without explanation is out of character for Katy. You know that."

"Something musta come up." Clearly distracted.

"Her car is in the garage. Her phone is here."

"Maybe she—"

"Are you listening to me?"

The crowd murmur swelled to a roar. Leather groaned as Skinny's ass scooched forward across it.

"Kill that damn TV," I demanded.

"Christ a'mighty. Don't get your shorts in a twist."

I heard plastic scrape wood, then blessed silence. I suspected Slidell had muted but not abandoned the game.

"There. You happy? Now roll that by me again."

I did.

"You checked her crib? Tried her—"

"I'm standing in her kitchen. Her phone is here but she's not. That's wrong. Katy never goes anywhere without it."

"On my way," Slidell said, tone unreadable.

Ten minutes of pacing and cuticle gnawing, then my mobile rang.

I snatched it up. *Unknown number* again.

"What do you want?" I said, trying to conceal the terror I was feeling.

"You haven't figured it out yet?" The voice was high and nasal, the words clipped with noticeable spaces between. Mechanically altered?

"Who is this?" I asked.

"If I told you that, the game would be over."

"I'm not playing your game."

"But you are."

"Is Katy there?"

"Oh, she's here, all right."

"May I speak to her?" Heart racing, voice calm.

"I don't believe she's up to conversation."

I felt a hollowness open in the pit of my stomach.

"Tell me about this game," I said, stalling, hoping to keep the caller engaged until Slidell arrived.

"You know the one."

"I'm sorry, I don't."

"Already you've forgotten our little talk about phobias?" Delivered with a malevolent snicker.

My mind flashed to a recent underground conversation.

Dear God!

Was my captor now targeting Katy? Using my daughter to get at me?

Seeing Slidell's Trailblazer pull onto the drive, I tiptoed across the room to open the door. As he approached, I silently mouthed the words "abductor" and "Katy." Then, fearing a switch to speaker might alert the caller, I angled the phone so Skinny could hear the conversation.

"Tell me what it is you want," I said as Slidell punched a number, then whispered into his cell.

"Acknowledgment that I've won."

"I don't understand."

"Pure evil."

"You'll have to explain that."

"You know what I mean."

"Help me out."

Slidell's mobile buzzed. Looking embarrassed, he strode off a few yards and answered.

"Who's that?" the robotic voice demanded

"Someone is calling my cell," I lied.

"Who?"

"I don't know."

Dead air.

We've all watched the scene on TV—investigators trying to keep the bad guy on the phone long enough to trace a call. Good for suspense, but hardly accurate. Since the eighties, as soon as a landline connection is made, the phone company can immediately locate the origin.

Due to requirements that cellphone networks feature location-tracking technology, like GPS chips, to assist 911 services, the same holds true for mobile devices. An IT cop once explained the tracing process, saying that pinpointing a call's origin was based on triangulating which cell towers were pinged to allow the phone to pick up signal and transmit data.

Thanks to those FCC regs and that technology, thirty minutes later Slidell and I were racing, lights blazing, toward an address in the Marlwood neighborhood in east Charlotte. Just past an outfit called Tim the Tile Man, Slidell hung a tire-squealing right, then another onto a modest residential street.

Quick take.

Every home was one story, with a long, narrow lawn hosting a curbside mailbox and a gravel driveway hosting a gaggle of cars. Most gaggles included at least one pickup, some appearing reasonably new, others looking like they'd last been driven in the eighties.

The usual chaos had already engulfed the block. Squad cars with their light bars flashing and radios spitting. Fire trucks with their hoses gushing and their engines rumbling. Onlookers with their cell phones raised above their adrenaline-pumped faces.

This time the focal point of the action was a brick ranch-style house with dingy white shutters and a dark-shingled roof. A sun-fried vegetable garden separated the home's narrow front lawn from the street on the left. An old crepe myrtle was trying its best on the right.

Slidell screamed to a stop amid the hodgepodge of vehicles parked willy-nilly along the curb, jamming the brakes so hard I wondered if I'd broken ribs slamming forward into my belt.

We both flew out of the SUV, leaving the doors winging wide.

I smelled it before I saw it.

Not trusting my voice, I pointed.

A dark cloud was spiraling upward into the sky, a tiny smoke twister rising from the back of the house.

Heart pounding in my throat, I ran.

Skinny followed, wielding his badge like a crusader brandishing a sword.

CHAPTER 33

Hoses snaked the lawn, held by men and women in impossibly bulky gear directing high-pressure jets onto the structure. I saw no flames, but the air was thick with ash. With the acrid stench of scorched wood, metal, and plastic.

Not wanting to distract any of the first responders, I searched the crowd on my own. One hand covering my nose and mouth, I plunged through the onlookers, scanning faces and silhouettes. I didn't know and didn't care where Skinny had gone.

No Katy.

Finally, desperate to establish that my daughter was safe, I approached a firefighter who'd retreated to one of the trucks.

"I'm sorry to bother you," I said, voice shaky.

The person turned to look at me, features obscured by a full-face SCBA mask. Given a height exceeding six feet, I assumed male gender.

"My daughter phoned me less than an hour ago from this location. I'm worried she might be inside."

Moving a mic from his collar to the voice port on his mask, the man said, "We did a sweep. The house is empty."

"You're sure?"

The man nodded.

"Did you check the basement?"

"If the place has one, I'm sure someone did."

Hardly encouraging.

"My daughter could be down there," I pressed.

"Look, lady. You gotta step back."

The man raised a gloved hand in the direction of the police cordon.

Struggling to keep my composure, I retreated up the block, my brain firing a barrage of questions.

Was Katy still in that house?

Was she alive?

Had Katy been abducted by the same person who'd called trying to terrify me, and succeeding?

If Katy was no longer here, had her abductor moved her elsewhere, perhaps suspecting his call had been traced?

My gaze never rested, at one point landed on a truck. On a logo with a familiar swooshing arrow.

My steps slowed as I felt a nudge from my lower centers.

What?

I studied the truck.

Noted spiderweb cracking on the rearview mirror.

A driver in a billed cap.

Again, the subliminal *psst!,* more adamant this time.

I'd seen the truck before. Where?

Pulse drumming, I looked around, anxious to find Slidell. I spotted him among the barricaded onlookers, between a kid in a Hornet's jersey and a blue-haired granny clutching a canvas bag.

Digging my mobile from my purse, I hit Skinny's speed dial number.

"Where the fu—" he began.

"I'm worried that the firefighters didn't check the basement. One of them gave me a runaround. We need to check if—"

"I'll take care of it. Your ass goes back to the car." The intensity of his command left no room for protest.

I did as Skinny ordered. Sat on the passenger side, worrying the damn cuticle and checking the time every few seconds.

Tapping my mobile to be sure it was on. Of course, it was on.

Ninety minutes later, the call finally came.

Hand trembling, I snatched the device from the dash.

"The kid's fine." Slidell's breath was striking the mouthpiece fast and raspy.

"Where is she?"

"On her way to an ER."

"Ohmygod! What—"

"I said she's fine."

"If she's *fine*, why is she in an ambulance?"

"I didn't give her no choice."

"Where *was* she?"

"The perp left her tied up in the cellar, then hauled ass."

"With the house on fire." The fury I felt was like a flamethrower piercing my chest.

"Whoever it is will pay for this. But you need to see this. The basement where this handiwork went down is a real freak show."

I needed no urging.

Flying from the car, I raced up the street. Skinny met me on the porch and handed me a Maglite, saying that the lighting on the stairs was shit. With that colorful admonition, he led me into the house.

The front entrance gave directly onto a parlor. Cheap factory rug on the floor. IKEA-type chair and sofa trio facing a flat-screen TV. Everything bland and normal.

Until we entered the kitchen and crossed to an open door.

The odor hit me before we reached the threshold, a familiar blend of cedar and oil.

The tiny hairs rose on the back of my neck.

Where had I encountered that smell?

An image flashed.

Boots with yellow laces slogging across flooded concrete.

But this aroma included something else. Something organic.

The heavy thud of Slidell's feet snapped me back.

I followed his retreating form down the treads. He'd been right about the bulb. A lame forty watter above and to the left was casting eerie copies of my movements onto the wall to my right.

Thirteen steps, then I felt hardness beneath my sneakers.

New smells took over. Mildew. Mold. A hint of damp concrete.

A furnace occupied the center of the room. Three doors surrounded it, roughly ten feet out. All stood open.

With a gesture that could have meant anything, Slidell disappeared through the farthest door on the left. I trailed him into a surprisingly well-lit room and looked around.

Ropes crisscrossed the small space, looping a few feet below the ceiling. Clipped to the lines by old-fashioned wooden clothespins were dozens of animal paws and several human hands, each neatly severed from the limb to which it had once been attached.

A counter ran along the back wall, tiled on top, with a small sink at one end. Metal shelving stretched floor to ceiling on both side walls. I crossed to inspect the unit on the left.

The shelves held scores of lidded plastic tubs in varying sizes. Each was marked by hand with a black Sharpie.

I scanned the labels at eye level. *Degreasers. Picklers. Tanners. Deodorizers. Neutralizers. Preservatives.*

My gaze dropped to a lower shelf.

Glass eyes. Ear liners. Jaw sets. Tongues.

"Follow me."

Not waiting to see if I'd heard, Slidell strode from the room.

As before, I scurried after him.

The second room was identical to the first.

A set of clothing lay in crumpled disarray on the speckled laminate surface covering the back counter. A pair of jeans. A blue polo with black collar and sleeves.

I felt the edges of my mind go fuzzy.

Could it be?

I didn't want to know.

I had to know.

Barely breathing, I stepped closer and lifted the shirt with a pen that I drew from my purse. Saw a logo. A single word with an arrow swooshing below.

Frantic strobe shots slammed together in my brain.

Suddenly, it all made sense.

An Amazon truck on the circle drive the day I fell.

An Amazon truck blocking the nun's view at Cordelia Park.

An Amazon truck now parked outside on the street.

I tried to swallow but found that my mouth had gone dry.

I whirled to face Slidell.

"It's an Amazon driver," I said.

"There you go agai—"

"An Amazon truck has been present every time something's gone down."

"You got any idea how many of those truck—"

"There's one outside on the street right now."

Slidell's features rearranged into an expression I couldn't read.

"The person who abducted me smelled of this crap." I jabbed a finger at a six-ounce bottle of Van Dyke's Finishing Deodorizer. "I'm guessing that the driver of the truck out there lives in this house, and that he probably reeks of this stuff."

"I'll be goddammed."

Face graveyard grim, Slidell yanked his mobile from his belt, whirled, and charged up the stairs.

I was right on his heels.

CHAPTER 34

Only one thing was missing from my vision.

The windows were covered with old-fashioned wooden blinds. Not a square inch of chintz in sight.

The resort was called Echoing Pines on Lake Lure. Unlike Harvard Boynton's trailer park, the place was delivering on everything promised in its name. And it was a welcome escape from the heat still holding firm in Charlotte.

Our room was large enough to accommodate paired double beds, bureaus, and side tables, all made of over-varnished blond oak. A brick fireplace filled one wall, faced by rockers whose backstory might have involved the Amish.

A week had passed since the events at the Marlwood house. Days filled with police statements and lineups—and with a zillion reassurances to friends and family that I was okay.

Ryan and I were sharing a swing on the inn's enormous front porch. He had one long leg stretched out to the railing and, now and then, was giving a gentle shove to encourage the movement that was making me slightly queasy.

"Très scénique, oui?" Ryan drew me close with an arm already wrapping my shoulders.

"Beautiful," I agreed.

Teakettle-teakettle-teakettle.

"What bird is that?" Ryan asked.

"I think it's a Carolina wren."

"Talented fellow."

"How do you know it's a guy?" I asked.

"While you were doing whatever *toilette* it is that you do, I flipped through the magazine provided by our kindly host. According to some Audubon enthusiast, only the males sing."

"Did he introduce himself as Jedediah?"

"The bird?" Ryan said, smiling.

"Our host."

"He did."

"Quite the mountain-man name."

"It is."

Jimmy-jimmy-jimmy.

"Is that the same wren?" Ryan asked.

"I don't know. Would you like me to request ID?"

"Hilarious."

"I try."

Teakettle-teakettle-teakettle.

"Birdie would enjoy this place," Ryan said.

"Birdie would enjoy eating that wren." As I said it, I reflected that my cat wasn't exactly the big game–hunting type. He much preferred the treats I purchased from the grocery store.

"We could have brought him."

"He loves staying with the neighbor. She feeds him canned tuna."

"Is that good for cats?"

"Doubtful."

We fell into a comfortable silence, listening to the birdsong and admiring the peaceful tableau spreading out below us. The glistening lake. The shadowy hills fading into the deepening dusk.

Ryan was the first to speak again.

"There are still some details on which I'm unclear."

"Nice grammar," I said.

"Thank you," Ryan said. Then, after a pause. "Let me recap. The guy's name is Turner Long. He's from Mobile but has worked as an Amazon driver in the Charlotte area for over three years. He's unmarried, has no partner, no kids."

Jimmy-jimmy-jimmy.

"Correct on all points."

"Did Long ever serve time?" Ryan asked.

"According to Slidell, he did five years in Alabama for stealing a handbag."

"A snatch-and-run got him a nickel stretch?"

"The old lady fell and broke her hip."

"That'll do it."

Teakettle-teakettle-teakettle.

Ryan gave the swing another gentle shove. We rocked backward. After swallowing, I continued the thread.

"Also according to Slidell, Long gets his jollies decorating and nailing dead animals to trees. He started out using roadkill, eventually shifted to snatching pets, then to robbing graves."

"Long admitted to those things?"

"Yes," I said. "With considerable encouragement from Skinny."

"What about Quaashi Brown?"

"Long says he had nothing to do with Brown or the corpse at Cordelia Park."

"Does Slidell believe him?"

"Not for a second. He's running down the evidence that will nail him on both."

"Where is Long now?"

"Central lockup. And, according to Skinny"—I hooked air quotes—"'the scumbag ain't going nowhere any time soon.'"

Another round of *teakettle-teakettle-teakettle,* then,

"How did this loser come to focus on you?" Ryan was trying to hide his anger, not really succeeding.

"Several weeks back, I admonished Long for making a sloppy delivery to my neighbor."

"The asshole took offense and decided that *you* needed admonishment." Ryan's free hand went to his shirt pocket, came away empty, the move a holdover from his years as a smoker. A sure sign of agitation.

"Long told Acorn that he'd bided his time until he had a delivery for me," I went on. "When I answered the door, Birdie fired through the gap. Fearing he might dart into the traffic on Queens Road, and totally focused on recapturing the escapee, I instructed Long to leave the package in the front hall. While he was inside the Annex and I was outside in cat pursuit, Long raced upstairs, shot a quick video, then stuck a recording device under the sideboard in the front hall. A good one, sensitive enough to pick up conversations on most of the first floor."

"That's how he knew what scared you, what scared Katy."

"No. That conversation took place at a picnic in a park. During his stealth strike inside the Annex, Long also dropped a device into my purse."

"Which was conveniently accessible in the hall."

I nodded.

"What a bastard."

"Agreed. Get this. Among other things, when Acorn ran his background check he learned that Long was a grad student in psych at the University of Alabama for about two heartbeats."

"Meaning?"

"He was booted from the program after one semester."

"On what grounds?"

"That info is sealed. But apparently, Long's interest in human behavior never waned. He took to nailing up grisly displays to observe how people reacted."

"Bear," Ryan said.

"Yes." The jolt of anger I felt startled me.

"Did Long shoot the dog?"

"He refuses to discuss it."

"Ralph Balodis?"

"He denies killing anyone. Skinny's certain he'll eventually get Long to crack."

I thought back to my conversation with Adina and our definition of evil. An act that is horrific, intentional, inexplicable, and the cause of extreme suffering.

After so much cold-blooded killing—of animals and people—and so much elaborate orchestration meant to terrify, Long, in my view, met every qualification.

Flash image. The letters *PE* carved into flesh.

Suddenly, I understood the meaning of the cryptic message.

Pure Evil.

There followed another long stretch of silence interrupted only by the bird. Then Ryan posed a series of questions.

"Ruthie never was missing, right?"

"Not to her thinking. She'd gone off on the spur of the moment with her UNCC pals, sans Meloy and Hall. In her haste to connect with them on time, she'd failed to leave a note. Figured she'd phone from the car."

"But forgot."

"Yep."

Another slow back and forth, then Ryan asked, "If Long was offing people for fun, why didn't he kill you?"

"I asked my friend Adina her opinion on that."

"The psychologist?"

"Yes. She compared Long's behavior toward me to that of a cat toying with a mouse."

"Long enjoyed observing your reactions when you were under duress."

"That was *her* theory."

Another pause. Then,

"Danielle Hall. What's the story there?"

"Just a grad student who took a liking to Ruthie."

"Do you find that weird?"

"Hall told me she'd had a rough time fitting in her freshman year of college. She thinks because of her size. Now, when she gives campus tours, if she spots a kid that looks iffy, she tries to mentor a bit. Ruthie fit the bill with her vociferous bad-mouthing of higher education."

I did some tweaking in the translation of Hall's account. Her language had been more colorful than that.

"Who was the guy with the neck tattoo?"

"Lester Meloy. His club really did call itself Live, not Evil. Nothing sinister, just a group of idealistic students wanting to change the world."

Teakettle-teakettle-teakettle.

"The black Honda you suspected was following you. What came of that?"

"Slidell tracked the owner. The car belongs to the grandson of a neighbor at Sharon Hall. Its presence near the Annex had nothing to do with me. Same goes for the one I spotted behind me in traffic."

"What about all those hang-up calls?"

"That was the lovely Mr. Long, blocking his number. Apparently, the prick loves playing with gadgets that he learns about while doing deliveries. He used a voice modifier when talking to me down in the tunnels."

"Does Slidell think it was Long who shoved the thumb drive up Quaashi Brown's butt?"

"Long denies doing it. But yes, he does."

"Why?"

"Clearly, the man has issues."

"I hate that you had to go through what you did. But I'm still pissed off that you took so long to confide in me. And Slidell."

Teakettle-teakettle-teakettle.

"I didn't want Skinny getting his shiny polyesters in a knot."

"And me?"

"You abhor synthetics."

Ryan rolled his eyes, then asked, "Has Skinny recovered from his little fun run?"

Triggered by my ID of Turner Long based on the deodorizer scent, Skinny had sprinted up the stairs and out the front door. Seeing a scowling red-faced man bearing down on him, Long had attempted to flee in the truck. When the engine failed to turn over, he'd flown from behind the wheel and dashed up the street. Panting and sweating, Skinny had been hot on his heels.

"I thought we might need a respirator," I said, picturing Slidell's inelegant takedown of Long into a hedge. "Skinny is tougher than he looks."

"Why the hell did the dolt hang around that long?"

"Seeing people react to the chaos he created was the point of his game."

Another slow undulation, then,

"What now?" Ryan's voice had gone softer.

"What do you mean, what now?"

"Will you continue your unending fight against the forces of evil?" Delivered in a superhero announcer's baritone.

"As long as my powers hold out."

"Abilities far beyond those of mortal men."

"And women."

"That's not how the intro went," Ryan said.

"It should have."

Ryan rubbed his eyes with the heels of his hands.

"Ready to call it a day?" he asked.

"I am," I said.

Teakettle-teakettle-teakettle.

"But I fear that wren may be warming up for an all-night gig."

ACKNOWLEDGMENTS

Although my name appears on the cover of *Evil Bones*, as usual, many other talented people contributed to the making of this book.

I owe special thanks to my editors: Rick Horgan in the US, Brittany Lavery in Canada, Katherine Armstrong in the UK, and Anthea Bariamis in Australia. What a super team!!

I must recognize all those who work so very hard on my behalf. At home in the US, Marysue Rucci, Elina Veysbayn, Addie Gilligan, Jaya Miceli, Sophie Guimaraes, and Katie Rizzo. North of the border, Nicole Winstanley, Lisa Wray, Kaitlyn Lonnee, and Rebecca Snoddon. On the other side of the pond, Ian Chapman, Suzanne Baboneau, Perminder Mann, Joe Christie, Pip Watkins, Justine Gold, Polly Osborn, Maddie Allan, Rich Hawton, Jonny Kennedy, Nicholas Hayne, Alice Twomey, and Olivia Allen.

Thanks to Ervin Serrano for the wonderful jacket.

Paul Reichs offered constructive editorial advice.

Big hugs to Kevin Hanson for his help and encouragement across so many years and so many books.

I appreciate the expertise of Deneen Howell, my legal representative at Williams & Connolly LLP. Hats off for keeping me lawful!

Melissa Fish was always there to check details and facts. And to set me straight on backstory from earlier Temperance Brennan novels.

Roy and Archie kept me company dozing in their respective places, dog curled in my office chair, cat stretched out on my desk.

My interest in the concept of evil came from reading *The Anatomy of Evil* by Michael H. Stone, MD.

I know there are scores of others too numerous to name. If I failed to mention you, I apologize. Your constant support and occasional criticism are appreciated!

I send a big hug to all of Tempe's loyal followers. You are the reason I write these books! I hope to see many of you at upcoming signings and other live events.

Please continue to visit my website (KathyReichs.com), like me on Facebook (@kathyreichsbooks), and follow me on Instagram and X (@kathyreichs).

If this book contains errors, they are my fault.